I0706333

PENSIONS, TENSIONS, AND HOMICIDE

A GRIME PAYS MYSTERY
BOOK 3

TRICIA L. SANDERS

First edition February 8, 2020

Second edition November 21, 2023

Copyright © 2020 Tricia L. Sanders.

ISBN: 978-1-962175-09-8

Cover Design by Mariah Sinclair

This book is a work of fiction. The names, characters, places, and incidents are the products of the author's imagination or are used fictitiously. Any resemblance to actual events, business establishments, locales, or persons, living or dead, is entirely coincidental.

All rights reserved. No part of this publication may be reproduced, stored in a retrieval system, or transmitted in any form or by any means (electronic, mechanical, photocopying, recording, or otherwise) without the prior written permission of the copyright owner. The only exception is brief quotations in printed reviews.

The scanning, uploading, and distribution of this book via the Internet or via any other means without the permission of the copyright owner is illegal and punishable by law. Please purchase only authorized electronic editions, and do not participate in or encourage electronic piracy of copyrighted materials.

Your support of the author's rights is appreciated.

DEDICATION

To my sister-in-law Maryellen May. You are missed, but your legacy will last forever.

ACKNOWLEDGMENTS

My family, first and foremost, I owe everything to you.

To my readers, thank you for following along on Cece's journey. The cooking and cleaning can wait. Cece has another adventure. Please keep reading, and I'll keep writing.

The Lit Ladies - Margo, Brandi, Grace, Camille, and Sarah thank you for helping me flesh out Cece and keep her stories going.

Thank you to Tatiana at Vila Design for my cover art.

Thank you to my advance readers for my last book, Death, Diamonds, and Freezer Burn — Mary Ingmire, Lacey Harrington, Michele Wicker, Lee Dunn, Janet Graham, Maggie Herrel, Meg Gustafson, and Dee Doub.

To my editor Cayce Berryman, you do not know how much I appreciate your comments, suggestions, and eyeballs. You, my friend, are a gem. I am so glad I found you. Or you found me.

To Barb Schmidt, I miss our Wednesdays, but you are in my heart seven days a week.

To Dixie Dart, we need an adventure. One of these days, friend.

Deborah Schott, my snark-sister, we'll have that writing retreat one of these days. In the meantime, keep those essays coming.

Jenna St. James, my guardian angel, this book would still be sitting on my hard drive if it weren't for you and your gentle prodding and guidance. Your willingness to share your wisdom and experience means the world to me.

To the Squad (you know who you are), thanks for letting me tag along. You ladies are an inspiration.

CHAPTER ONE

"I know it's going to be a good day when I wake up to a desperate call from a potential client."
Cece Cavanaugh

Ed Jennings's emergency phone call in the wee hours of the morning interrupted my much-needed beauty sleep. I was typically a morning person but on my own terms—after a shower, a cup of tea, maybe even a bagel slathered with cream cheese. Then, and only then, could I greet the day.

Today I didn't have time for any of that. When I parked my car and trudged into Wickford High School, I was not a happy camper. Nor was I chipper and ready to face the world. I wanted—make that needed—caffeine or something energizing to jump-start my day. Instead, I spotted my former friend, Liz Blevins. She wiggled her fingers in a pretentious wave. My judgmental self kicked in and tried to ignore her. She hadn't called me once in the seven months since I'd separated from my husband. None of my friends from the country club had called—not one. I had reached out to several, but my calls were either met with icy chills or not returned. At least Liz had recommended me for this job. My conscience made me wave back. A grim-faced man stood next to her. I assumed he was the new principal, Ed Jennings.

My recent separation had pushed me to the brink of poverty, and I was slowly clawing my way out of the never-ending black hole of bills. Jobs like this one helped tremendously. In between the bigger, more lucrative jobs, I had a steady gig cleaning condos for a local developer.

I relied on friends and acquaintances to spread the word about the new business I'd recently started. I specialized in cleaning in the aftermath of catastrophic events. The money those types of jobs brought in helped much more than any other positions I found. My résumé was a bit blank since I'd been out of the workforce more than seventeen years.

Liz used to be my doubles partner at the country club—before my pending divorce from Phillip Cavanaugh, the grandson of one of the founding members. Liz was also the school nurse at Wickford High.

"Hey, Cece," Liz greeted me. "Hope you don't mind me giving your contact information to Ed. I was surprised to learn you'd started a business. Why didn't you go back to nursing?"

"Long story." I forced a smile, unwilling to share my down-on-my-luck story. "Thanks for the recommendation. I appreciate you thinking of me." Which was not what I thought at all since she hadn't bothered to call even once to check in. Angie, my best friend, was at my house minutes after Phillip walked out and had been by my side since.

Liz introduced me to her boss and continued to hang around—a fact that irked me. I'd hoped to avoid her. Her snub still smarted. I thought I had put all those feelings aside, but seeing her brought them all to the surface. I had lost my husband, my standing in the community, and most of my friends in one fell swoop. The only thing I'd managed to hang onto was our family home, which I now shared with my seventeen-year-old daughter.

"Morning, Mrs. Cavanaugh." Ed extended a beefy hand. "Sorry to drag you out of your cozy bed on this rainy morning."

I shoved my keys in my pocket, shook his hand, then pulled my coat around me to ward off the chill. "No problem. And call me Cece, please."

Even though we were standing in the front hall, the frigid temperature felt like I was still in the parking lot. I clenched my teeth to keep them from chattering.

"Sorry about the cold." Ed pulled a flashlight from the pocket of his jacket. "Maintenance is working on getting the heat back on. With the storm last night and all the rain, we lost power. No power equals no heat. The rest of town seems to be fine. We must have blown a circuit or something."

I shivered and looked around. "So, what's the emergency you alluded to?"

Ed clicked on the flashlight and pointed to the stairwell, which descended to the terrace or first-floor level of the school. "Come take a look."

I followed him and Liz to the railing and peered over. He swept the beam of light around the area, revealing a water-flooded hallway.

"The rain came down so fast, it had nowhere to go." Ed's light flickered and he slapped it against the palm of his hand. When the light steadied, he continued. "Water and mud poured in through the doors in the atrium like a dam had burst. The entire first floor is covered in about six inches of muck. Plus, all that rain has wreaked havoc on the storm sewers. Everything's backed up."

Liz made a face like she'd been asked to scrub a gas station toilet.

Ed sighed. "My janitor's out with a slipped disc. That's why Liz recommended you. And Zella seconded it."

"Zella? Is she still working in the cafeteria?" I'd gone to school at Wickford High many years ago and remembered she made the best chocolate chip cookies. After school, my best friend and I would sneak into the kitchen where Zella always left a fresh batch. We'd gorge ourselves and vow never to eat another one. At least not until Zella baked more. She always feigned anger about the missing cookies, but she wore a big grin while pretending to search for the culprits who had snatched the goods.

"Still cooking. Hate to lose her when she and Tommy retire, but she deserves to enjoy some time off. We'll be contracting out food service. With the proposed budget cuts, we're in a real mess." Ed shook his head.

I nodded in commiseration. "It's a shame about the tax increase failing. I saw an article in the paper about the budget shortfall and the number of positions being eliminated. Must make it tough on you. And now this."

"It's sad, but every dollar counts these days. Every day the school is closed is money lost. That makes getting this muck cleaned up my number one priority. You can make it your priority, right?"

"Yes, it won't be a problem. I have an assistant I can bring in to help, but I have to ask, is there going to be a problem finding resources to pay me? As much as I'd love to volunteer my services, I can't afford to work for free."

"Not a problem. There's a special fund for emergencies," Ed said. "Come on. Let's take a walk, and I'll show you what I'm talking about. Liz, follow us. Since you and Cece know one another, you can be the point person if Cece needs anything."

"About the water . . ." I shivered. "Is sewage involved? Because that's a whole different issue."

"No. No, no, no," Ed said. "The sanitary sewers are not involved. This is rainwater and mud. That's all."

"Good." I relaxed a bit. "Makes my job easier." I wasn't in the mood for the problem sewage presented or the time required to do the cleanup. Any other time, I'd be all over it. The money those kinds of jobs garnered was twice what I could charge for simple cleanups. Jobs like crime scenes raked in big bucks. But I wanted this one done so I could concentrate on planning and paying for my Thanksgiving celebration.

I glanced down the shadowy hallway. The familiar smells of stale sweat, industrial-strength cleaners, and floor wax assaulted my nose, along with the damp earthy smells of mud. My mind filled with scenes of endless corridors jam-packed with chattering students, lockers slamming, and the ever-present pealing of the class bell urging everyone on to next period. I'd never witnessed the school this dark or deserted.

Ed dug two more flashlights from his pocket and switched them on. "Maintenance should have the lights working soon, but I brought a light for each of you."

Shaking off my stroll down memory lane, I took the proffered light, adjusted my purse across my shoulder, and followed him down the steps. Liz lagged behind. I was glad I'd taken Ed's advice and worn boots, because before we reached the bottom step, we were ankle-deep.

"Watch your step. It's slippery." He splayed the light across the darkness. Double-stacked lockers lined both walls.

My own locker was long gone, replaced with these tiny versions, but that didn't stop me from reminiscing about Jordache jeans, slouchy socks, and mile-high hair. I could almost see myself primping in front of the mirror I'd taped to the inside. Not that I was bragging, but my hair had been spectacular—naturally blonde, thick, poofed, and gelled in all the right places. To obtain the height and fullness, I'd endured torturous moments wrapping my hair around steaming hot rollers while trying not to burn my fingers. Thirty years later, I was still blonde—with a whole lot of help from my stylist. The poofing and gelling disappeared with the eighties replaced by mousse, styling spray, and blowouts. Thank goodness for fading fads.

"We've canceled classes for the day and possibly into next week too. I've also assembled the staff whose classrooms and offices are on this floor. I've called a quick meeting, and I'd like you to attend, Cece. And of course, you too, Liz." The principal turned left into the school's east wing.

Despite the flooded hallway, his stride was long and his pace brisk. It took everything I had to keep up without slipping and sliding. Today wasn't the day to take a mud bath, though a soothing soak in my Jacuzzi sounded tempting. Scratch that. My leisurely days had ended when my husband cleaned out our bank accounts and left me with a mortgage six months in arrears. Club luncheons and tennis dates had given way to bill collectors and long days of back-breaking work. That was why a soak in my Jacuzzi would feel great at the end of the day when my muscles cramped and ached.

The school was built on a sloping piece of property. The main entrance, where I'd come in, was actually the second floor. The first floor, or atrium level, had a wall of windows and doors in between the east and west wings overlooking the commons area, which led to the football field.

Liz raised her flashlight and shined it at a door. "This is my office."

"Come ladies, we have a meeting to get to." The principal led us down the hall and stopped in front of the maintenance room. "Let me check the status of the generator." He turned the knob, but the door didn't budge. "Odd. That door's not supposed to be locked." After a moment, he sighed and waved at it dismissively. "I'll take care of it later. Let's get to the meeting."

Even before we reached the cafeteria, I heard a cacophony of voices. It sounded like a smaller version of the standard lunch period, with the exception of clattering trays and utensils.

Ed stopped short and took a breath. He pushed open the door, and a group of adults on the verge of mutiny met us. Floor-to-ceiling windows stretched along two sides of the cafeteria admitting what little light there was from the gloomy morning.

"All right, people. I need your attention," Ed's principal voice boomed across the room.

The chattering did not abate. Instead, it grew louder. I pictured the angry mob scene from the movie *Frankenstein*, but instead of torches, this group carried flashlights.

"How do you expect us to get anything done in the dark?" a short wisp of a woman shouted. "Why can't we go home?"

"You canceled school. It seems silly to make us come in." This from a tweed-jacketed man with a stringy, gray ponytail. "Especially in the wake of the so-called budget shortfall."

"Folks, calm down," Ed said. "I understand your concern, but until we get electricity and get the water out of here, you all need to work in your classrooms and offices making sure your supplies and books aren't ruined. We certainly can't afford to replace everything, and insurance only goes so far."

The group let out a collective moan, and those who were standing shuffled to the nearest chairs and sat down.

"Everybody, this is Cece Cavanaugh. She's going to help us get this mess under control. She'll be in charge of the cleanup. Liz recommended her. Thanks Liz." He tipped his head in her direction. Liz nodded back.

I recognized Zella, the head cook for Wickford High, but the other faces were unfamiliar.

"As soon as maintenance figures out what the power situation is, we can get the water pumped out of the hallways, then Cece can work on getting rid of the mud," Ed said. "The last thing we need is someone slipping and filing a lawsuit. Understand?"

The group pummeled Ed with questions from all directions.

"Ed, my office is a wreck," said the small woman who wore a gray sweater over black slacks. "It needs priority. Can't she start in there?"

"I've got a ton of experiments in the science lab," said the tweed-jacket guy. "If they're ruined, there goes our shot at the state science fair."

"You're the woman who found Delores Redmond's dead husband," said the woman in black slacks, directing her attention to me.

Her declaration brought a whole new volley of questions and outed me as the solver of Lloyd Redmond's murder. My face grew hot, and I felt sweat collecting at the nape of my neck despite the chill in the air. In June, Delores's daughter had asked me to clean out Delores's home so it could be sold. Elderly Delores had turned into a hoarder after her husband abandoned her. Turned out he hadn't. A couple days into the job I discovered his body buried under a frost-bitten stack of frozen dinners in a freezer in their garage. After finding a stash of diamonds and books filled with hundred-dollar bills, I'd inadvertently confronted the killer, almost gotten myself killed, and unraveled the tangled murder.

Ed leaned toward me. "What are they talking about?"

"Please, it's nothing, really. Can you get them to focus on your meeting?"

"All of you, listen up," Ed said. "Let's get on track."

"I've got produce to put away," Zella said. "You wanna talk

budget? If that stuff gets ruined, you got no food to feed these kids. May I be excused?"

Ed nodded. "Go ahead, Zella. As for the rest of you, Cece only has two hands. When our meeting is over, you all need to pitch in too." He pulled a paper from his pocket and handed it to me. "I have a list of priorities. Work your way down the list with Liz's guidance." The principal paused and scanned the room, a frown tugging at the corners of his lips. "Where are Steve and TJ?"

I didn't have a clue who Steve and TJ were, much less where they were.

Heads swiveled in Liz's direction.

"What?" Liz said. "I'm not his keeper."

"Steve was talking to TJ earlier near the library," the woman in the gray sweater offered.

Tweed-jacket guy mumbled something under his breath. Those closest to him laughed nervously. Liz ignored him.

"I saw Steve too," Tweed-jacket said. "I saw you talking to him outside your office, Liz."

Her face flushed bright red. "You must be mistaken."

Ed blew out a breath. "The first one to see either one of them, tell them to find me right away. Now if you'll excuse us, I've got to get an update on the generator." With a wave of his hand, he dismissed the group.

"Let's get going," Ed said to me. "I can't imagine what's taking so long. We'll check the maintenance room, then get you situated."

The staff continued to grumble as they dispersed.

Liz caught up with me. "Sorry I haven't kept in touch." She smiled, but her eyes hadn't received the message from her lips.

I shrugged. "Don't worry about it."

Ed was almost out of sight. I picked up my pace with Liz following close behind.

"No, really. I am sorry. I've been a bad friend, and I want to make it up to you. You could come over this weekend. Bill's hunting—" Liz stopped mid-sentence.

I knew exactly where her husband would be this weekend. It was deer season. Bill and several of his friends, including my soon-to-be ex-husband, had partnerships in a lodge near the lake. Deer weekend was a notorious party weekend for the guys and a source of constant complaint from the wives— only this year I didn't have a care in the world. If Phillip wanted to tromp around in the woods and shoot Bambi or *do* Bambi, more power to him.

The weekend also gave way for Liz's annual sleepover bash for the deer hunters' wives. The last place Liz wanted me was in the middle of her gabby girls' weekend. I had to admit she always put on a good spread, hiring the best caterer. Last year's extravaganza included a chocolate fountain, every kind of canapé imaginable, and enough liquor to loosen even the stiffest tongue. Gossip flowed almost as freely as the booze. No, spending the weekend with the country club set was definitely not my idea of a fun weekend, especially since my mother-in-law would be there. Plus, the grapevine would be eager for the latest Cavanaugh gossip.

There would, of course, be the requisite questions, asking if Phillip was still seeing Willow, the woman he'd left me for. My former friends would disguise their questions as concern. If the Wickford rumor mill was working properly, there would be surreptitious attempts to find out about my love life or lack of one. I was sure word had spread that I'd been seen having coffee with Grant Hunter, the local developer I worked for. And I knew my mother-in-law had broadcasted the word about seeing me on a few occasions with Case Alder, a detective I'd met during a murder investigation.

"I've got plans," I lied.

Liz breathed an audible sigh. "I totally understand. Maybe we can get together for lunch during the holidays."

We both knew we wouldn't. My life had changed directions. She probably thought for the worst, but I knew my future already looked brighter without Phillip. Though, it had taken me several months to figure it out. Now that I had, there was no looking back. No regrets. No crying over spilled Dom Pérignon.

Ed tapped the flashlight against his leg. "I don't have all day."

"If you'll excuse me, I've got to go," I said.

"Stop by my office when you're ready." Liz clicked on her flashlight. "Or shoot me a text. You have my cell number."

"No," I said, "I don't." I'd deleted her number. In a moment of self-pity, I'd gone through my phone and deleted the numbers of everyone who'd turned their backs on me. Freed up a lot of memory on my phone, but it was more an act of freeing myself.

Liz grimaced. "Oh, let me give it to you."

While she recited her number, I tapped it into my phone, then slid it into my coat pocket.

When she turned the corner and headed toward her office, I caught up with Ed. "Sorry." I nodded after Liz. "We haven't talked in a while."

He continued down the hall, the beam of his flashlight bobbing ahead of us. We stopped at his office and he picked up his keys. Just as we entered the maintenance room, the generator rumbled to life and the lights flickered on.

Ed stopped, and I bumped into him. "What the devil?"

Across the room, a man slumped over a workbench. The hair on the back of my neck prickled.

"What are you doing in here?" Ed addressed the man. "I've been looking for you."

A feeling of dread washed over me.

"Steve?" Ed sloshed through the water and touched the guy's shoulder. "Trupeli, what's going on?" The man tilted precariously and toppled onto the mud-covered floor.

Crap! Crap! Crap! I closed my eyes and prayed the guy had just fallen asleep—a really deep sleep. Maybe a coma. I knew better. I'd recently been privy to two other murder scenes—Brian Anderson who was murdered at Harmony Inn back in the spring and Lloyd Redmond whom I'd found stuffed into a freezer in early summer. This scenario had all the markings of foul play.

The maintenance man, whom I recognized as Tommy King, walked in wiping his hands on a grubby towel. "Didn't think I'd ever get that mother working, Ed."

Ed's face paled. I inched closer to the workbench with him. Ed jumped back like he'd been electrocuted. Which wouldn't have been out of the question considering he was standing in six inches of water, and Steve Trupeli had an electric cord wrapped around his neck. Fortunately, the dangling plug indicated the drill was not connected to an outlet.

Still clueless, Tommy kept talking. "Everything in this place is falling apart or dying. You gotta find a way to cut loose with some money."

The only thing that needed to be cut loose was the power cord wrapped around Steve Trupeli's neck.

CHAPTER TWO

"I really did consider Cece a friend. It just was not in my best interest to take her side against Phillip."
Liz Blevins

I stared at the scene unfolding, not certain whether I should take charge or not. Ed was the principal, after all. I didn't want to usurp his authority, but on the off chance the guy wasn't dead, we needed to act.

"Is that Steve Trupeli?" Tommy asked. "What's he doing here? Daggum teachers got no respect for a person's space."

"G-Go call 9-1-1!" Ed yelled.

Fortunately, Ed had decided to take charge.

Tommy continued to stare. "What's wrong with him?"

"Now!" Ed shouted. "He's not responsive."

Tommy scrambled over to the phone hanging by the door and placed the call. I kneeled and checked Steve for a pulse.

The principal eyed me suspiciously. "Should you be doing that?"

"I used to be a nurse." I slid two fingers along Steve's radial artery.

"I guess that explains why you're not freaking out."

"Been there, done that. Doesn't do any good to panic," I said. "But I'm not getting a pulse."

Ed bent over and took deep breaths. "Oh boy. This is not good."

I glanced at Tommy, who had plastered himself against the door. His eyes were wide and his hands trembled. "You okay?" I asked.

"No ma'am. I seen way too many dead guys when I was in Vietnam. I don't need to be seeing one in my own room. On TV, yeah. But in real life . . ." He shook his head rapidly. "No ma'am, I am not okay."

Steve was not the first dead man I'd come in contact with either. I scanned the room, looking for anything out of place or unusual—other than the drill cord wrapped around his neck. The bench he'd been sitting at had a large to-go cup from Café du Soleil, one of my favorite hangouts. Next to the cup a prescription bottle lay on its side with a few pills scattered about. The last and oddest thing I noticed—one earring consisting of a dangly silver feather with turquoise and coral stones inlaid along the center leaning against the coffee cup. Very odd in a maintenance room.

"We need to get out of here," I said.

Ed straightened. "Shouldn't we at least get him out of the water?"

"Absolutely not," I said, eyeing the drill at the end of the power cord. "He didn't just accidentally get a cord wrapped around his neck. We'll need to wait for the ambulance, but I think it's too late." I pulled myself to a standing position and wrapped my arms around myself. "We have to wait outside."

"Ya don't have to tell me twice." Tommy scrambled into the hallway.

My stomach did a little somersault when I envisioned Detective Alder arriving on the scene. I hadn't seen him since July. He and I had made a connection, but until my divorce was final, nothing could come of it. Phillip, my husband, was holding a prenup with a morals clause over my head. If I as much as looked cockeyed at Alder or any other man, I could kiss a divorce settlement goodbye. The kicker here being the divorce was precipitated by my husband having an affair. Several affairs, I'd learned after the fact. Because he came from a wealthy family and I didn't, his mother had insisted on a prenup in an effort to scare me off. It hadn't, but the morals clause was one-way and not in my favor. Phillip's indiscretions didn't alter the prenup one iota.

Ed pushed me aside. "What are you talking about? He can't be dead. Steve, buddy, wake up. This isn't funny." Ed jostled the dead man to no avail. His entire body shook, and his voice rose in pitch. "This is horrible." He sank to a bench and buried his head in his hands.

I motioned toward the doorway. "Come on. This is a crime scene, and we're contaminating the evidence."

Ed jumped up. "This can't be happening."

Before I could get him out the door, he pointed to the coffee cup on the workbench. "Is that yours?" he asked Tommy who was hovering right outside the door.

"Nope. Don't drink the stuff. It gives me the shakes."

Ed reached for the cup.

"Don't touch that. It might be evidence," I said.

Ed made a growling sound. "This makes no sense."

I started to explain about the chain of evidence and all the police stuff I'd learned during the last two situations I'd been involved in, but he cut me off.

"I understand that. What makes no sense is I saw Steve this morning when he came in grumbling about not having time to stop for coffee. And now here's a coffee, and if it's not Tommy's, whose is it?"

I didn't say what I was thinking—that it probably belonged to whoever killed poor old Steve. "Come on. Let's go." I herded Ed into the hallway and pulled the door shut with my sleeve. "Call your faculty and staff to a central location, so they aren't roaming all over the building. I'm sure the police will want to question everyone."

"Police?" Ed gave one last look over his shoulder then turned to Tommy. "Lock the door and give me your key. No one goes in until the police arrive."

Tommy did as ordered and dropped the key in Ed's hand, then mumbled, "You can keep that key. I ain't ever going in there again."

———

"Everyone, please proceed to the cafeteria for a mandatory staff meeting," Ed announced over the school's P.A. system. "Immediately!"

Bewildered faculty and staff trekked past me on their way to the cafeteria.

"We just had a meeting," someone complained.

"Maybe he's sending us home."

"Now of all days. What is wrong with him?" said another.

As we found seats, the blaring of approaching sirens changed the trajectory of comments from joking and annoyance to fear and apprehension.

Liz approached my table with two cups. "Mind if I join you? You still a tea drinker?"

"Sure." I scooted over to make room. "Thanks." I wrapped my hands around the cup for warmth.

She sat down and nodded toward Ed. "What's going on? He looks like he's seen a ghost."

Before I could answer, Ed rapped his knuckles on a table-top. "Take a seat, people. I've got some news and it's not good. Steve's been located. I can't share any details until I talk to the police. But until we figure this out, you all need to stay put. Am I clear?"

Grumbles and groans echoed around the room.

"What is he talking about? Is Steve ill?" Liz asked. The concern in her voice was unmistakable.

I evaded her question. "We called an ambulance. We'll know more when they get here."

Liz's eyes narrowed. "That's an evasive answer if I've ever heard one. Is he okay or not?"

"We probably shouldn't speculate. We'll know soon enough." I glanced around the room, pretending to sip my tea. The staff had settled down and murmured anxiously among themselves.

"I have a right to know," Liz said. "Especially if he needs an ambulance."

"Really?" I asked. "Why's that?"

Liz frowned. "Steve is my ex."

"Seriously, how did I not know that?" I couldn't imagine working in the same building with Phillip.

"I suppose it never came up. It's not like I'm proud of having a failed marriage."

If the town of Wickford was a soap opera, Wickford High would be rumor central. Liz had shared tons of gossip about the school employees, herself notwithstanding. Her ex-husband dumped her more than a decade ago, but she'd never once indicated that she worked with him. She'd quickly rebounded and married Bill Blevins.

"I totally understand," I conceded.

"And we had an amicable split. If you can say that about divorce. I've known him all my life, and we work together," Liz said, her voice quivering. "We're still friends."

Her news left me speechless. I couldn't imagine being friends with Phillip—ever again. Not after what he did to our family.

Ed made his rounds chatting and engaging his staff, trying to keep them calm. Tommy and Zella sat huddled in the kitchen. I could see them through the glass partition. Tommy reminded me of the cartoon character Popeye, thin and grizzled but strong. Even though he was wiry, you could tell he still had muscle tone. And Zella was his exact opposite. She was a jolly Mrs. Claus-type. Her hair was white and cottony and framed her pudgy, pink face—an instant contrast to Tommy. If opposites attracted, you could say that about the two of them. North and south poles to be exact.

An air of class difference pervaded the room: blue-collar workers on one side, white-collar on the other. It was a sad commentary on life but pretty much mirrored my own experience since my separation. Once I'd been a woman of leisure with tennis dates, spa appointments, luncheon engagements, and no money worries. My friends lived similar existences. Now that my lifestyle had changed, they had drifted into oblivion, just like Liz. If I ran into one of them, the excuse was always the same—been too busy, but let's do lunch sometime. Of course, we never did.

Angie Valenti, my neighbor and best friend, had remained my only constant. She stood by me through my marriage, impending divorce, and ensuing money problems.

Liz interrupted my thoughts. "Do you see TJ anywhere?"

That caught me short. "Huh? Who?"

"TJ. Just curious why he's not here. I know he was in the building today. I spotted him when I first came in this morning."

"I wouldn't know him if I saw him. Who is he?"

Liz shrugged. "The new athletic director. He replaced Steve at the beginning of the school year."

"Your ex was the athletic director?"

"*Was* is the operative word. Oh, there he is. See the guy over there?" She nodded in the direction of an attractive young man who had just walked in the door carrying a sack and a cup of coffee from Café du Soleil. "That's TJ Gordon. With all the budget cuts, and the fact that our football team didn't win a game the last two seasons, Steve lost his title of athletic director. The district brought in this guy at the beginning of the school year."

And now Steve is dead. "The district fired Steve for two bad seasons?" I asked.

"No, they took away his responsibilities and the money that goes along with being athletic director. He's still a coach and art teacher, but it was a big blow to his ego and his wallet. There's a huge stipend for being the athletic director. Not to mention the celebrity status. At least when the team is winning."

The woman in the gray sweater approached our table and bent in low. "Liz, what's going on?"

"You know as much as I do," Liz said to her without even looking up.

The woman pulled out a chair.

"If you don't mind, Marni, Cece and I have a lot of catching up to do."

The woman backed away without a word and joined a group at the next table.

"Who's that?" I asked. "She looks familiar."

"The woman Steve left me for—Marni Caruthers," Liz said. "The bane of my existence."

"I don't understand. I thought you said you and Steve were on friendly terms. Bygones and all that."

"Right. *Steve* and I are friends," Liz said. "We settled our grievances a long time ago, but I will never be friends with a woman who goes after another woman's husband. But she can't seem to get that through her thick head. Like wanting to sit with us. But what is it they say about paybacks?"

"What do you mean?" I asked.

"I've heard she's getting a taste of what it's like to be cheated on."

"Do tell."

"Rumor has it that Steve's got another fling going on. Now mind you, I don't know this firsthand." Liz leaned back and crossed her arms over her chest. "Once a cheater, always a cheater."

"You think she knows?" I glanced back at Marni, who had her gaze trained on Liz's back. When she saw me, she averted her eyes. A part of me felt sorry for her, but the jilted woman in me wanted to lash out.

"I doubt it. Even if she did, she'd be in denial. Aren't we all? Deep down I knew long before Steve confessed, but I wouldn't admit it to myself. No, she's clueless."

It's not like he hadn't done it before. Liz had told me once before that her ex had a penchant for the ladies. Even though he and Marni were an item and had been for more than ten years, he liked to play the field. When Liz and I played tennis, she'd told me on more than one occasion that was the only thing keeping him single. The girlfriend, as Liz had always referred to her, wanted commitment, and he liked their relationship just the way it was. No strings. Kind of like mine with Phillip—only we were married.

The cafeteria door squeaked open and Detective Case Alder walked in. Saying he was a handsome specimen of a man didn't do him justice. It might have been his eyes, which were the color of my grandmother's Delft blue china, or the mustache dancing along the upper edge of his lip. He definitely made my heart skip a beat. The unfortunate thing about Detective Alder, or Alder as everyone called him, and me was the fact that we had a love-hate relationship. He loved to infuriate me, and I hated it, most of the time.

Since we'd crossed paths back in the spring, there had been an instant attraction. For me, not acting on my impulse was a no-brainer. My husband of thirty years had just left me for a woman almost half my age. I didn't know what hurt most, him leaving me or the fact that his girlfriend was young and perky and now sported boobs that my husband had paid for. I needed to start a new relationship like I needed a space-ship. My launchpad had been closed for business until Detective Alder expressed an interest.

It had taken every ounce of willpower I could muster not to act on my feelings, especially when he'd almost told me he was falling in love with me. At least, that was what I thought he was going to say. Because as soon as the words started coming out of his mouth, I'd squashed the notion. We were currently in a holding pattern until my head and my heart could get on the same page.

"Uh-oh." Liz shifted in her seat. "The cops are here. Let the inquisition begin. This should be fun. Not."

I slunk down and tried to make myself inconspicuous. Alder would not be happy to see me, especially since he was probably dealing with a homicide. In the seven months since I'd met him, I'd helped solve two crimes. *Helped* was probably not the word he'd use, since I'd almost gotten myself killed both times. So, let me just say, the crimes were solved, and I'd played an important role in bringing the perpetrators to justice.

Ed met Alder at the door, chatted a minute, and then Alder exited the cafeteria without noticing me. No doubt heading to the maintenance room.

"Everyone, listen up," Ed said to the group.

The buzz of conversation in the room quieted.

"The police have asked that you all remain seated until

they've had an opportunity to do a preliminary investigation. Once they're finished, they'll want to question each of you."

"Question us? Why? What aren't you telling us?" Marni asked in a shaky voice. "It's Steve, isn't it." Her voice cracked. "He's dead or else the police wouldn't be 'investigating.'" She made little quote marks with her fingers. "Tell us the truth." Marni slumped in her chair and sobbed.

Beside me, Liz drew in a wobbly breath. "Oh my God. Is that true?"

A low murmur circulated as the news sank in, and the staff realized we were witnesses or possibly perpetrators of a potential crime.

"Can we get some heat in here?" an elderly gentleman near the tray return asked, oblivious to the news we'd just been given. He had not been at the earlier meeting. Several new faces had joined our group.

"The generator's running. Give it a little while, and we should start getting heat soon," Ed said.

The science guy leaned back in his chair and waved his hand. "Tell us what's going on. We have a right to know."

Heads nodded in unison until Ed slammed his fist on a table. "I can't discuss it. You all sit still until the detective comes back and tells us what to do." He rubbed his hand, pulled a chair up to the door, and sat down.

"Steve's dead, isn't he?" Liz asked. Despite the chill in the air, beads of perspiration clustered on her forehead. "It wouldn't surprise me one bit."

I wondered if she was having a hot flash. They had invaded my personal comfort zone a while back, and I still struggled to keep them at bay. A couple months ago a friend had suggested herbal supplements, but they didn't help.

"How come?" I scanned the room, trying to pick out faces I'd seen earlier.

"Steve was in trouble," Liz offered.

I leaned in. "What kind of trouble? Besides woman trouble?"

"I hate to speak ill of Steve. Especially when he can't defend himself." Liz lowered her voice to a whisper. "You didn't hear this from me. Okay?"

I nodded.

"Financial trouble. Big time. That's why losing the directorship was such a blow. It cost him a chunk of money when they brought TJ in. And Steve was so angry. Hopeless, really." Liz shrugged. "Steve's been up to something. He's been acting very oddly. Hey, you never answered my question."

"What question?" I asked.

"Is Steve dead? You were with Ed, so I assume you know what's going on."

Liz reached for her cup and it went flying. Tea splashed on the table and streamed across the surface right into my lap. "Oh my." She lunged for the cup, splattering the puddle onto my sweatshirt.

I jumped from my chair and patted my jeans. "It's okay. Just a little tea."

Zella arrived with a handful of napkins and a wet rag. "Here, blot your pants with this, honey." She pushed the cloth into my hand and went to work wiping the mess from the table.

Liz continued to wring her hands and apologize.

"Don't worry," I said. My jeans felt clammy against my legs as I soaked up the tea. Lucky for me, I'd worn old clothes —my standard apparel these days when it came to cleaning.

Zella gathered the soppy napkins into a pile. "It's good to see you again, Cece. Looks like we got a bigger problem on our hands than this here little flood. Don't we?"

I agreed and handed her the rag.

"That Steve got himself into some mess this time, didn't he? If it's not one thing with him, it's something else. And

Marni over there, pining away for the likes of him. I swear some women don't know when to call it quits." Zella shook her head. "If you ladies will excuse me, I've got chores to do in the kitchen. Mr. Jennings never said I couldn't work, just that I had to stay here."

After Zella left, Liz and I returned to our seats.

"Is Steve dead?" Liz pleaded.

She'd find out anyway as soon as Alder came back. "Yes. I'm sorry, but it appears so."

"Why didn't Ed come get me? I'm a nurse for crying out loud. Are you serious?"

"I used to be one too, remember?"

"I know." Liz looked around. "That means the killer is most likely in this room."

I followed her gaze, searching each face for a clue.

"From what Zella said, it sounds like Marni might be a candidate. Do you think she's capable of murder?"

Liz swiveled around to get a better look at Marni, who had moved to the back of the room—alone. I didn't know her, but I felt sorry for her. She looked so forlorn sitting by herself.

When I turned back around, Liz's lip was trembling. "I'm so sorry," I said.

"Cece, I think I'm in big trouble."

"What are you talking about?"

Liz wiped the perspiration from her forehead again. "The cops are going to think I killed Steve. I've got a motive, and he was at my house this morning."

CHAPTER THREE

"It's not that I don't want to see Cece. I just don't want to see her at my crime scene."
Detective Case Alder

Detective Alder walked in after Liz made her stunning announcement. I stared at her, but before I could ask her to elaborate, Alder spotted me, did a double take, and walked to my table.

"Can I have a word with you?" he asked.

I gave him a good, long look, and yes, he still made my insides tingle. But, just like old times, the frown on his face made my nerves prickle. "S-Sure."

His jaw twitched. When I didn't move, he bent over and said, "In private."

"Excuse me, Liz, but the detective here requests the honor of my presence." I rose from the table.

Her eyes pleaded with me not to tell Alder what she'd just shared. With him standing right there, I couldn't do anything to reassure her. Besides, it didn't matter whether I opened my mouth or not. He'd find out soon enough. It was just a matter of time before he lined all these people up for the inquisition. If there was hanky-panky going on between Liz and her ex, the rumor mill would rat them out. Was there hanky-panky going on between Liz and Steve? Why had he been at her house this morning? Pretty gutsy. Her husband was out of town with all his hunting buddies. And the science guy said he'd seen Steve and Liz talking outside her office this morning. I didn't like the thoughts racing through my mind.

"Let's go into the hallway." Alder took my arm and led me through the double doors and down the ramp.

I sloshed beside him, careful not to kick mud on the khakis he'd carefully tucked into rubber galoshes. His light touch sent a major quiver to a location just south of my navel. He had a way of making me feel all twitchy and nice. It was a severe contrast to the way I'd felt before my separation from Phillip.

My hormones kept me in a constant state of confusion. Usually, I'd sweat like a construction worker, but since the weather had turned chilly, my feet and hands felt like I'd injected them with liquid ice. What I wouldn't give for a hot flash. Well, not right now, not while I followed Alder. I didn't want him to see me all red-faced with my hair plastered to my head. That was normally how I looked when I was in the throes of a personal heat wave—gross and disgusting.

"Don't tell me. Let me guess. You've given up cleaning and taken up teaching?" His salt-and-pepper mustache—more pepper than salt—wiggled along the top of his lip as he spoke.

My knees trembled remembering how it felt the last time he'd kissed me. It had been months. My fault, not his. But I hadn't forgotten that kiss. With my divorce pending, I was still reeling from a cheating husband and not ready to fall into a relationship with another man so quickly—not even with one who made me weak in the knees. An added complication to the equation was Grant Hunter, the developer I worked for. Grant, a widower, had shown a desire for a relationship—one I wasn't ready to pursue or might never be ready to pursue. Grant was an amazing man, but I didn't know if we had the chemistry to make it work. Not like the electricity that constantly zapped between me and Alder. First, I had a man who didn't want me and was willing to throw away our family and thirty years, and the next thing I knew, two equally handsome men were competing for my attention.

"You're quite the funny man, aren't you?" I crossed my arms, aware of the grubby sweatshirt I'd worn this morning. "I'm here on a job."

"The body is barely cold." He climbed the stairs to the entrance door and stopped in the main hall. "Are the criminals calling you before they commit the crime?"

In April, I'd unintentionally accepted a job to clean a murder scene, and I met Alder during the investigation. Then, in June, a friend hired me to unclutter her elderly mother's house where I'd found the woman's estranged husband in the freezer—dead. Alder had worked both cases and loved to needle me about my habit of getting involved with the less desirable aspects of my occupation.

"If you haven't noticed, the school is slightly flooded." I waved my hand in the direction of the water-soaked hall we'd just tromped through. "Ed Jennings hired me for cleanup."

Alder laughed, his blue eyes twinkling. "I'm joking with you. Don't get so defensive." He leaned against the wall and shoved his hands into his pockets. "You doing okay? It's been a while."

What he wanted to know without asking was how my divorce was progressing. I stared at the floor, not trusting myself to meet his gaze. The man had a way of melting my core. "I'm fine. It's been since June." I bit my tongue. Why had I said that? It's not as if I'd been counting the days until I saw him again, but that's exactly how it sounded. After he'd wrapped up the case where I'd found the frozen stiff, he'd told me he respected my need for space but assured me he was all in and willing to wait. Then he disappeared. Not literally, but after a few late-night phone calls, we'd put the brakes on, pending my divorce.

"Angie told me your court date is right around the corner."

Next week to be exact, but I didn't trust myself to tell him. My feelings were all over the map where Alder was concerned, and he wasn't making this easy. If he only knew how many times I'd picked up the phone and started to call him. Resolve wasn't my strongest attribute, but I felt the only way to get my head together after Phillip was to put distance between me and anyone who permeated my space.

"Don't you need to be investigating?"

"Good try, Cece Cavanaugh." He pushed off the wall and laid his hand on my cheek. "You're right. I have work to do, but we need to talk. I'm tired of waiting for you to call."

I backed up, and his hand slid from my face. "We'll see. You're going to be busy. What with this investigation and questioning all those suspects, you won't have time to breathe much less worry about me."

"Don't you fret. I find time for the important things in life." He waggled his eyebrows.

I loved it when he did that. His eyes crinkled a bit. Not enough to make him look old, but enough to give his face character and appeal. Just enough to make me want to reach out and caress his—*stop it, Cece. You need to get your train of thought going in a different direction.* I hated it that he had that effect on me.

Weakness had killed my marriage. I needed to become a stronger, more independent person before I let myself get involved in a relationship again. I also needed my divorce decree so Phillip had nothing to hold over my head. The divorce hadn't been my idea. Phillip had served me. When I learned he was leaving me, I'd been crushed. When I learned he'd had multiple affairs during our thirty-year marriage, I'd been livid. When I learned he wanted to work on our marriage and was *willing* to forgive me for something I hadn't even done, I'd signed the divorce papers and told him not to let the door hit him in the butt. It still stung, but I knew I was doing the best thing for my own peace of mind. I deserved better.

"What about the dead guy?" I shivered at the thought of my grisly discovery. Maybe it was time to find a new line of work. Who knew cleaning would be so disastrous? A nice little boutique sounded lovely. If I ever got my finances straightened out, I might invest in a little storefront down on Main Street and sell herbal teas or socks. Yes, designer socks, that could work. How much trouble could I get into selling pretty footwear?

"He'll be on his way to the morgue shortly. The crime techs are still processing the scene."

"I hate to ask, but when will you release the scene? Ed has me on a tight deadline." Not to mention, I needed the money. Between the work slowing down at Hunter Springs and having to pay Nancy, my finances were still on the bleak side. The sooner I got back to work, the less I would dwell on the fact that I'd found another body. Instead, I mentally ticked off the other items on my to-do list. Two condos in the Hunter Springs development were ready to be cleaned, and I'd gotten a contract for a dentist office out near Wolf Run Road. Neither of which paid big money, but they paid.

My little endeavor continued to grow thanks to word-of-mouth from Grant Hunter. He must have sent out emails to the world telling them about Cavanaugh Cleaning—CC for short. I'd picked that name to irritate my husband and his nasty mother. They both held the Cavanaugh name in high esteem, much higher than it deserved, and it gave me great pleasure to drive around in my new-to-me fluorescent pink van with my cleaning company name plastered on both sides in lime-green lettering. I loved seeing heads turn when I drove through town. I loved even more that my company specialized in jobs that were not run-of-the-mill. No maid service for Cavanaugh Cleaning. I took the nasty jobs that other services didn't want. With my nursing background and additional training in protective gear, I could handle most any type of biohazard cleanup—including trauma and crime scenes.

"Probably tomorrow at the earliest," Alder said. "Let's get back to the cafeteria. I've got me a whole bunch of suspects to question."

"Do I need to stick around?"

"Yeah, I need to interview everyone, including you. I could stop by later, but then, I probably shouldn't." Alder smiled. "Or should I?"

"No, I can stay, but I could be working out at Hunter Springs until I can get back in here." The minute I mentioned the condo development, I regretted it.

"Hunter said you were still out there." A tinge of jealousy edged his voice. "Didn't put much distance between you and him, did you?"

Alder and Grant Hunter had clashed back in the spring when both had shown an interest in me, but much to my dismay, they had become fast friends during the summer. Thanks to Hunter's season tickets to the St. Louis Cardinals and Alder's affinity for baseball, they'd bonded at Busch Stadium. Grant had been my saving grace by hiring me as an independent contractor to clean condos when I was scrambling to get my finances under control. He had made an overture or two but understood my need for independence.

"Don't be pouty," I said. "It doesn't become you. The only reason I'm still there is for the money. And Nancy does most of the work. I just go around once in a while to check up on her and lend a hand. Having her around has given me the ability to concentrate on marketing my company. In fact, I can't remember the last time I've even talked to Grant."

Nancy, my assistant, needed a constant eye. Her work ethic rivaled that of a rock. Not to mention, it didn't take much to distract her. But she was getting better.

Alder shook his head. "I can't believe you hired that kook. You still got her living at your place?"

"Yes. It's temporary. Until she gets back on her feet."

"She's been there since June," he said. "Doesn't sound temporary to me."

I hiked my lip in a sneer. "Point taken."

It had been a while since I'd asked Nancy how her apartment search was going, but I didn't need the space over my garage where she was living. It was bad enough I had to deal with her at work, but coming home to find her rummaging through my refrigerator made me want to pack her bags and put her out on the street.

"Let's go. The folks will be getting restless," Alder said.

We waded back down the hall, neither one mentioning our earlier conversation. When we reached the cafeteria, he paused and opened his mouth, then closed it and shook his head.

I knew that look. It always preceded a lecture. "Don't even."

Alder laughed. "You're getting wise to me. I know you won't listen to me if I tell you to stay out of this, so instead . . ." he trailed off.

"Instead what?" I asked. "You want my help, don't you?"

"Oh, just shoot me now." Alder pretended to pull the trigger on an imaginary gun. "Yes. I mean no. I don't want you to do anything but keep your ears open. Do not instigate anything, and for crying out loud do not interrogate people. Let them do the talking. You listen. That's all."

I stared at him, not believing what he'd just said. "You want me to spy on them?"

He pointed to his ear. "Listen. Ears only. There's going to be a lot of speculation going on and a lot of waggin' tongues. So, just listen to what they're saying."

"Is that sort of like you're deputizing me?" I mocked.

"Absolutely not. Never mind! This was a bad idea. Poor judgment on my part. Don't even know why I brought it up." He shrugged. "You just stay out of it. Okay?"

"No, you did bring it up. And you're right. I'm going to be around for a while, and some of these people know me and will open up. The rest will ignore me. Since I'm the hired help, it'll be like I'm a fly on the wall. They won't pay me the least bit of attention, so I can listen, and they'll be none the wiser." I liked where this conversation was going. Other than the obvious side-effect of almost getting killed, I'd enjoyed running down clues in the two previous murders. It was like piecing together a jigsaw puzzle—a giant puzzle with moving parts and guns and murderers.

Alder sighed. "This better not come back to bite me in the butt. Listening only, okay?"

"Roger that," I said. Then I realized what I had agreed to. *Heaven help me.* I'd done well to keep my distance, but now that fate had brought us together again, I didn't know how long my resolve would hold out.

CHAPTER FOUR

"Cece wasn't a troublemaker in school, but she had a spunky attitude."
Tommy King

Alder conducted his interviews in the school library. After he'd questioned me, I headed to my car but remembered I'd left my purse in the cafeteria. Staff who had already been interviewed had to leave the facility—all except Ed and Tommy. Ed could stay in his office until the last interview wrapped up, then he would have to leave too. Tommy was Zella's ride, so he was allowed to stay until Zella finished her interview.

On the way down the hall, I passed Marni and the science guy, who I'd learned was named Keith Preston, being escorted by a uniformed officer to the library for their interviews. Liz was already there.

I zipped into the cafeteria, got permission from the officer standing guard, and went straight to the table where I'd been sitting. My purse was nowhere to be found. I looked under the table—nothing. A quick glance around the room, just in case someone had moved my chair, revealed no purse. I was positive I'd left it draped over the back of the chair.

The room had cleared out with the exception of TJ, the athletic director, who sat near the back of the cafeteria eating a muffin and nursing his coffee.

"Have you seen a purse?" I asked. "I thought I left it here."

He startled when I spoke. "What?"

I repeated my question, motioning to the chair where I had been sitting.

"No, sorry. I haven't been paying attention. Too much commotion going on."

He hooked his thumb in the direction of the kitchen where Tommy sat waiting for Zella and said, "Try him. He's the go-to guy for that sort of stuff."

"Oh, thanks, I'll do that." I glanced at TJ. Since my cleanup was on hold, I might as well start my detective work. "It's really sad about Steve. Did you know him well?"

He shook his head. "I've only been here since August, and since I kind of replaced him, it's not like we were on a friendly basis. I think his last words to me were something about wanting to smash my face in."

"Yikes! What brought that on?" I pulled out a chair and sat down.

"I needed some training videos he still had. When I asked for them, he went off on me."

"Guess he was still bitter," I said.

"Even brought him a coffee this morning. Knew he was coming in before the coffee shop opened to get ready for a holiday art show his students are participating in. We're almost always there the same time every morning. When I got to Café du Soleil, I grabbed an extra one hoping to make a truce so I could get those videos without a big ruckus. I thought he was going to punch me."

"What happened?"

"I was afraid to give him the coffee, afraid he would throw it on me. After he stormed out, I left it on his desk as a peace offering."

A cop cleared his throat beside me. "Ma'am, you're going to have to leave."

"Oops." He'd probably rat me out to Alder.

"Can I check with the maintenance guy to see if he's seen my missing purse?" I asked the officer. "He's already been interviewed."

The cop nodded.

It wouldn't hurt to see if Tommy had a clue about my purse or if he had any idea who might have killed Steve.

"Hey," I said to Tommy when I entered the kitchen. "You haven't seen a stray purse, have you?"

He was perched on a stool at the long stainless-steel prep counter. "Can't say I have." He gave me the squinty eye and then said, "Don't I know you?"

"I'd hope so. It's only been a couple hours." Did the guy have severe memory loss or what?

"No, I meant you sort of look familiar. Like I know you from somewhere else."

"I used to go to school here," I said.

"Must have been a long time ago," he muttered.

"I beg your pardon. I'm not that old. Besides, look who's talking. You're not so young yourself."

"I do know you," Tommy said. "You're that little hellion, Cece Buchanan. I'd recognize your attitude anywhere." He jumped from his stool and pulled me into a hug. "How ya doing, Cece? It's been a long time."

I pulled back abruptly. My face must have registered what

my mind was thinking. Who was this guy? And why was he hugging me like a long-lost friend?

"Shoot fire, girl. I can't believe you don't remember me. Course, I wasn't maintenance back then. I had janitorial duties. Did that for about ten years, then after taking some night school classes, I got promoted to maintenance. Been here ever since."

I smiled. "It's Cece Cavanaugh now, and it's been a while, but now that you've refreshed my memory, I do remember you." How could I have forgotten Tipsy Tommy. He'd come to Wickford my junior year fresh from the army. Rumor had it he had a drinking problem. Back then I had more important things on my mind than paying attention to the school janitor who weaved and stumbled around the hallways.

"Changed my ways a lot since then. Married Zella a while back, and she set me on a better path." Tommy's face brightened. "Now we're getting ready to retire. Just bought us a big RV. Unless the district tries to screw us out of our retirement." Tommy blew out a breath. "If they can find a way to mess with our benefits, it wouldn't surprise me none. Cut this. Take away that. Save a dime and spend a dollar to do it."

"Congrats on retirement. Zella will be a great travel companion," I said.

"Don't I know it."

"Surely the district won't mess with you."

"Yeah, that's what Trupeli thought. Then they brought in him." Tommy pointed to TJ, who was still sipping coffee waiting for his interview. "Paid him half of what Steve was getting. Steve had more experience in his little finger than that jerk has in his whole body. Waste of good oxygen, if you ask me."

I thought about what Liz had said. "I heard the issue was with Steve's performance and how Wickford hadn't won a game in a couple seasons."

Tommy laughed. "That's the excuse they're using. Steve had a huge stipend for being the A.D. They're paying that kid practically nothing. They cut the salary but doubled the stipend. He's got a master's degree and all just like Steve, but . . ." Tommy let his words trail off.

"But?" I asked.

"Nothing. I done said too much."

"Do you think that has anything to do with what happened to Steve?"

"*Hmpf*! Wouldn't surprise me. Can't fire a tenured teacher, but if he croaks, well, it saves the district a ton of moolah, if you know what I mean."

"Yeah, I guess so." Not that I wanted to see her again, but I'd have to ask Liz more about TJ and his background. Ed would know, but I doubted he'd share that information with me.

Zella had finished her interview and walked in. "You ready to go?" she asked Tommy. "Oh hey, Cece. You doing okay?"

I shrugged. "I'm fine. It's definitely not how I like to start my day."

Tommy pulled a coat off the counter and helped Zella into it. "Hey, honey, you haven't seen a pocketbook, have you? Cece's misplaced hers."

Zella buttoned her coat and retrieved a pair of gloves from her pockets. "I don't recall seeing one. But with all the craziness that's happened today, my brain is all scattered."

"You didn't leave it in the maintenance room, did you? You'll never get it back with all those cops collecting evidence." Tommy grimaced. "They better leave my dang tools alone. Some of those are my personal ones."

I retraced my steps in my head and thought for a minute. "Pretty sure I left it draped over the back of my chair." I patted my coat pocket. "No worries. I have my keys anyway. I'll check with Liz later. She may have rescued it."

"Did you check your car?" Zella asked. "I'm forever getting in a toot and leaving mine in the seat. It's a miracle my car hasn't been vandalized to get to it."

"Good point. I'm on my way out now."

"All righty, guess we'll see you around. Good luck with your pocketbook," Tommy called over his shoulder as he ushered Zella out the backdoor.

When I went back through the cafeteria, TJ and the officer were both gone.

———

Marni stood in the front hallway weeping. My heart squeezed at the sight of her. She might be the reason for Liz's marriage falling apart, but she didn't deserve to be going through this alone.

"Marni," I said. "I'm so sorry about Steve. Is there anything I can do?"

She swiped her eyes. "Oh, that's so sweet of you. Did you know Steve?"

"No, I didn't meet Liz until . . . well, she was dating her current husband when I first met her. I didn't even know Steve was her ex. I knew she had one, but I'd never met him."

Marni sniffled. "She's been so good to us. Always including us so Steve and I could share holidays and other family events with the kids and grandkids."

"Yes, it sounds like you all had an amazing family dynamic. Pretty uncommon." Not likely to happen with me and Phillip. Our daughters were grown and could make their own decisions about spending time with their father. They didn't need my involvement. But I could guarantee Phillip and Willow wouldn't be invited to share my holidays.

"She's one in a million. I'm so fortunate to have her as a friend."

"Indeed." *That's what you think.*

"Do the police have any idea who could have done this to Steve?" Marni asked.

"What?"

"Suspects. Do they have any suspects?" She looked over her shoulder. "You know it's kind of creepy knowing that one of your coworkers killed your boyfriend."

"Uh. I don't know. It's really early in their investigation."

Marni leaned in. "You're on the inside track, right? I mean, you solved that case this summer."

I laughed. "Some would say that was just dumb luck on my part."

"Oh, give yourself credit. What you did sounds very brave."

"Thanks."

Marni's expression turned sad. "I don't know how I'm going to cope with all this. Poor Steve. Who would want to hurt him?"

"Unfortunately, I didn't know Steve. What was he like?"

A smile flickered across Marni's face then disappeared. "He was very kind. A great father and grandfather. Once he lost the director position, his attitude soured, and he started lashing out at anyone he thought had wronged him. But who could blame him? I'm sure everyone here will be telling the police all kinds of things to discredit his name."

"I don't think you have to worry about that. The detective assigned to this investigation is very thorough," I said. "He'll find out who's responsible."

Marni's hands trembled. "I hope so. There are so many people who had motive."

"Really?" I asked. "Like who?"

"Look around," she said. "TJ for one. It was just a matter of time before the school board saw through him and gave Steve back his athletic director position."

"Why so?" I asked.

"TJ doesn't have the experience that Steve had. I mean, Steve had a couple bad seasons, but TJ doesn't have any leadership skills." Marni laughed. "He's not going to be able to whip that team into shape. Especially with Steve being here. The kids have so much respect for Steve. Now that he's gone, TJ might have a chance. See what I mean? Really, two motives. TJ knew he was on a short leash with the board and with the team."

"That's an interesting perspective," I said.

"There's also Keith and Zella. They've both been on the outs with Steve. And as much as it pains me to say it, Liz might have a motive. Please don't tell her I said that, but I know she still harbors a grudge against Steve."

"But I thought you said you all had such a great relationship."

"Oh, we do. I shouldn't have said that. Liz is a dear, and I shouldn't speak badly about her. Sometimes I think she just pretends to put on a front for the family. Not that I could blame her." Marni adjusted her coat. "No, truly. Liz would never hurt a fly. Ignore what I said. It's the grief talking. I can't . . . I don't know what I'm talking about. It's just too overwhelming." Tears streamed down her face. "I'm sorry. I have to go." Marni fled through the front door, leaving me standing with my mouth agape.

"Excuse me, ma'am." The officer who I'd seen in the cafeteria earlier walked toward me. "You'll have to leave."

I sent a forlorn glance over my shoulder. "I still haven't located my purse. I don't guess there's any use in asking if I can keep looking, is there?"

"No ma'am. I'm sorry."

———

After giving the van a thorough search for my purse and not finding it, I started the engine and saw Liz walking out the front door.

She pulled her coat tightly around her and started across the parking lot with her head down. I tapped my horn to get her attention. When she saw me, she waved and trotted over.

"Dang, it's cold out here," she said when I rolled down my window.

"You got a minute?" I asked.

She shivered. "I'm freezing."

I pointed to my passenger door. "Hop in. It's starting to get warm in here."

When Liz was seated next to me, I turned the heater blower up to full blast. "This should help."

She pulled her gloves off and rubbed her hands together in front of the vent. "If all this water freezes, it's going to be a mess out here."

A few awkward moments passed. For me, because I knew my friendship with Liz had never been about being friends. It had been about who I was married to and about being half of one of Wickford's power couples. For Liz, who knew?

Bill Blevins was the son of Mavis Blevins, one of my mother-in-law's best friends. Their family was a powerful force in the wine industry in Wickford. By marrying Bill, Liz had cemented her social standing in Wickford—as long as they remained married.

But her ex-husband had just been murdered, and she'd told me she had a motive. Several thoughts crossed my mind. Why had Steve been at her house this morning? Convenient that her husband was out of town. What did I really know about her, other than she had a wicked tennis serve. And she was hosting all my former "friends" for her annual deer hunters' wives' weekend tomorrow. All my old friends would be there except Angie—my one true friend—who had stuck by me regardless of my social, financial, or marital standing.

Liz spoke first. "What did you want?"

I wanted to tell her about my encounter with Marni but kept my mouth shut. At this point, everyone was a suspect, and I wasn't going to screw with Alder's investigation by telling one suspect what another suspect had said. "I misplaced my purse and haven't been able to locate it. Have you seen it by chance?" I asked. "Spice-colored shoulder bag."

"Sorry, can't say that I have. Did you check the lost and found?"

"No! They won't let me back in. How'd your interview go?" I felt a hot flash coming on and turned the heater down a notch.

"Routine, I suppose, but darn that detective is good-looking. I can see why you'd be attracted to him." She gasped and clamped her lips together. "Oops. You know how the rumor mill is around here."

I waved a hand in dismissal. "No worries." I knew better than to deny it. Especially with her band of biddies getting together. My ears would ring all weekend, and I didn't need to fuel their interest. "You were getting ready to tell me about Steve being at your house this morning," I said. "What's that about?"

Liz turned in her seat so she was facing me. "Oh that. Nothing."

"But you said—"

"And I just now said it was nothing." Liz chuckled and opened the car door. "No need getting another rumor started. Now I better go run my errands. With all this extra time, I can add the finishing touches to my menu for girls' wee—" She slammed the door before finishing her sentence.

Another rumor indeed.

CHAPTER FIVE

"I hope Mrs. Cavanaugh's divorce doesn't mean I'll be looking for a new job."
Beatrice Giovannetti

I rolled into my driveway at three thirty. Alder had spent the better part of the morning questioning everyone. After he released me, I made a trip out to Hunter Springs, took lunch to Nancy, and gave her a hand. With both of us working, we'd finished both condos, and I gave her the rest of the afternoon off. Nothing new to report on her behalf. She had done a good job today and deserved to be rewarded. I had to admit she really was getting better. I was sure my not-so-gentle prodding helped.

We still had the dentist office but couldn't get in until after hours. Nancy said she'd tackle it tonight because she needed the money. With the rest of the afternoon free, I was at odds with myself. It was too cold for outdoor activities. Thanksgiving was almost a week away, much too early to grocery shop for the family get-together, but I could work on my menu. This would be the first Thanksgiving without Phillip. Jessie, my oldest daughter, had a new man in her life, and that was reason to celebrate.

Brad worked for Hunter Construction, and the minute I introduced him to Jessie, the two had hit it off and become inseparable. I knew it was too early to anticipate wedding bells, but this was the longest relationship Jessie had ever had. A mother could hope. He was employed, he was good to her, and I liked him. All points in his favor.

The house was quiet when I walked in the front door. My youngest, Michelle, a senior at Lakeview Academy, had already come and gone. Today, of all days, made me grateful I'd kept her at Lakeview instead of transferring her to Wickford High when Phillip and I separated. As long as he continued to pay the tuition, that was where Michelle would stay.

She'd recently taken a job at the recreational center giving swim lessons. Prior to my separation, Michelle had never worked and pretty much acted the part of her daddy's spoiled princess. But after getting caught shoplifting, and once the cold, hard reality of my divorce slapped her upside the head, she'd turned an about-face and seemed to be handling responsibilities much better. I knew we'd have more mother-daughter squabbles, but I really felt like the tough times were behind us. Her whole demeanor seemed to mature overnight.

Beatrice, my housekeeper, looked up from scrubbing the kitchen sink when I walked in. "Good afternoon," she called, waving her dishcloth.

I smiled. "Hi Beatrice." She'd been such a blessing. Hazel, my mother-in-law, had hired her to clean my house after Phillip and I separated and not because Hazel felt sorry for me. She had really hired Beatrice to snoop on me and report back about my activities in case I was doing anything lewd or lascivious that Hazel could tell Phillip to help in our divorce. When Beatrice slipped and let me know the housekeepers where she worked had nicknamed my mother-in-law "The Barracuda," we'd become allies in a single war—to best my mother-in-law.

Beatrice and I had turned the tables and fed Hazel all sorts of innocent and blemish-free information. Not that I had a bad reputation or anything, but by the time Beatrice got finished with our false reports, I looked like Mary Poppins. I practically was Mary Poppins, but that was beside the point. I lived a pretty boring life, other than my recent uptick in the man department, but then what Hazel didn't know wouldn't hurt her.

A beautiful vase of rust-and-yellow chrysanthemums sat on the breakfast bar. I pulled the card from between two blooms.

"Looks like your admirer is still at it," Beatrice said. "Those aren't as pretty as the roses he used to send."

The card read: HOPE YOU HAVE A HAPPY THANKSGIVING —GRANT.

Grant had been sending flowers since we met. He'd started with roses. Once we'd had the talk about not getting involved, he'd begun sending less romantic flowers.

"I really need to talk to him." I sighed, dreading having another conversation. He was such an amazing man, but I hated that he might still be holding out hope for something more to develop between us. The last thing I wanted to do was hurt his feelings or lead him on. I had to admit the flowers were a sweet gesture and it touched me deeply. I couldn't recall one instance in thirty years when Phillip had sent me flowers.

"How's the menu coming for your big dinner?" Beatrice

rinsed her cloth and folded it over the sink. "If my son hadn't invited me to come up for a visit, I'd have been glad to cook for you."

"No need for that, but I appreciate the thought. This is the first time I've done Thanksgiving and I'm pretty excited. I scoured the Internet and found a couple recipes for dressing or stuffing. I'm not sure which one I'm going to try."

Beatrice held her hand up. "Let me give you my granny's. She was the best cook in the county. I'll write it down and leave it on the counter for you. Nothing can beat it."

"Fantastic. Honestly, I didn't know which one to use. One calls for white bread, the other cornbread."

"Granny's uses cornbread. It's as southern as they come. Gets a crispy top, but the inside is moist and tasty. It makes me homesick just thinking about it. My daughter-in-law makes that stuffing in a box, and it's not the same, but she rules the roost in their house, so I just keep my mouth shut and do as she says. That way my son doesn't catch any flack."

"You're one smart lady." As an afterthought I added, "I thought you were Italian through and through."

Beatrice winked. "Only on my papa's side. My mother was a southern belle."

I reached into the fridge for a bottle of water then sifted through the mail. Bills, bills, and more bills. That was the story of my life. I no sooner paid off one and three more showed up.

"Oh, there's a message for you on the desk. Mr. Cavanaugh called." Beatrice scrunched her face in a disapproving scowl.

"Thanks." I picked up the note from the desk in the nook next to my kitchen and tossed it in the trash—he didn't deserve the recycle bin. In less than a week, I wouldn't have to listen to his threats to enforce our prenup.

The phone rang while I was opening envelopes. I glanced

at the screen to make sure it wasn't Phillip. It wasn't. I answered and wedged the phone between my ear and shoulder, so I could continue reading my mail.

"Hello?" I wadded up two advertisements and tossed them in the recycle can in the pantry.

"Cece," the voice squeaked. "Have you got any clear soda?"

"Angie, you sound horrible. What's wrong?" I glanced at the three bills, all with current balances. Not bad for a woman who'd almost filed bankruptcy just a mere six months ago. My mortgage wasn't out of hot water yet, but after long talks with the bank and my husband's attorney, it was almost caught up.

"I've got food poisoning." The phone clattered, and I heard an unmistakable sound in the background.

My stomach did a little flip-flop. In my younger days, I'd been a nurse and most sickness didn't bother me, but that sound always made me queasy. I waited for Angie to come back to the phone. When she didn't, I grabbed a can of Sprite from my fridge.

"I'll be right back. I'm going over to Angie's," I called to Beatrice as I grabbed Angie's spare key from my desk drawer and headed next door.

Angie was still slumped over the toilet when I arrived. I got her back to bed, pressed a cold washcloth to her forehead, and found a glass.

"Take a few sips of this." I held the tumbler to her lips and urged her to drink.

"Argh, I can't." She slid under the blanket and pulled it over her head. "Just the thought of putting something in my mouth gives me the heebie jeebies," she muttered from under the covers. Angie had a smattering of freckles sprinkled across her nose. Her usually rosy pink complexion matched the white of her bedspread, making her freckles even more obvious.

"Come on. This will settle your stomach." I pulled the blanket aside and sat on the edge of the bed. "Have you taken anything?"

Angie leaped from the bed and rushed to the bathroom. From the sounds she made, it wasn't a minute too soon. She padded back to bed and crawled in.

"How long have you been like this?" I asked, holding the glass to her lips. "You look like crap."

"I was kind of queasy yesterday, but this morning it hit me with a vengeance. Dave cleaned out the fridge last night, and we ate all the leftovers we'd been stockpiling."

She hated to cook, and so did Dave. They lived off restaurant takeout and meals they could scavenge from friends and family. When they ran out of willing friends, they heated up frozen pizzas. I'd contributed more than my share to their collection of leftovers. Michelle and I hadn't been sick recently, so I felt confident it wasn't something I gave them.

"Where's Dave?" If it was food poisoning, he would be holed up somewhere in much the same shape as Angie.

"He had an early surgery." Angie continued to take baby sips. "He was fine when he left."

Dave Valenti owned a plastic surgery practice in town. We always joked that he'd seen most of the boobs in the county. Lately, I wondered if my cheating husband held that same distinction.

I tested her forehead with my wrist. "No fever. You had any chills?"

She shook her head. "Nope."

"How about achy muscles?"

Another shake. "The only achy muscle is my abdomen from all the barfing."

I placed the glass on the nightstand. "Probably something

you ate. You all need to be more careful with leftovers. There's a reason they put expiration dates on the stuff you get from the store. It would surprise me if Dave isn't hunched over a toilet at the hospital."

The color had started to return to her face. "Can you wet my washcloth?"

I did as asked. When I returned, she was sitting upright. "You look a little better. Are you still feeling nauseous?"

"Not so bad." She touched her matted hair. "I must look a fright. I haven't even combed my hair today."

Her chemically altered burgundy hair had certainly seen better days. When she was on patrol, Angie wore it slicked back in a bun at the nape of her neck "to keep the bad guys from grabbing it and yanking me bald," she always said. Off work, she wore it loose, falling just below her shoulders and with enough curl to have body. Today, she looked like she had a bad case of helmet head.

"Can I get you something to eat? Dry toast or crackers. I'm fresh out of chicken soup, and I know you don't have any. At least not any that hasn't been around for a while."

She blanched. "No. No food yet. I'll be okay. Just keep the clear soda coming. That seems to be helping."

"You missed all the hoopla at the high school. With all the rain we've had, the storm sewers backed up into the school. They canceled classes because of all the water. The new principal hired me to clean and was giving me the grand tour. When he opened the door to the maintenance room, one of the teachers was slumped over a workbench. Dead. He had a power drill cord wrapped around his neck."

Angie sat up a little straighter. "No way. All the good stuff happens when I call in sick. Who was it? Do I know him?"

"Steve Trupeli. He used to be married to Liz Blevins, my doubles partner from the club." I liked that Angie was getting her color back. She didn't look as pasty-faced as she had when I first came in.

"Oh, I recognize the name. Didn't know he was Liz's ex. I think he's involved with one of the dispatchers at the station."

"Seriously? He's in a long-term relationship with the guidance counselor at the high school."

"I'm pretty sure that's who she was seeing. Maybe I'm mistaken. I just heard a couple of the gals talking about him in the breakroom. What else? Who did it?" She threw her feet over the side of the bed. "Come in the bathroom and keep me company."

"No way. I can't stand watching anyone hang over the toilet. I'll stay right here, thank you very much."

"I'm gonna brush my teeth. That soda seemed to settle my stomach. I almost feel human again. Sit on the side of the tub and fill me in on all the dirt."

I told her what I knew, which didn't amount to much, but I left out the part about Steve being at Liz's house this morning. I needed to gather some information before I could form an opinion. Also, Liz had never answered my question about Marni's motive, so I still needed to ask about that. Then I could ease into a conversation about Liz and Steve.

I was still miffed at Liz for dumping me after my divorce, but I truly hoped she didn't kill Steve.

Angie spun around, toothbrush in hand, wagging it at me. "You're leaving something out."

I feigned ignorance. "*Moi*? I don't think so. The school flooded. We found a dead teacher in the maintenance room. Oh, you're right. I did leave something out. Zella still works there, and she married Tipsy Tommy the janitor, but they're retiring at the end of the semester. And he's the maintenance man now."

"Don't play coy. I'm a cop. Remember? It doesn't work

with me. My interrogation skills are superb." She wiped her mouth and padded back to the bedroom.

I followed. "You and Dave still coming over for Thanksgiving?" It was a stupid question. Of course, they'd be there. I was serving their favorite—food.

"Don't change the subject. Alder drew the case, didn't he?"

"Yep."

She straightened the sheets and pulled the spread over the pillows. "Well?"

"What do you want me to say? It was awkward. We haven't seen each other since summer." I smoothed a wrinkle from the spread and considered pulling a disappearing act. Seeing Alder again had dredged up feelings I wasn't willing to deal with yet. I didn't know if I'd ever be able to deal with them. My failed marriage had left me gun shy.

Michelle still lived at home, and I had to worry about her welfare and getting her through school. Even though Jessie was on her own, now that she was in a relationship, I saw less of her and constantly fought to maintain contact. It's not that I didn't like Brad. I did. But they were always on the go, and between visiting his parents and grandparents and the time they spent with friends, it seemed like Jessie didn't have nearly as much time for me as she used to. *Waa. Waa.* I sounded like a spoiled baby, but the truth was I felt left out.

"You're going to screw around and wind up letting him slip away. Honestly, you can't do better than Case Alder. He's hard-working and loyal to a fault." Angie threw open her closet door and rummaged around, pushing hangers back and forth.

"I know. He's a real catch. But . . ."

Angie turned around and planted both hands on her hips. "It's that Hunter guy, isn't it? You're steering clear of Alder because he doesn't have a trust fund or a big house. He earns a pittance compared to Hunter."

"Oh, for Pete's sake, you know me better than that." But I wondered if she might have a point. I'd been spoiled by my opulent lifestyle, and since I'd had to eke out a living, I didn't like it one bit. I missed getting manicures and pedicures. Now every cent had to be scrutinized to make sure I really needed to make the purchase.

"You've been spending a lot of time with Grant Hunter, and you're getting used to him taking care of your every whim. Don't think I haven't noticed the flower deliveries." Angie continued her tirade, and I tuned her out.

She didn't know anything about Grant Hunter. That's one part of my life I'd managed to keep away from her. Grant was safe. He and I had already had the "not ready for a relationship" conversation. And truth be told, I hadn't seen him in ages. His wife had been dead for years, and he was ready to dive back into dating, but he totally understood where I was coming from. A bear of a man, he made me feel safe and comfortable. He was a friend, someone who had helped me when my life sucked.

"Are you listening to me?" Angie flung a hanger in my direction.

I didn't realize I'd been biting my lip, but when the hanger hit me, I drew blood. "Jeez, look what you did." I pulled a tissue from the box on her nightstand and rubbed my mouth.

"Oh, good grief, you're such a baby."

"Takes one to know one," I quipped. "Hey, do you remember anything about Tommy from when we were in high school?"

"Nothing. Other than him going into rehab our senior year."

"What?"

"Don't you remember?" Angie pulled a pair of jeans out of

the closet and stepped into them. "I think it was our senior year. He was gone most of our last semester. Zella played cards with my mom and told her he'd had some problems when he came back from the army."

"It's starting to come back," I said.

Angie dropped the T-shirt she held. Her face went ashen, and she dashed to the bathroom.

My cell phone vibrated with an incoming text message.

PHILLIP: DON'T IGNORE ME. WE NEED TO TALK.

Leave it to my husband to harass me even when he was supposed to be hunting.

My phone vibrated again.

PHILLIP: JUST REMINDING YOU WE'RE STILL MARRIED UNTIL THE JUDGE MAKES IT FINAL.

ME: TELL THAT TO YOUR GIRLFRIEND.

PHILLIP: MEET ME FOR A DRINK MONDAY NIGHT.

ME: GET REAL. I'D RATHER EAT GLASS.

I shoved the phone in my pocket where it continued to vibrate and buzz like a giant, annoying gnat.

When we'd first separated and he'd started his quest to catch me violating the morals clause in our prenup, I'd been intimidated. Now I was just counting down the days until Tuesday. I had done nothing to violate that clause. After Tuesday, I would be a free woman—a free, single woman at the age of forty-eight. And . . . just like that I felt like an utter failure, just like my mother.

When Angie returned, she climbed back into bed. "Guess I'm not feeling so good after all."

I poured her another glass of soda and decided to take my loser-self home. "I'm out of here. If you've got the flu, I don't want any part of it."

"You stay out of this," Angie called behind me. "Let Alder do his job."

"Speaking of Alder," I said, "I need your advice."

Angie rubbed her hands in a scheming manner. "Lay it on me."

"Down, girl. I misplaced my purse at the school. Can you pull any strings? I know they won't let me in to look for it."

"For pity's sake, just call him. Then cancel your credit cards, if you haven't already."

CHAPTER SIX

"Cece's taste in clothing is definitely nothing to write home about, but she does know how to accessorize."
Nancy Lustbader

The next morning, Ed Jennings called and told me the police had given him the go-ahead to allow employees back in.

When I entered the building, it was apparent someone had already been hard at work. The water in the halls was gone, and big fans were blowing air around to aid in the drying effort. My job today was to get rid of the mud, and it was a big one.

The cafeteria, gymnasium, and front foyer hadn't been damaged. From the main entrance, I took the stairs down. The cafeteria and gym were on opposite sides of the hall with each entrance being elevated. It didn't seem like a logical layout, but Wickford High was old. I'd graduated in 1989, and it was old then. To accommodate the growing population, every couple years a new addition appeared. Nothing was ever torn down, just rearranged to make room for another classroom here or office there—a real hodgepodge of space.

I had just opened the door to the maintenance room to check for my purse when I heard my name.

"Cece, wait up."

I turned to see Alder jogging toward me. "It's okay to go in here, isn't it? Ed said you released it."

Alder nodded. "Sure, the team is finished."

"Any news on my purse?" I'd called him last night when I returned from Angie's.

"Sorry, I took a look around and didn't find it."

"Rats! I loved that purse, plus my wallet, identification, and credit cards were all in it."

"I'm sure it'll turn up, but I'll make a report just in case. Don't forget to cancel your cards."

"I did. I can't afford an unexpected shopping spree at my expense. I have enough of those with Michelle."

"Where's your sidekick, Nancy?" He glanced down at his watch. "Still at home getting her beauty sleep?"

"For your information, she ran out to Hunter Springs to pick up some supplies then she'll be here." I turned up my snark. "You're welcome to stop by and chat her up." Two could play his game.

I hoped to run into Liz to continue the conversation we'd had yesterday, but with Alder in the building, my investigation would be limited to "listening" to what she had to say. I'd tried to call her last night but got no answer. I'd left a message, and she hadn't returned my call.

"Um, no thanks. I'm out of here. You're on your own with the dingbat." Alder backed out of the room but then stuck his head in. "Call me if you learn anything."

I pounced. "Got anything in particular you need me to find out? I mean, is there anything I need to be *listening* for."

Alder grimaced, walking back in and giving me a worried look. "Oh, I'm going to be sorry for this. I can already tell."

"I'm kidding," I said. "I'll be on alert. Silent alert. Promise." *Sort of.* If he hadn't been standing right there, I would have crossed my fingers. Truth be told I couldn't wait to dig in and find out what I could. It was foolhardy, I knew, but I'd pay more attention this time around.

"Okay, I'll check in later. Take care and stay out of trouble." Alder gave my forearm a squeeze. His hand lingered a bit too long, and I felt the familiar zing.

I wiggled my arm from his grasp. "Go on, scram. I've got work to do."

Even though Nancy was growing on me, she still drove me nuts. She had a horrible gum chewing habit, which she made worse by constantly blowing enormous bubbles and then popping them. It wouldn't have been so bad, but the smacking was intolerable. And the constant cracking when they exploded gave me a headache. I'd begged her to stop, even offered her incentives. But since I'd forced her to quit smoking, she relied even more on the gum.

After checking in with Ed and inquiring about my purse to no avail, I went to work scrubbing the atrium area. It wouldn't do any good to start in the offices or classrooms. As long as people were tromping through the hallway, they'd drag mud on their shoes everywhere they went.

When I finished the atrium and hall, I took a break and headed to Liz's office. The room looked like a huge garage sale in progress. Every surface held boxes upon boxes of books, supplies, and files. She was on her hands and knees, head stuck in a cabinet when I walked in. I cleared my throat to get her attention. She rose too quickly and bumped her head.

"Oh, good grief," she said. "You scared the dickens out of me." She'd been busy this morning. The floor looked clean enough to pass a Martha Stewart inspection. One less floor for Nancy and me to clean.

"Sorry, I tried not to scare you." The room brought back memories of my years at Wickford High. The nurse's office hadn't changed much. Still the same pale green color—soothing. Back in my day, Nurse Sally had run the office with an iron fist. No one faked an illness, or she'd give you a dose of some nasty-tasting medicine. Times had changed. Now they couldn't give kids pain meds without a permission slip from a parent. "Hey, what do you do with the fakers these days?"

She stood and wiped her hands on her pants. "What?"

I laughed. "The ones who pretend to be sick to get out of class."

Liz pointed to a locked cabinet. "Between doling out prescription meds, administering insulin to diabetic students, and reviewing health history questionnaires, I don't have time for fakers. But if they come in with a complaint, I'm not allowed to ignore them." She shook her head. "Don't get me started. You got time for a cup of tea?" She pulled two mugs from a stand.

"Sure. I can't stay long. My assistant will be here in a little while."

"Any luck finding your purse?"

"Not yet. I canceled all the cards, so I'm not as worried. But I was hoping we could talk." I slung my coat over a chair and sat down. "Have the police made any headway in the investigation?"

Liz laughed. "I was about to ask you the same thing considering you have an inside track."

I didn't say anything. Again, the less said, the better.

Liz set the cups down and pulled out her chair. "That wasn't funny. Sorry. And no, I haven't heard a word. The detective was talking to Ed earlier, but that's all I know. It's kind of creepy around here. Everyone is walking around either looking at each other suspiciously or wearing a huge guilt trip."

It was entirely possible one of Steve's coworkers had killed him, and until the police arrested a suspect, everyone was under suspicion. To that end, I needed to remain vigilant and not let my guard down.

"I understand being suspicious, but why the guilt trip?"

"Steve wasn't well-liked. Ever since we divorced, he's been stringing Marni along. She's just too infatuated to see that he was never going to marry her. People around here are like family. We take care of one another. Everyone has tried to get her to see how hopeless her relationship was. I've kept my mouth shut, because I'm sure my advice would appear to sound like a jealous ex-wife. But Zella constantly hounds her to give him the boot. And lately Keith and TJ have started in on her too. And there's other stuff." She squeezed a stream of honey into her tea and offered the container to me.

I waved it off, preferring my tea *au naturel*. "Like what?"

"Take Zella for instance," she continued. "Everyone loves Zella. She'd do anything for you. When someone has a birthday, she always does up a cake and makes the day into a celebration. Not in her job description, but she does it anyway. Steve did something that upset her. I assume it had to do with Marni. Zella hasn't spoken to him for a month. His birthday came and went—no cake. Nothing. And Keith and Steve had a huge argument a couple days ago. Steve had him in a headlock. Tommy had to break it up."

"Which one is Keith again?" I asked.

"The older guy with the ponytail. Teaches science. We were all just holding our breath until Steve retired. And with his reduction in pay, that wasn't going to happen anytime soon."

"I remember seeing Keith yesterday," I said. "What were they arguing about?"

"Not a clue. Tommy might know. He was there when the argument started." She paused for a moment. "Or maybe he just came along while they were arguing. You'd have to ask him."

"How was your relationship with Steve? You mentioned yesterday that he'd been at your house."

Liz placed her hands around her cup and looked down. "It's not what you're thinking."

"I'm not thinking anything. You brought it up yesterday, remember? You're the one who indicated you might have a motive. Do you?"

Liz got up and shut the door. On the way back to her desk, she said, "Half the staff here has a motive."

I noticed how weary she looked, like something was weighing on her mind. "That's not what I asked."

"Lordy, can't you leave it alone?"

"Okay, so who else had motive? Marni? Keith? TJ? What about Ed?"

"Yes, yes, and yes. Probably Ed too. Who knows? Don't forget Zella and Tommy while you're at it. They all had run-ins with Steve at one time or another. Enough to kill him? I don't know, but I'm telling you—everyone's had a skirmish with him."

"What about Bill?"

Liz held up a hand. "Don't even think it. Bill went to the lodge yesterday morning—early. And all the guys are there, including Phillip."

Ack! Would Alder be questioning my soon-to-be ex to check out Bill's alibi? Talk about awkward. "So, start with Marni?"

"Like Zella said yesterday, Marni is pining away for a man who would never marry her. But lately she's stepped up her game. Started wearing more makeup, and her clothing style has definitely improved. She used to look pretty dowdy. Now her styles are current and attractive. She's even gotten flirty with a couple of the faculty members."

"Anyone in particular?" I asked.

Liz chewed her bottom lip. "I don't think it's anything really. I mean, Marni is harmless and really over the top for Steve, but lately I've seen her playing up to Keith and even TJ. And TJ is like twenty years younger." Liz shivered. "*Ack!* That kind of makes my stomach queasy. TJ laps up her attention. No one has much to do with him because they kind of feel if Steve could be railroaded, they could too. So, TJ's pretty much *persona non grata*."

"Making Steve jealous perhaps?"

"Either that or trying to get his attention." Liz paused for a sip of tea. "I was in that same spot one time—trying to get Steve to focus on me instead of whatever or whomever had his attention. Doesn't work with Steve. Once he focuses on someone or something else, he's a lost cause. No amount of dolling up would have helped Marni."

I needed to figure out what had Steve's attention. Possibly that dispatcher Angie told me about.

Nancy burst into the room. "Well, there you are. I've been looking everywhere." She breezed in wearing skintight jeans and a ruby red sweater with a plunging neckline and boots. Not rubber boots, but my Jimmy Choo lizard print boots. I knew they were mine, because I'd seen her eyeing them.

"Those are my boots!" I screamed. "Have you lost your mind? They cost a small fortune." In the days prior to my separation, I'd never thought about what I spent on shoes, or anything else for that matter. I loved those boots.

Nancy's lips turned down into a pout. "You said I could

wear them sometime. I figured now was as good a time as any."

"*Sometime* is not when you're working. Please take them off before they get ruined." I cringed. This wasn't the first time Nancy had raided my closet. I had told her time and again living over my garage didn't give her the right to go into my house unless I invited her.

Nancy unzipped my boots and slid them off. "What am I supposed to wear?"

Holy cripes! She didn't even have socks on. Her bare feet had been in my boots. "You should have thought of that before you helped yourself to my closet."

Liz looked from Nancy to me, a grin plastered on her face. "This must be your assistant."

I nodded and snatched my boots. "Liz, this is Nancy."

Nancy had plump, pouty lips, high cheekbones, and the nose of a veteran hockey player. Frizzed out hair, the color and texture of a withered sea sponge, framed her face. I had previously guessed her age to be about thirty-five but had since learned she was closer to forty-three. Her flawless skin and absence of laugh lines had caused me to underestimate her age. That and the fact that she acted like a hormonal teenager.

Nancy alternated lifting her feet. "Brrr. It's cold in here."

"You really going to make her walk around barefoot?" Liz asked.

I took a sip of tea and leaned back in my chair. "You got a better idea?"

"There's always the lost and found. Surely, we could scrounge up a pair of stray gym shoes for her."

Nancy grimaced.

"What? Wearing someone else's shoes didn't seem to bother you when you had mine on a minute ago." I turned to

Liz. "Speaking of lost and found, we can check for my purse while we're there."

"Good idea. Maybe someone turned it in."

As we headed to the office, Liz leaned in. "Please don't repeat what I told you to anyone. I'm sure it's probably nothing anyway. And I sure don't want to get Marni started."

"Did you tell Detective Alder any of this when he interviewed you?"

"No," Liz said. "I answered all his questions but didn't volunteer anything. I know better than that. I watch the police shows on TV."

CHAPTER SEVEN

"You can't blame a man for looking."
Keith Preston

My purse had not made its way to the lost and found. I knew I'd left it in the cafeteria. I had been sitting with Liz, but she claimed not to have seen it. The only other place I had been was the maintenance room and it wasn't there. My only conclusion was that someone had taken it. But why? It wasn't like I had any money.

We outfitted Nancy in stylish purple-and-orange-striped socks—school colors—and the grubbiest pair of tennis shoes I'd ever seen. Liz pressed her lips together, but I busted a gut laughing.

Nancy frowned. "This is so not nice."

"She kind of has a point." Liz giggled.

I waved them off dismissively. "Don't wear my stuff next time."

After I took my boots to the van, I armed Nancy with a mop and a bucket of soapy water.

"I've done the atrium and main hall." I pointed to a secondary hall close to the cafeteria. "I'll head down to the other end and meet you in the middle. When your water gets muddy, there's a janitor closet at the end of the hall where you can dump it out."

Nancy leaned against the mop, chomping an oversized wad of gum. "We'll be here until morning."

I exhaled, snatched the mop from her, and pushed it into the bucket of suds. "If it takes all night, then we'll be here all night too. That's what we get paid to do. And get rid of the gum. If Ed catches you, he'll have a coronary."

"I guess now wouldn't be the time to tell you that your mother's here," Nancy said.

I spun around so quickly, I tipped the bucket, sending soapy water across the floor. The hall behind me was empty.

"Not here, here. She's at your house, silly. Right after you left, she rang the doorbell." Nancy righted the bucket and began to push the mop around in long strokes.

There was so much wrong with what Nancy had just said I didn't know where to begin. First, she was not supposed to be in my house, but since she'd raided my closet, it was pretty obvious why she'd been there to answer the door.

Second, my mother lived in Tucson with husband number five or six. I couldn't keep track. I hadn't talked to her since Phillip left. The last time we'd talked, she assured me that Ned or Charles, whatever his name was, was a keeper. They were soul mates, destined to spend the rest of their lives living the good life. That was code for "he's rich, and I got myself a sugar daddy."

Third, how did Nancy know it was my mother and not some crazed, stalker lunatic?

Fourth, the thought of my mother being alone in my house scared the crap out of me. *Boundaries* was not a word she understood. She'd snoop just for the heck of it. I hadn't told her about my separation, because frankly, I was none too proud that my marriage had failed. My mother and I now had that in common along with our diminutive bustline.

"You left her alone in my house? How'd you even know who she was?" I pulled my phone from my pocket and punched in Angie's number. If she was home, she'd distract my mother until I got home.

"You're kidding, right? You look just like her. You've got more gray hair than she does, but she's probably got a better hairdresser." Nancy smacked her leg and cackled.

Angie took forever to pick up.

"What?" Her tone indicated whatever was ailing her yesterday still had a grip.

"Not any better?" I asked.

"Uh-uh." She emitted a low moan.

I couldn't ask her to ride herd on my mother. Angie would do anything for me, even if it meant hauling her sick butt out of bed and trudging next door to keep my mother from finding out all my intimate secrets. "You called the doctor yet?"

"It's just a stomach virus. I'll be okay." Her voice sounded weak.

I ran through my options, only to discover I had none. I'd have to leave Nancy here and go home. Once I figured out what my mother wanted, I could decide how to handle her. "I'm on my way home. Can I get you anything?"

"No, I'm okay. I just want to sleep." Angie's voice trailed off until I heard the familiar click of her disconnecting.

Nancy scowled and shoved the mop in the bucket. "You're not leaving me here with this whole mess, are you?"

"Yep. I'll be back when I find out what my mother wants. I'll make it up to you." I pocketed my phone and called over my shoulder, "Don't forget to change your water when it gets dirty."

I retraced my steps to Liz's office to grab my coat. At this rate, it would take all weekend plus some to get this place cleaned up. When I passed Marni's guidance office, I was surprised to see her sitting behind her desk with TJ sitting opposite. Her boyfriend had just been murdered—yesterday. And she was with TJ, of all people.

"You spying for the opposition?" a voice behind me said.

I jumped and let out a squawk. "What? No, I mean . . ." My words would not come.

Keith, the ponytailed science teacher, laughed. "Just teasing you. But seriously, what are you doing?"

Think fast. "I misplaced my purse and wanted to check with Marni to find out if she's seen it. But she has someone in her office, so I was just leaving. Have you seen it by any chance?"

"Umm, let me think." He tapped his forehead with a finger, delaying my exit.

Seriously, either you have, or you haven't. "Well?"

"What does it look like?"

"Long strap, rust-col—" This guy was screwing with me. I turned to leave.

"Hey, don't rush off. I haven't seen your purse, okay?" Keith caught up. "Don't get mad. We haven't been introduced." He whirled around in front of me, blocking the hall.

I pulled up quickly so I didn't run headlong into him. As much as I wanted to hang around and chat—*not*—I needed to get home. "I kind of thought Ed did that yesterday when he called all of you together in the cafeteria."

"So he did. My mistake." He stepped forward and extended a hand. "I'm Keith. If you need anything, give me a holler. My classroom is just down a ways. Be happy to show you around. Not often we get a pretty face in the place. Not one over eighteen anyway." His eyes focused directly on my chest.

Not that my chest is anything to look at, Mr. Obvious! Was he hitting on me or was he just creepy? I ignored his attempt to shake my hand. The last thing I needed was a creeper trying to pull me in for a hug. Or trying to cop a feel. You'd think a teacher would know better than to give off stalker vibes. "Thanks," I said. "I'm familiar with the school. Spent a few years here myself."

He didn't budge.

"Um, do you need something?"

"No, just offering a friendly face in this sea of backstabbers. You know where to find me."

"Okay then, good to know." I started around him, but he moved in front of me again. My nerves were already on edge and this guy wasn't helping. "If you don't mind, I have to go." I screwed up my courage and stepped around him and practically raced to Liz's office.

"Hope you find your purse!" he called after me.

———

"You're back," Liz said. "I'm just trying to straighten up my supply closet. Did you get your assistant squared away?"

"Yes. Sorry for her interruption. There's a long story about her, but I don't have time to go into it. My mother has shown up unexpectedly, and I need to get home and deal with her." I scanned the room looking for my coat.

"Did you need something?" Liz pushed a box aside with her foot.

"Left my coat here, but I don't see it." Lately, my memory faded about as fast as my energy level. "Must have left it in my car."

"Oh, I hung it on the coat rack behind you. Do you have a few minutes to finish our conversation? I do need to talk to someone."

Crap, of all the times, why did it have to be now. "I need to get home. How long are you going to be here?" I patted my coat pocket for my keys and breathed a sigh of relief when I felt them. "Maybe I can make it back in time for lunch. Would that work?"

"Sure, I need to scrub out the bottoms of all the lower cabinets before I finish emptying these boxes. I'll probably check in with some of the others to see if I can lend a hand." She ran a hand through her hair.

Liz had aged in the several months since we'd played tennis. And she didn't seem to be moving as effortlessly. Then again, neither did I. Age had a way of sneaking up and zapping looks and physical attributes.

"Great. I'll look you up when I get back." Curiosity more than anything made me want to stay and chat, but I couldn't risk leaving my mother alone. For a minute, I thought about calling Jessie to see if she had time to swing by the house, but she had a crazy schedule and my mother wasn't her responsibility. No, this was one job I needed to handle.

As I was headed to my car, I saw Marni sitting alone in her office. I tapped on the doorframe.

"Do you have a minute?" I asked when she looked up.

"Sure, come on in."

No telling what kind of havoc my mother would cause before I got home, but I couldn't let this opportunity pass me by. The guidance office hadn't changed much since I was in school. College posters of Harvard, Yale, and several other Ivy League schools lined the walls. I guess, to make the students aim high. I'd always wondered why the state schools were absent. Still wondered, because they were still absent.

Marni lifted a pile of brochures from the side chair next

to her desk. "Sorry, I piled stuff all around to keep it off the floor so you could clean."

"No problem. I appreciate you making it easier on me."

"I know you're friends with Liz," she said.

"We used to play tennis together, but that was a while ago." If I played down our friendship, she might open up to me.

"I don't know if you were aware, but everyone here has been trying to get me to break up with Steve. Everyone except Liz. She's never once said a word to me. It makes me wonder why. I knew he was never going to marry me, but if everyone else was so against him, why wasn't she?" She wrung her hands in her lap.

Marni was a slip of a woman, not more than five feet and barely one hundred pounds. I only knew what Liz had told me about her, and she hadn't painted a very good picture of the woman.

"Maybe she thought it would sound like sour grapes coming from his ex-wife," I said.

"Is that what she said?"

I asked for this. Now I was planted squarely in the middle. "Have you talked to Liz about how she felt?" Asking a question with a question always proved to be a good deflection.

"No. I don't know if I could trust her answer. Steve's been acting really strange lately. He was up to something, but he wasn't sharing it with me. I'm pretty sure it involved Liz."

I leaned in. "Any clue what was going on?"

"He's been getting a lot of calls on his cell that he takes in private. He never had any secrets from me. But a couple of weeks ago, something changed that. The calls started and he began acting nervous and secretive. And I found a business card for a private detective."

"Do you think it has something to do with him being removed as athletic director?"

"I don't know what to think. Why would he be in contact with a private detective?"

"Do you still have the card?" I asked.

Marnie shook her head. "No, the name was unique like Quentin or Quinlan Investigations."

The morning he was killed, he stopped by my place for breakfast on his way to work. While we were eating, he got five calls. His cell phone never rings that often in a week, much less in a mere half hour. Something was up, sure as I'm sitting here. And I'd lay money that Liz is involved."

"Do you think he was investigating Liz or maybe her husband?"

"I can't imagine him not telling me if he was, but that's what I'm leaning toward. I followed him after he left my house, and he went straight to hers. Well, not straight. He sat at the end of her street until her husband left. Then he went. She was standing on the porch waiting for him. She knew he was coming." Marni's face flushed and her hands trembled. "I know losing the athletic stipend has caused him financial difficulty, but he told me not to worry about it, that he was taking care of it. But I worry at what cost."

"Maybe it had to do with one of their kids." Who knew? Divorce or not, once you had kids together, you were connected for life whether you liked it or not. The thought of dealing with Phillip the rest of my life made my stomach hurt.

"I thought about that, but Steve tells me about his kids. We've never had secrets or parts of our lives that were off limits. It had to be something else, and the only thing I can think of is they were having an affair."

"But the private detective, what do you suppose that was about?"

"Who knows? I was losing traction in our relationship. But there was something up with him and Liz. I do know that."

"Liz and Bill seem happy together. I can't imagine her taking up with Steve again. She'd never do anything to hurt her husband."

"Steve and Liz have always had a relationship, maybe not sexual, but they've been way chummier than most divorced couples," Marni said.

Sounded like jealousy to me. "Maybe so, but I think it's great that they've been able to maintain their friendship. That's a hard thing to do after a divorce. And it's even harder to have an amicable split."

Marni laughed. "Sounds like you're speaking from experience."

"Oh, yes I am. It's still pretty fresh too. I don't know if I'll ever be able to maintain a friendship with my almost-ex. I'll do what I have to for my kids, but it's for them. If I didn't have to see him again, it would be too soon. And I will never be able to have a relationship with his new girlfriend."

Marni gave me an icy stare.

I'd gone too far. "Look, I didn't mean to come off sounding so bitter, but it just spilled out. This whole situation with my husband is new, and I haven't fully processed it."

"No worries," she said.

Before I did more damage, I excused myself.

CHAPTER EIGHT

"Cece needs her mama's touch to get herself organized."
Gigi Evans

No car in my driveway was a good sign. Maybe my mother had thought twice about dropping in on the spur of the moment and decided to check into a hotel. My hopes died a painful death when I opened my front door and smelled the faint odor of cigarette smoke. Georgie Evans, or Gigi as my girls called her, was in the house.

The nickname bestowed on my mother came from my older daughter. Mother had been adamant that she was too young to be a grandmother and insisted Jessie call her by her first name, only Jessie's version came out Gigi. It stuck.

I followed the stench, passing five bulging suitcases and a rolling duffle bag. This was no ordinary visit. I recognized the telltale signs of escape. Gigi's sugar daddy must have turned off the charm. My most vivid memories of childhood included some form of escape carrying all our worldly goods in paper sacks and cardboard boxes. Anytime the going got tough, Gigi got going, either down a fire escape in the middle of the night while some alcoholic boyfriend slept off his drunken rage or sneaking off when the rat went out to buy more liquor. The result usually remained the same; we'd wind up at my grandpa Earl's trailer or in a fleabag motel always with my mother promising it would be different next time. It never was.

All my kitchen cabinets were open and the contents stacked on the breakfast bar, counters, and every available surface. Another telltale sign Georgie Evans was in the house. Apparently, my organizational skills were still not on par with her expectations. If she stayed here long, she'd have my whole house turned on end, because putting all that stuff back would be on me—under her direction. Nothing I did pleased her. I shoved a stack of bowls back in the same cabinet they'd been in and then went to look for her.

Gigi, all five-foot-two of her, perched on my sofa with her feet propped up on the coffee table—shoes and all. A smattering of ashes trailed along the leather-covered arm of the sofa, and she was using my favorite teacup for an ashtray. It hadn't escaped me that she'd rearranged the display of photos on the mantel over my fireplace.

I gritted my teeth.

"Lordy, you look all wrung out, Cece," Gigi said. "You need to be taking better care of yourself, honey."

The age lines she'd once sported around her eyes and mouth were gone. Nancy had been right about the hair color. Gigi's hair was a beautiful honey blonde, styled in a perky swing bob. Instead of her usual polyester pants and thrift store top, she wore a pair of gray wool slacks and a tasteful ivory-and-gray sweater set.

"Mother, you know I don't allow smoking in my house." I took the cigarette from her, carried it to the kitchen, and held it under the faucet. "It sets a bad example for Michelle," I called over my shoulder. "Not to mention it's an unhealthy habit."

"Still playing nurse, aren't you?" She set the cup on the sink and leaned in to kiss my cheek. "Nice to see you too, Cecelia."

I backed away, smelling not only cigarettes but also alcohol on her breath. And it was barely ten in the morning. "Have you been drinking?"

"I just had one little scotch," she mumbled. "A little pity party for me, and apparently for you too."

I spun around. "Wh-What are you talking about?"

"When were you going to tell me that you're getting divorced?" Gigi shook her finger in my face. "I have to come all the way to Wickford to find out that my baby girl's got big troubles. Big troubles in River City."

Gigi's reference to her favorite musical almost made me laugh, but I held firm. When I was growing up, on the numerous occasions we'd find ourselves adrift in a seedy motel, we'd amuse ourselves by taking in the musicals at The Muny in St. Louis. Lucky for us, the outdoor amphitheater had free seats in the nosebleed section for those willing to come early and wait in line.

"I had to hear it from a complete stranger. And by the way, who was that? I thought I had the wrong house."

I thought about telling her to mind her own business, but I remembered all the nights she'd cried on my shoulder promising me a better life. She meant well. She just never got it right. "It's a long story, Gigi."

She pulled me into a hug. "I've got all the time in the world, baby girl. Come on and tell me what's going on."

If it hadn't been for the noxious odor, I might have snuggled in and accepted her comfort. Lord knew I ached for a little sympathy, but not when it came with cigarettes and my scotch.

"How about I fix us tea while you put my cabinets back together," I said, backing away. "It looks like we've both got some talking to do."

"I'll help you get organized later." Gigi made herself comfortable at the breakfast bar while I busied myself making tea. When she reached for another cigarette, I shot her a disapproving look. "On the patio. I won't have you fouling my house with your nasty habit."

She shoved the pack aside. "Okay, okay. I'm trying to quit anyway. This will be just the thing I need to force me to give them up."

I emptied the teacup she had been using for an ashtray and placed it into the dishwasher, shivering at the thought of ever sipping tea from it again. I set two cups of tea on the breakfast bar and pulled up a stool across from my mother.

"Where's your car?" I asked. "I didn't see one in the driveway."

Gigi waved her hand dismissively. "I caught the red-eye flight from Tucson. Then called a cab when I got to St. Louis."

"Criminetly, that had to cost a fortune."

"Pish posh, Ned can afford it."

"Tell me what happened," I said, watching the steam from my cup swirl until it disappeared. Kind of what I was hoping to do—the disappearing, not the swirling.

Gigi sipped her tea and frowned. I knew she'd have preferred coffee, but since Phillip left, I had none. Tea and diet soda fulfilled my need for caffeine, and I refused to let Michelle get hooked. At seventeen, she displayed enough of her dad's habits. But I remained steadfast about the coffee.

"Where to start?" Gigi's green eyes flashed. "Ned's a good guy. The best. One in a million, but he's turned into a golf addict. Ever since he retired, that's all he wants to do, play golf or go to the range and hit a bucket of balls. I want to go to the movies once in a while. And the worst part is he wants me to go with him—every stinking time. He wants me attached to him like a tick. And when he's not dragging around a golf bag, he's camped out in his recliner waiting for breakfast, lunch, or dinner. Since he retired, I've become a short-order cook." Gigi sighed. "You know me, Cecelia. I hate to cook. I'm certainly not a nurturer."

Truer words were never said. In our relationship, I'd been the nurturer. I was the one who kept her from falling apart after each breakup. I cooked, cleaned, and kept our laundry up—never good enough for her approval. But if I didn't do it, it didn't happen. She sometimes worked two or three part-time jobs to keep us afloat. Household help was out of the question. We could barely keep a roof over our heads as it was.

"Sounds like Ned's at odds with himself since his routine changed." I thought about how my own routine had changed since Phillip left. At least I stayed busy. If I didn't, I'd probably have gone mad, or driven Michelle or Jessie crazy wanting to latch on to their lives.

Gigi laughed. "I feel like Pac-Man following him around biting at his heels."

"What are you going to do about it?" I hoped she just needed a break and that before the end of the week she'd be on her way back to Tucson. I had enough worries without having to play nursemaid to my mother. We could maintain a good relationship as long as it was from a distance, and I wanted to keep it that way.

"I left him. That's why I'm here, and it looks like I'm not a minute too soon. It'll be like old times, baby girl, only with my grandbabies around." She swept her arms in a grand gesture.

I cringed and swallowed hard. That was what I was afraid of. I'd grown up since our "old times." Gigi hadn't.

I pushed away from the breakfast bar and paced to the sink and back. "Oh, no. No. No. No. You are getting right back on a plane and going to Tucson. You and Ned need to work this out. He's the best thing that's happened to you in . . . well, in forever, Gigi. Do not ruin it this time. He's a good man. You said so. How many times have you told me that if only you could find a good man, you'd never let him go? This is him. He treats you like a queen. I'm not going to allow you to destroy this." I spilled the desperate words so quickly, if drool had sputtered from my mouth, I wouldn't have been surprised.

My mother had a way of turning me into a crazy woman. I pulled the phone from its cradle and shoved it at her. "Call him. Now! You call him and apologize. Get down on your knees and tell him you're sorry and that you will be on the next plane to Tucson. I'll take you to the airport. Better yet, I'll drive you to Tucson." I stopped and took a breath. God, I hated when I got like this. An intense heat enveloped my cheeks, neck, and face as a hot flash reared its ugly self.

She waved off the phone. "Calm down. Look at you. You've worked yourself into quite a tizzy." She tipped her cup and drained it. "I am not calling Ned. You can just forget it. Now, do you have any more of that tea?"

Ack! "How long . . . umm . . . how long are you staying?" My palms began to perspire.

"It's not like I have anywhere to go. I thought I'd hang around here. Keep you company. The holidays are right around the corner, and I haven't seen my grandbabies in ages. I heard Jess has a man. That's a feat in itself. Thought that girl would turn into an old maid. And without Phillip to nag me, I'll be quite comfortable for as long as you want me to stay." Her eyes narrowed to slits. "Is there a reason you don't want me to stay? You got yourself another man, Cecelia? Or a woman? Have you turned into a lesbian? There ain't no shame in that, baby girl."

"I am not a lesbian, Mother, and I do not have a new man. Phillip's side of the bed is barely cold."

"Well, if you aren't swinging the other way, who was that woman who let me in? Nancy—was that her name?"

That's what I disliked most about my mother—twenty questions—and each question begat another question. Her mouth motored endlessly. I had to figure out a way to convince her to go home to Ned. "Nancy lives over the garage. She works for me." I groaned. Now why did I have to tell her that?

Gigi seized the opportunity I'd just tossed her. "Works for you? What the what? You got you a little business? That's perfect! You can put your mama to work." She sidled up to me at the sink. "I'm a good worker. You know that. Who worked three jobs while you were growing up?" She smiled a wide, toothy grin and flashed recently capped teeth.

Uh-oh, major guilt trip in progress. But honestly, she was a good worker, and I had my hands full with the mess at the school.

What was I thinking?

Maybe just until after Thanksgiving. Now that she was here, it seemed cruel to make her leave. But after the holiday, she was gone. And no way was she staying until Christmas. If I gave in on that, she'd never leave. "I started a little cleaning business. Maybe you could help me out for a couple days. We're kind of busy right now and with the holiday coming up . . . well, you could hang around until Thanksgiving, see the girls and catch up with them. But after that, you and Ned need to work out your problems. How does that sound?"

"The job and the holiday sound great, but I'm not going

back to Ned, so you can put that idea out of your head. He's got golf on the brain, and I want my independence."

I wanted to point out that working for me and living in my house wasn't my idea of independence, but rather than argue, I nodded. This predicament required a well thought out plan, and frankly, my brain was too frazzled to figure out what I was going to do. But I'd do something. Gigi wasn't going to be camping out at Chateau Cavanaugh any longer than necessary.

"Help me get this kitchen back together and I mean help. Don't just tell me where you think it should go. I want it all back where it was."

CHAPTER NINE

"Cece always brings a smile to my face."
Grant Hunter

After Gigi and I replaced the contents of my cabinets, I searched my house and van again for my purse and came up empty-handed. I decided it had to be at the school, but just in case, I took my stash of mad money that I kept in the safe in my closet. I wasn't about to let a missing purse deprive me of finding out what Liz had to say. My purse would eventually show up. I'd just misplaced it, and as soon as I could retrace my steps, I'd find it. With Gigi in tow, I headed back to the school.

Miraculously, Nancy had made headway in her cleaning efforts. She was outside Liz's office when I returned to school.

After I formally introduced her to Gigi, I asked, "When you were helping yourself to my boots this morning, did you by any chance see my purse?"

Nancy put her finger on her chin as if in deep thought. An

oxymoron if ever there was one. "Um, there's a cute leather crossbody one in your closet that I'm dying to use."

"You'll be *dying* if I ever catch you with it," I said. "And I meant the one I've been using—leather spice-colored shoulder bag."

"Nope," she said and continued to drag her mop around in large swirls. "Oh, Grant called and said they released two more condos for us."

"He called you?"

"Yeah, I've been doing most of the work out there, so I guess he figured he'd just cut out the middleman." Nancy grinned. "It's okay, isn't it? He knew you had your hands full here."

"Sure," I said, but I wasn't so sure at all. I made a note to call Grant and check in when my schedule slowed down. Nancy was too much of a goofball to trust her to handle scheduling details with the one job that consistently brought in money. "Okay, you head out there and get started. I'll work here today."

"What about me?" Gigi asked.

Nancy frowned.

"You stay with me. We've got a ton to do here," I said.

Nancy's deeper frown made her look like some sad clown. "What?"

"Is she helping?" Nancy asked. "Grant wants these condos done before the weekend because they have a big sales promotion going on. If she helped me, I'd get done faster."

"I don't think so. We haven't even started in the classrooms or offices."

"That's the beauty of it. It doesn't take a lot of effort out at the condos, but it takes a while. If she and I knock it out, then we could all team up back here."

I thought about it and agreed it was probably the best solution.

After Nancy and Gigi left for Hunter Springs, I went to work in the classrooms off the east wing. At noon I stuck my head in Liz's office. She wasn't there, so I sent a text message to let her know I was ready for lunch. Just to cover the bases, I decided to leave a note. I grabbed a sheet of paper from a blank notepad on Liz's desk and saw an earring lying next to her phone. A dangly silver feather with turquoise and coral stones inlaid along the center—a twin to the one I had seen in the maintenance room next to Steve's body.

I pulled my phone out to call Alder but heard voices coming from the hallway. Alder said to listen and see what I could find out. I pocketed my phone and peeked out Liz's door. Marni and TJ stood outside Marni's office.

"Pull yourself together," Marni said, pushing him inside with a shove. "Everyone's going to hear your whining. You don't have anything to worry about."

"But, everyone's going to think—"

"Oh, there you are," Liz said. "I got your text. You ready to go?"

"Uh, yeah." I glanced over her shoulder just as Marni shut her door. "They didn't look so lovey dovey just now."

"Who? Marni and TJ?"

"That's the second time I've seen them together today."

"Meh! Marni is such an insecure twit, it's no telling. TJ feeds her insecurity. Come on. I'm starving." Liz took her coat from the hook and grabbed her keys. "I'll drive."

I glanced over my shoulder at the earring, wishing I had snatched it up when I had the chance. "Maybe I should stay here. I got a good start on the classrooms and probably shouldn't break my momentum."

Nancy had finished the entire hallway in the wing where

Liz's and Marni's offices were located. At this rate, we might have a shot at finishing before the holiday. Ed Jennings had told me that was his one requirement for me taking the job. He needed to get the school back in operation, and I didn't want it hanging over my head during my Thanksgiving celebration.

"Did you hear me?" Liz snapped her fingers.

"What?"

"I said, don't be ridiculous. It will be waiting when you get back." She gave me a gentle nudge. "What sounds good?"

"How about Café du Soleil?"

"Perfect!"

Grant had introduced me to the little restaurant a few months back. It sat on Main Street, overlooking the Missouri River.

As we exited the building I said, "I can drive."

"In that van? I don't think so. We can ride in style in my birthday present."

Liz jabbered all the way to her car—a shiny new Lexus.

"Which way? I've heard of the place but never been there," Liz said.

After I provided directions, we arrived at our destination. Liz parked and we made our way across the cobblestone streets of the older section of Wickford. The buildings along this stretch dated back to Lewis and Clark days, and the ambience was befitting. With Thanksgiving less than a week away, most merchants were gearing up for the Christmas shopping season. Lampposts were bedecked with greenery and bright red ribbons. Twinkling lights edged windows frosted with fake snow. I dreaded the holidays, the first since Phillip left. I'd miss the gala parties at the country club, festive open houses laden with fattening sweets, and the pompousness of the Cavanaugh Christmas that my mother-in-law always insisted on.

The hostess had seated us before I recognized my mood for what it was—pity. I shrugged it off, hoping I could make it through the holidays without bringing the rest of my family down. I owed it to Michelle and Jessie to make it the best holiday ever. As if I could erase their dad's shortcomings. I couldn't make up for the errors of his ways with money, but I could push aside my feelings and embrace the spirit of the holidays.

"Earth to Cece," Liz said. "You look like you're a thousand miles away. You okay?"

The closeness I'd once felt for Liz had dissipated just like my marriage. In the past I would have shared my feelings. Now I felt like our friendship was history, evaporated when my status as Phillip's wife had been jerked out from underneath my feet. It was clear that Angie, the friend who had stuck by me regardless, was the only person with whom I could share my pain.

"I'm fine. My mother arrived this morning. As if the holidays aren't stressful enough, now I have to keep her from reorganizing my house. She excels at pointing out my shortcomings and making me feel inadequate." I laughed, hoping Liz didn't see the real reason for my distraction. She'd been through divorce, so she'd probably had some of the same feelings I felt now. Except by marrying Bill Blevins, she had moved up in the world and acquired status, instead of the other way around.

"Mine is happily ensconced in a retirement village in Florida. She complains if the temperature falls below seventy, so I don't have to worry about her setting foot in Missouri before April."

"Apparently, weather isn't an issue with mine. She lives in Tucson and left Arizona to come here in November."

A tinkling bell at the front of the café announced another customer. I glanced up and saw Grant Hunter with Brad,

Jessie's boyfriend. They both nodded to me and angled their way to my table. Grant bent and deposited a hasty kiss on my cheek. I felt a blush rise and watched for Liz's reaction. She opened her menu and peered over the top. Grant and I weren't seeing each other, at least not in a romantic way, but he had a way of making me feel special—the flowers for instance. I needed to speak to him about that, but this was not the time.

"Morning ladies," Grant said, his Texas roots showing in his voice.

Brad stood to the side, looking nervous. I suppose his boss kissing his girlfriend's mother was a bit unnerving. I had been ecstatic when Jessie and Brad hit it off. Jessie dated a lot but had never had anyone serious in her life. Meeting Brad had changed that. They'd been seeing each other exclusively, and I even began to imagine that Jessie had met "the one."

"Grant. Brad," I said. "This is Liz Blevins. Liz, this is Grant Hunter and Brad James."

"Nice to meet you." Liz motioned with her eyes to Brad.

I laughed. "I was just about to tell Liz that Jessie was dating the nicest young man. Isn't that so, Brad?"

Brad turned red all the way to his ears. "If you say so, ma'am."

Grant cuffed him on the shoulder. "Of course, it's the truth. Don't be modest, boy."

Brad smiled a wide smile that a future mother-in-law could be proud of. Not that he and Jessie were near making an announcement, but a mother could hope and offer encouragement whenever necessary.

"I was going to give you a call later. You've been pretty scarce out at the project," Grant said. "It's short notice, but a client had a spare set of tickets for *The Nutcracker* Sunday afternoon. Would you be interested?"

Liz raised an eyebrow.

"I'm sorry. I can't. My mother showed up unexpectedly." I squirmed in my seat knowing that I'd get the third degree from Liz after Grant and Brad left.

Grant pretended to pull a knife from his chest. "Rejected right here in front of my employee and your friend."

"Not rejection," I said. "I have to deal with her. I'm really sorry."

"It's not a big deal. I just didn't want to squander the free tickets. I don't know much about ballet but know how ladies like that sort of thing. If you change your mind, let me know." He turned to Brad. "Come on, son. Let's let these gals eat their lunch in peace. We've got business to discuss. Maybe you can use those tickets to take Jessie."

We said our goodbyes, and Grant flagged down the hostess.

"Wow, he's a smooth talker," Liz said. "And real good-looking too. Is there something going on I need to know about?"

"No. He's a good friend. Nothing else." I left out the part about me working for him. I still had my pride. Liz might have been a friend at one time, but she still belonged to the country club and hob-nobbed with all my other so-called friends who had turned their backs on me. Plus, she had a direct pipeline to Hazel, my mother-in-law. And the whole lot of them would be together tonight for her girls' get-together. I did not want to be the center of attention.

"I don't think I've ever seen him around. Does he live in Wickford?

"I'm not sure where he lives," I said. "He's originally from Dallas or Houston or somewhere down there."

"Ever since that show *Dallas*, I've loved Texans. Is he an oil man or cattleman?"

"Actually neither, he's a developer. That huge development out near the county line is his."

"Hunter Springs. That place is amazing. Bill and I looked at a house out there. Very palatial. This one had a pool and five bedrooms and a stunning view."

I picked up the menu and changed the subject. "What are you having?" Besides gloating.

Liz took the hint and we made small talk until the server took our orders. Liz told me about her newest grandchild, a baby boy born to her oldest daughter. I told her about Brad and how Michelle's grades were the best they'd ever been. I neglected to mention Michelle's new job, a sure sign the tide had turned on our friendship. Liz and I had never been close like Angie and me, but as tennis partners for five years, we'd shared plenty of ups and downs along the way.

When our salads arrived, I dug in, grateful for a chance to take a rest from trying to come up with stuff to talk about.

Liz picked up her fork and hesitated. "Steve was going to take me to court."

I stopped mid-chew, not quite sure what her revelation meant. They'd been divorced more than ten years. What purpose would he have to sue her?

"When we divorced, we divided everything equally. Since we were both employed by the district, we had roughly the same salary, so there was no alimony. We had joint custody of the kids, so there was no child support. An amicable split—that's what everyone, even the judge, called it." She paused and took a drink of water laced with lemon. "We'd even managed to remain friends, celebrating holidays and birthdays as a family, even though we weren't. After I married Bill, we still tried to include Steve in our holidays. It took a while for Bill to warm up to the idea, but he did it for my kids' sake. Then Steve started wanting to include Marni, and she wanted to be my best friend. I drew the line at that. They were welcome at family events, but she and I will never be chummy."

Her revelation set me on edge. I wasn't sure what any of this had to do with me. As much as we'd talked in the past, we'd never shared this type of detail. Mostly our conversations had been the benign chit-chat about the irritating stuff our spouses did. We'd shared recipes, gossip, and the latest exploits of our kids, not financial stuff and certainly not information about the relationship between her spouse and ex-spouse.

"Steve never acted like it bothered him that Bill had money or that I now had the kind of house I'd always longed for. Bill sprang for a trip to the Caribbean last year when the kids decided they wanted a tropical Christmas, and we invited Steve and Marni along. Did Steve refuse? No, he sat on the beach just like the rest of us, drinking tropical drinks and enjoying the break from winter. Now the ingrate has the nerve to sue me." She stabbed a chunk of lettuce and shook it at me. "That's what I get for creating an amicable split. I should have left him alone to stew in his own misery instead of including him and making like we were one big, happy family. My behind." She shoved the lettuce in her mouth and chewed furiously.

"Did something happen?" I imagined that Steve had injured himself at Bill and Liz's house or perhaps a car accident with Liz at the wheel.

"He was going to reopen our divorce case and sue me for alimony and half my retirement. Can you believe it?" She forked a grape tomato and swirled it around the plate. "What's this world coming to?"

Their divorce had been finalized more than ten years ago. I'd never heard of such a thing and couldn't imagine what lawyer in his right mind would take on such a suit. "Wait, can he even do that? Take you back to court, I mean. I thought once the divorce was settled, it was over and done with."

"Apparently there was some loophole, and the pensions

were not part of the divorce decree. We didn't even think about it, and now he's claiming his attorney was incompetent. Anyway, he's been investigating if he can still claim a part of mine, and his new attorney seems to think he can and even get alimony." Liz leaned in. "Please, please don't say anything to anyone."

I was pretty sure my mouth was hanging open. Would my divorce be dangling over my head for the rest of my life like a guillotine waiting to slam down and decapitate me? "Unbelievable."

"Apparently it's the new trend. A former spouse falls on hard times and wham, he or she goes after what their ex has."

"Surely after this long, he doesn't have a prayer of getting anything. Does he?" In her case, she had a ton of assets, or at least Bill did. The Blevinses weren't hurting financially. Steve, on the other hand, was losing a good portion of his income and not nearly eligible for retirement, and with his track record, landing a position at another district as athletic director was out of the question.

"That's what I thought, but after I saw a lawyer, I'm not so sure. There's been a couple of recent cases where the ex-spouse has been made to pay or divvy up the retirement. With Bill's income, Steve could take us to the cleaners."

"Oh, Liz. That seems so unfair. I mean after all the hospitality you and Bill have shown him. Why would he ever consider that you and Bill should support him?" My lunch sat in a lump in my stomach. Who would think that a decision made so long ago would have after-effects even today. Would it come to that with Phillip and me? Not if I had anything to do about it. I didn't need Phillip's money. It hadn't done much to keep me happy in the thirty years we were married, and I couldn't imagine being dependent on him the rest of my life. What, indeed, was this world coming to?

"Do you see my dilemma?" Liz asked, wiping at the corner of her mouth with her napkin.

"Not really. With Steve out of the picture, you should be relieved." The minute the words were out of my mouth, I knew exactly the dilemma Liz faced.

The image of the earring burned a hole in my brain.

CHAPTER TEN

"They always say the spouse did it, but what about the ex-spouse? I couldn't look any guiltier."
Liz Blevins

Liz must have noticed the light bulb going off over my head. "Now you see what I mean." She nodded. "I had motive and opportunity. He'd been at my house that morning."

I decided to keep the little tidbit about the earring to myself. But I also needed to call Alder before Liz got back to her office. "Liz, anyone could have had the same opportunity. I mean it's not like they found you standing over him." I thought back to everyone who had been at the school when Steve's body was found. Since he'd been discovered after he'd been to Liz's house, that made his time of death sometime that morning.

I mulled over the suspects in my mind. There were only a handful of people at the school when Steve's body was discovered. I guess I'd have to count myself too. Though, I didn't even know Steve Trupeli, so in the eyes of the police that had to mean something.

With what she'd just told me, Liz popped to the top, along with TJ, Keith, and Marni. Ed, Tommy, and Zella were next. The thing that bothered me was the sheer force it would take to kill someone by strangling them with a cord. Marni barely weighed a hundred pounds. Tommy was muscular but really small and old. Zella was old and not in good shape at all. And Liz didn't look so fit either. Keith looked like Ichabod Crane with no upper body strength. TJ was the only athletic one in the bunch.

Liz and I hadn't met until she married Bill. My doubles partner had just moved to Dallas about the time that Bill started bringing Liz around. When I found out Liz had played tennis in college, we made fast friends and started playing twice a week at the club. The only knowledge I had of Steve was what Liz told me, and I'd never met him or even known his name. She'd always referred to him as her ex.

"I need your help," Liz whispered across the table.

"Help with what?" I thought I knew where this was going but hoped it was something else, like maybe she needed me to finish cleaning her office. Though it sparkled, so that wasn't it. I gulped.

"Someone at the school killed Steve. I just need to find out who else had a motive. The police aren't going to look beyond me." Tears sprang to her eyes. "He brought this on himself, and I'll be darned if I go down for it."

"I don't know what I can do. I didn't even know him." I had a bad, bad feeling. If I got involved with another one of Alder's cases, he would find a way to lock me up. Actually, if it hadn't been for me, the last case would have never been solved; the evidence would still be lying at the bottom of the county dump. The case before that would have probably resulted in Jessie's best friend going to prison if I hadn't found evidence that linked the real killer to the murder. However, Detective Alder didn't see things quite the way I did.

"You've got access to the whole school. You can look around in places that I can't. Plus, you can ask questions, and the staff will never get suspicious. If I start poking around, everyone will wonder what I'm up to, especially if it gets around that Steve was trying to get hold of my retirement." Liz reached into her purse and extracted a tissue. "Cece, you've got to help me. And you've got experience in solving murders."

"Well . . ." I hedged. I felt sorry for Liz, and we did have a past. I was already helping Alder, and I did have access to everyone involved. But there was the issue of that earring. I needed to bring that to Alder's attention before Liz and I left here. I wondered if Liz was trying to get me on her side to throw me off. Seven months ago I wouldn't have hesitated, but our friendship had taken a dive off a cliff. Did I dare put myself out there?

"Please," Liz pleaded. Her tears had subsided, but the sadness in her eyes tugged at my heart.

"I guess I could look around, keep my ears open, but that's as far as it goes. I'm not exactly on the best terms with the cops. They weren't happy with my involvement in the last case. I have to keep a low profile. Do you understand?"

"I do. Oh, Cece, you don't know how much this means to me. Thank you so much. I don't know how I'll ever repay you."

The look of relief on her face told me I'd made the right decision. "You could start by picking up the tab for lunch."

"Gladly. If you can get me out of this mess, I'll owe you a lot more than lunch."

"I'm going to visit the restroom before we leave." I prayed Liz wouldn't follow along. When I got to the bathroom, I called Alder's cell and told him about the earring in Liz's office and how it matched the one on the workbench in the maintenance room where Steve Trupeli was found. There might have been hope for salvaging my friendship with Liz. But first, I had to know if she was guilty of killing her ex-husband.

CHAPTER ELEVEN

"I feel bad for telling Alder about Liz's earring, but he would have found out sooner or later."
Cece Cavanaugh

When we returned to school, Alder met Liz at the door. He asked to speak to her in private, so I headed to Marni's office. He'd promised me that he'd keep my name out of it. I felt like a snake for throwing her under the bus, but if that earring was a vital piece of information, then Alder needed to know.

I had just swept Marni's office and was getting ready to mop when Liz rapped on the door, her face whiter than chalk.

My stomach sank with dread. I hoped Alder had kept his word.

"This is not good," Liz said. "Not good at all. Cece, I am so screwed."

"What happened?"

Liz dropped into a chair. "Your detective asked if he could look around my office. I told him certainly. I mean, I had nothing to hide."

"And?" I prodded, knowing full well what she was going to say.

"He went through my medication cabinet and made me take an inventory. The ones I dispense and keep under lock and key, which are prescribed to the students. One of the bottles was missing."

This was not good news for Liz, but I breathed a tiny sigh of relief. "I don't understand."

"Neither do I. I checked my log, and I dispensed a dose to the student Wednesday, so it was there then. Today it's gone." Liz sagged in a chair by the door. "The detective took an earring I had on my desk."

I feigned surprise. "What? Why?"

"Beats me. It was one of my favorites, but I lost the mate to it a couple days ago." Liz reached up and tugged an ear. "Anyway, when someone pointed out that I only had one earring on, I tossed it on my desk hoping the other one would show up. It never did. And now a detective takes it into custody. It doesn't make any sense. Unless . . ."

"Unless what?" I asked.

Liz's eyes widened. "What if someone is trying to set me up?"

Her idea made sense. But I wanted to hear who she thought the prospects might be. I also wondered if the prescription that was missing from her cabinet was the same one that had been on the workbench next to her earring. "Who would do that? And why?"

"I don't know," Liz whined. "I just don't know."

"Do you remember who noticed you'd lost the earring? Maybe they picked it up." I knew this was stretching it, but any information Liz could give me would be beneficial.

"No." She shook her head. "Wait, I do remember. It was Zella, during lunch Wednesday. I was at the salad bar, and she was replacing some of the empty containers. She made a joke about how it had better not be in the lettuce bowl."

I nodded. "That's a start. Any chance it was in the lettuce and Zella found it?"

"No. The lettuce was almost empty too. I would have seen it. Zella even dug the tongs through it to make sure."

Thinking for a moment, I added, "Who else knew you lost it?" Another long shot.

"Marni was behind me in line jabbering away. Steve behind her. Keith and TJ were in line too. They were both in front of me." Liz sighed.

"Anyone else?"

"Not in line, but Tommy was nearby. There was a ceiling leak from all the rain, and he was setting out buckets."

"How about Ed?" I asked. "Or anyone else?"

"Nobody else. There were other teachers around, but most were already seated. The ones I mentioned were all late arriving to lunch because we'd had a quick meeting. Ed shoved us all on a budget reduction committee to come up with ideas for saving money. Wednesdays, he has a standing lunch at the district office. All the school principals get together for a meeting and lunch. So, he wasn't even there. Not that he'd notice a missing earring. He's got too much else on his mind to take notice of any of us."

Since my purse had vanished into thin air, I didn't have the little notebook I usually carry around, so I pulled out my phone and made a memo to myself. My main suspects were still the same, but I made a note about Ed not being around when the earring turned up missing.

"What about the medication?" I asked. "Who had access to your cabinet?"

"What do the meds have to do with all this?"

"You think it's a coincidence they went missing? What was the prescription for?" I asked.

"It's a seizure med."

"Again, did anyone have access to the cabinet besides you?"

Liz sighed. "I keep the key in my desk drawer. If I'm out for any reason, my replacement needs to be able to get to the meds. It's common knowledge among the staff."

Interesting. I made a note to tell Alder that some seizure meds can act as sedatives. Even though he should probably know that. This was a game-changer in my suspect list. If Steve had been sedated before he was choked, even the weakest suspect could have done the deed—even tiny Marni. At this point, I wasn't buying a set-up yet, but it was something to keep in mind.

Ed popped his head in the door and Liz and I looked up. "Oh, there you are. I'm calling another staff meeting. Come on down to the cafeteria."

I started toward the door and Ed said, "You're good, Cece. This is for staff and faculty only."

"Perfect. I just started in here. Then I'll move on down your list."

With the entire staff in a meeting, it left me time to snoop. I wasted no time. It wouldn't take much to scope out Marni's room while I mopped and cleaned up. I shut the door when Liz and Ed were out of sight. Since Marni was the closest person to Steve, it made sense that she'd be the prime suspect.

I rummaged through the papers she'd left on her desktop and found nothing of any consequence. The desk drawers also proved uneventful. Everywhere I looked— nothing. Nothing I had found pointed to one person. I kept hitting dead-ends. Yet, someone in this school was guilty. Frustrated, I dipped my mop into the soapy water and made a couple of swaths across the floor. The mop caught under the leg of the desk and refused to come loose. I gave it a good jerk and flew backward. I felt just like the mop —stuck.

I finished mopping the office and headed to the janitor's room to empty my bucket and fill it with clean water. My arms ached from carrying the thing. In the old days, the janitor pushed around a galvanized bucket on wheels. If I could locate it, my job would be much easier. I searched around and finally located the granddaddy of all rolling buckets, and as luck would have it, a faucet and drain in the corner made filling it much easier than trying to use the sink.

Keith's classroom was across the hall. As long as the meeting was still going on, I needed to take advantage. Who knew when I'd get the chance again. At the door, I stopped and looked behind me. Much to my dismay, I saw Alder walking my way.

"I've been looking all over for you," he said.

Dang, why did he have to look so good? I bet he even smelled good, but leaning in for a whiff would surely cause me to go up in flames. I was self-conscious enough with my disheveled hair hanging in clumps around my face. My jeans had muddy water splattered almost to the knees, and the Mizzou sweatshirt I'd grabbed from the rag bag had a three-corner tear in the sleeve. He, on the other hand, wore jeans with a knife-sharp crease down the center and a rust-colored, quarter-zip fleece. His salt-and-pepper hair looked freshly cut. I could still see the visible tan line where his barber had shaved the back of his neck. Not too shabby.

I ran a hand through my hair in an effort to tame the mess. "Sorry, I must look awful," I said. Nothing I could do about the outfit short of dashing to the lost and found in search of something a little less cleaning lady-like.

"Yeah, but you clean up good. That's the important thing." He waggled his eyebrows and my knees trembled.

"Ha! You keep me in stitches with your humor," I chided. "What can I do for you?"

He raised an eyebrow. "You really want me to answer that question?"

"Not if you're going to take it out of context." I felt the blood rise in my neck. Lately I never knew when I was blushing or fixing to have a hot flash. Not that it mattered, except I didn't perspire when I blushed. "I suppose you had a reason for tracking me down."

"I did, indeed. I find myself the lucky recipient of an invitation to a bonfire tonight. I'm not much for roasting weenies, but I am a sucker for a good s'more." He pushed his hands into the pockets of his jeans. "Would you know anyone who'd be willing to clean up real good and go with me? It's not fancy. You don't have to get all gussied up."

A twinge of adrenaline raced through my veins. "We talked about this. You know how I feel about getting involved."

"Oh, lighten up. It's just a bonfire. It's not like I asked you to go away with me for the weekend." He winked. "But, if you'd rather . . ."

The last thing I wanted to do was go away for the weekend. At least, that's what I told myself. A bonfire sounded safe. There would be other people, lots of conversation, sitting on logs. It's not like we were teenagers, for goodness sake. I could control myself for one evening to enjoy a crisp, autumn outing. And we'd be around other people.

"Well." He shrugged. "What'll it be, the bonfire or a weekend alone with me?"

"Why, Detective Alder, I do not know you well enough, sir." I faked a southern accent to match his authentic one. "I suppose it will have to be the bonfire. But no hanky-panky."

His snapped his fingers. "Darn. Hanky-panky is my specialty. I'll pick you up at six. Wear something sexy."

"Really, to a bonfire? Wouldn't that be a bit chilly?"

"I'll be sure to keep you warm." His voice was doing a good job of warming me up. "You don't need to worry your pretty little head."

"You keep talking like that, and you'll be attending that bonfire alone. This is just a friendly outing with two friends. No strings, no involvement." I reminded him what I'd been telling him since June. I was not ready for anything other than friendship. But it was me who needed convincing.

"Are you telling that to Hunter too?" His eyes turned serious.

"Not that it is any of your business, but yes I am. This isn't junior high you know—"

"No, it's senior high," he interrupted and laughed. "That was a pretty good one, huh?"

I giggled despite my misgivings. Things seemed to be escalating again between him and Grant. We'd gone through this a couple months ago, with one trying to outdo the other to win me over. I thought I'd put a stop to it, but since they were friends, they talked. Grant must have mentioned his invitation to the ballet, so now Alder was reciprocating with a bonfire. Apparently, Alder didn't know that I'd turned Grant's invitation down. Men—did they ever outgrow the teenage boy rivalries?

"You crack me up," I said. "But you better get out of here, so I can get to work."

He started to turn around but stopped mid-step. "Hey, what's up with Valenti? She's missed two days of work. That's not like her."

"She thinks it's food poisoning, but it sounds more like a twenty-four-hour bug to me. If she's not better tomorrow, I told her she needed to get to the emergency clinic. There's a flu bug going around."

"Ah, we had the shots a couple weeks ago. The department sprang for them for anyone who comes into contact with the public. Hope it's not some new strain that the shot doesn't cover."

I leaned against the mop. "Well, whatever it is, if she's not better tomorrow, I'll personally drag her to the doctor. It's crazy to be so sick and not do anything about it."

Alder pursed his lips. "Hope it's not something serious. It's not like her to miss work."

"Oh, thanks for not ratting me out to Liz about the earring," I said. "She told me about the missing prescription bottle."

"I wouldn't do that to you," he said.

"Speaking of that. The prescription missing from Liz's cabinet was a medication used for seizures. One of the side effects of some seizure meds is drowsiness. Maybe the victim was sedated before he was strangled."

"Good to know," Alder said. "She told you about it, huh?"

"Yes, but I just listened. Honest!"

"Perfect. Keep it low-key."

"You're not thinking Liz did it, are you?"

"I'm keeping my options open," Alder said. "You heard anything else of interest?"

"Maybe not heard but seen. TJ, the new athletic director, and Marni seem pretty chummy considering her boyfriend just died. And on a personal note, the science teacher is a creeper. He also had an argument with Steve that got physical. The maintenance guy had to break it up." I paused and tried to think of anything else I'd heard. "Not sure this is important, but apparently Zella's been giving Steve the cold shoulder for over a month. And Marni, the girlfriend, said he'd hired a private investigator. She had a name, Quentin or Quinlan Investigations."

Alder chuckled. "Well, aren't you a fount of information."

The meeting must have broken up, because Marni was approaching, and fast.

"I better go. See you at six." Alder swerved to get out of Marni's way and headed down the hall.

CHAPTER TWELVE

"Motive? Everyone had a motive to kill Steve. Some more than others."
TJ Gordon

Marni blew past me, not stopping even when I said hi. My pace quickened, worrying that she might slip on the wet floor, but after two days of it, she was probably used to choosing her steps wisely.

She stopped in her office long enough to grab her coat and purse, and then she took off out the side door like the devil was on her tail. Only it wasn't the devil, it was TJ. He caught up with her at her car, which was parked in the faculty lot right outside.

They both had their backs to me, so I eased out the door and squatted behind a row of bushes in a bed between the parking lot and the building. A very muddy bed. My feet sank, making it difficult to move without leaving a shoe behind. I spread the branches aside to get a better view.

"What was Steve up to?" TJ shouted.

Marni turned to face him. "What are you talking about?"

TJ pulled a paper from his jacket and shook it in her face. "This came in my mail yesterday. It's pure blackmail, and the only person I can think who would stoop to this is Steve."

Marni read it and pushed it back at TJ. "I don't know anything about this. It doesn't make sense. Why would he send this to you?"

Send what? Come on, Marni. Give me something to work with.

"Why do you think? He was trying to get me fired. This is so lame."

"Are you going to give it to the police?" Marni asked.

"You're joking, right? This gives me a motive. It makes me look guilty." TJ scrubbed his hands through his hair. "I can't even deal with this."

Marni backed up until she bumped into her car. "Did you kill him?"

"Marni, get real. Do you really think I could do that? What about you? Did you kill him?"

"Speculating and pointing fingers doesn't help. I have to go." She jumped in her car and sped away.

TJ stared after her.

I heard a light *tap tap tap* sound behind me. Still in my crouched position, I turned, lost my footing, and butt-planted in the mud. When I looked up, Liz was grinning at me through the plate glass window. I held a muddy finger to my lips, begging her not to give me away.

After what seemed like forever, TJ got in his car and left the parking lot.

Liz opened the door. "What in the world are you doing?"

I stood up and nodded to where Marni and TJ had been standing. "A little reconnaissance. Thanks for not blowing my cover."

"Get yourself in here and let's get you cleaned up."

"I'm not wearing lost stuff from that bin. I draw the line at that," I said, trying to muster up a laugh.

"There's a spare pair of jeans and a scrub top in my office. You never know when one of these kids is going to upchuck on you."

I pulled off my shoes and scraped them against the edge of the sidewalk to knock off the excess mud. "And to think I used to pay to have a mud bath."

"What was up with those two?" Liz asked.

"It appears Steve was holding something over TJ's head. Blackmailing him. And TJ confronted Marni to see what she knew. Any ideas?" I padded down the hall beside Liz.

"No. Nothing surprises me anymore."

"It looks like they're getting ready to turn on one another. She asked if he killed Steve and he threw the question right back at her."

"Interesting. At least that probably means they aren't involved in his death together."

When we passed Keith's classroom, we both did a double-take. He wasn't there, but his entire place had been tossed.

"Oh, my word." Liz stopped and gawked in the doorway. "Wonder where Keith is. He'll go ballistic. The weird just keeps happening."

"Especially since I was just here not ten minutes ago and everything was fine."

"We should get Ed," Liz said.

I started to agree, but I noticed my purse right in the middle of Keith's desk amid all the clutter. "Good grief. That's my purse." Without a second thought, I marched in and grabbed it.

"Do you think that's wise?" Liz asked.

"What? It's my purse. Do I need to show identification?" I laughed as I opened my bag to see if anything was missing. What I saw left me cold.

STOP SNOOPING OR YOU'RE NEXT was written on a paper napkin in bold, black marker with what appeared to be dried ketchup posing as blood smeared across the message.

I closed up my purse and ran to my car, leaving Liz standing open-mouthed in the disheveled classroom. Nancy pulled into the parking lot as I was leaving.

I honked my horn. Nancy pulled up next to me and lowered her window. "Where you headed?"

I told her about finding my purse and the note that was in it. "Why don't you guys knock off for the day? I need to go by the police station and talk to Alder."

"Meh! I'm not worried." She turned to Gigi. "Are you worried?"

Gigi shook her head.

"Seriously, let's at least let Alder check it out," I said.

"Whatevs," Nancy said, mimicking something Michelle would say. "We'll stick together and watch out for the bad guys."

I waved her on. "Be careful." Then I headed to the police station and told Alder about Keith's classroom being ransacked and gave him my purse and the note.

———

My hands trembled as I brushed my hair. I should never have agreed to go to the bonfire. What was I thinking? Obviously, I wasn't. At least I wasn't thinking with my brain.

Jessie had picked up Gigi and Michelle for dinner and a play. I begged off with a headache. It wouldn't do for Jessie or Michelle to know I had a date with Alder. A date, at my age. That sounded so juvenile. An engagement sounded better, except then it sounded . . . well it sounded like something official. I had plans. That was it. I had plans with Alder. Nothing less, nothing more.

The girls were taking Gigi to their favorite Chinese restaurant in St. Louis and then taking in a play at The Fox Theatre downtown. By the time they wrangled with traffic and made it back to Wickford, I'd be home none the worse for wear and they wouldn't be any wiser.

After they left, I filled the Jacuzzi and took a leisurely bath, shaved my legs, and slathered on my favorite jasmine body lotion. Who knew what might happen. My divorce would be final in a matter of days, I realized. There wasn't much Phillip could hold over my head anymore.

My casual clothing selection consisted of designer jeans, something my current budget didn't allow, and twinsets. I didn't have a sweatshirt in the bunch. Not one I'd wear to an outing anyway. Finally, I found a burgundy turtleneck sweater and pulled it over my head. A silver chain finished off the look.

The sweater accented my curves but didn't hug me too tightly. I'd layered on a tee underneath. And I'd found a pair of jeans that fit. I slid my feet into brown crop boots and called myself fit for a bonfire.

While I was messing with my hair, the doorbell rang. I dropped the brush, pinched my cheeks for additional color, and descended the steps.

Alder looked fit and handsome in brown cords and a beige-and-brown plaid flannel shirt. The shirt was open at the neck, revealing a beige thermal beneath.

The weather was unseasonably warm for November, and coats were not necessary.

"Wow, you look great," Alder said. "How about we skip the bonfire and do the town? It'd be a shame to waste your looks on a dark field with a flickering flame." He grinned a wicked smile and waggled his eyebrows. "On second thought, that sounds perfect. Let's get going."

"You have an evil side, don't you?" I said, trying to settle the butterflies in my stomach.

"Ha! We shall see. Oh, before I forget, I have your purse in the truck. Make sure there's nothing missing. I kept the note, obviously." He threw an arm around my shoulder in a protective measure. It felt good, like it was supposed to be there. Though, I did a quick glance around to see if any neighbors were out and about. I felt so illicit, yet I was doing nothing wrong. I felt a tad bolder since my divorce would soon be final. Just in time to really have something to feel thankful for. Though, it's not like I'd declare that when we went around the table and told our blessings.

He led me to a silver quad cab pickup, not his usual department-issued Crown Victoria.

"New?" I asked.

"Nope. Figured you wouldn't want to be riding around in my grungy car. This is my personal vehicle. I cleaned it up special for you." He opened the passenger side and waited until I was buckled in before he shut the door.

"Well, don't I feel special." He jogged around the truck and hiked himself into the driver's seat. He was a gentleman through and through, nothing like Phillip, but I wondered if the gentleman stuff wore off over time. Though, I could never remember a time when Phillip opened a car door for me. Maybe when we brought Jessie or Michelle home from the hospital. I nixed the thought when I remembered both times; it had been the discharge nurse who had held the door and baby while I got situated.

I had told Alder earlier about the conversation between TJ and Marni and the blackmail note. "This whole thing keeps getting weirder and weirder." I rummaged through my wallet and made sure my credit cards, driver's license, and the little bit of cash I had were still there.

"I suppose," he said, buckling himself in.

"Someone takes my purse, nothing is missing, then a day later it shows up in Keith's ransacked office. It's almost like someone is pointing fingers. First Liz and the earring and medication. Then TJ gets a blackmail note. Now Keith's classroom gets ransacked and my purse appears with a warning attached. By the way, TJ and Marni were practically accusing each other of killing Steve."

"You're not going to like what I'm going to say." Alder turned in his seat to face me.

I narrowed my eyes, knowing exactly what his next words were going to be. "Before you say it, the answer is no. I have a job to do, and I intend to do it."

Alder blew out a breath. "Seriously, you confound me. Can't you just stay away from the school until we wrap up this case?"

"No. I can't afford to turn down jobs." After I had met him at the station and given him my purse and the note, he'd driven out to the school. When he saw Nancy and Gigi there, he'd sent them home. "Unless you close the crime scene, we're going to be there. It's my reputation if Ed doesn't get the school open soon. If word gets out that I'm unreliable, the jobs will dry up. I need this to work."

"Cece—"

"I said, no. I'll take Nancy with me and we'll work together."

He laughed. "You remember how well that worked out the last time."

"I forgot to ask if we were supposed to bring anything to this shindig," I said, changing the subject. I wondered if it was considered etiquette to arrive empty-handed. I'd never been to a bonfire before. Were we supposed to provide our own marshmallows? Should I have brought a small gift for the hostess? The least I could have done was put together a small basket with a bottle of wine and maybe some cheese and crackers.

"Okay. Okay. You are one stubborn woman." Alder sighed and pointed over his shoulder into the back seat. "I've got everything we need. Don't worry. When you party with Case Alder, you do it in style. Maybe not the style you're accustomed to, but don't you worry about a thing."

Alder cranked the engine while I peered over the back seat. He had thought of everything. Two fold-up camp chairs lay next to a cooler on wheels. There was also a blanket. I shivered, and not from the chill in the air.

"So, where is this bonfire?" I wondered out loud.

We were heading west, leaving Wickford behind.

Alder left the highway and turned north. "Not too far. Be patient and you'll see."

I sat back while we rode in silence. Alder must have noticed the quiet and reached for the radio. He had a penchant for talk radio, and I absolutely hated it. I placed my hand on his to stop him. When I did, his breath caught. I startled and drew my hand back. "Don't ruin it with the radio. It's such a lovely night without all that rhetoric."

I was glad it was dark, so I couldn't see his reaction, but he left the radio off and focused on driving.

We drove for another twenty minutes or so when he pulled off onto a gravel road and through a set of gates. I looked around expecting to see cars and people and a bonfire. Instead, I saw nothing but a full moon shining over an open field. He stopped the truck and bounded around to my side and pulled open my door.

"Are we early? Where is everyone?" I asked.

He put a finger to my lip. "Shh, don't ruin it with talk." He took my hand and led me up a path, the moon lighting our way. The path ended at a sheer drop-off. Below I could see rippling water—a meandering stream.

"There is no bonfire. You tricked me." I frowned and started back to the truck.

"Wait," he said. He pulled something from this pocket and struck it against a rock outcropping. A match flickered to life. He tossed it into a circle of rocks stacked with kindling that I hadn't noticed before. I stopped and watched as the flame caught. Alder bent down and tended the fire until he had a blaze burning.

"Okay, so there is a bonfire, but you still tricked me." I feigned anger, but something in his manner touched me. He had thought of all this ahead of time down to having the fire laid and ready, just to bring me out here. The gesture was so romantic, it brought tears to my eyes.

He stood and brushed off the knees of his pants. "It's called End of the Road—fifty acres of solitude and nature. I signed the papers today. I've been eyeing the place for a couple months, but the time just never seemed right. Then the seller calls me out of the blue and lowers the price. I couldn't pass it up. It doesn't look like much in the dark, but in the day, the lane coming into the place is lined with towering oaks. You can't tell this time of year, but there are masses of dogwood and redbud. This cliff," he said, pointing to where we stood, "overlooks the river. This is the first time I've even been out here after dark. Can you just picture it covered in fresh snow?"

He took my arm and swung me around, so we had our backs to the river. "Can you see it?" he asked.

I squinted. "See what?"

"The log cabin. Two-story with a wrap-around porch. Stone chimney on the end."

He led me several feet and kicked his boots against a rock. "This is the porch; double doors lead into the great room." He stepped across the imaginary threshold and I followed. "The kitchen is back there, along with a guest bedroom and bath." He pointed into the darkness. "And up those stairs, the master bedroom."

I shivered and Alder put his arms around me.

"Now can you see it?" he whispered in my ear.

"I . . . I think so. It's beautiful." The tenderness in his voice brought another round of tears to my eyes, blurring my vision. He was a big macho cop sharing his dreams with me and I could feel them. I could see them. Right down to smooth, flat rocks laid out in a path to the overlook—imaginary daisies and lavender peeking over a split-rail fence. I was seeing a side of Case Alder I hadn't expected. A side I didn't know existed. A side that gave me hope that someday I might be able to let go of everything that was holding me back.

"Someday." Alder sobered. "Help me bring the stuff from the truck. I've got all the makings for s'mores, and a bottle of wine."

"What does one drink with s'mores—red or white?" I queried as we walked back to the truck.

"White, of course, what else would you drink with marshmallows?"

Alder had thought of everything. I unfolded the camp chairs and spread the blanket while he loaded marshmallows onto long sticks he'd sharpened with his pocketknife.

When they were golden brown, he pulled them from the fire. "Try this," he said, slipping one onto the graham cracker I was holding.

I slapped a piece of chocolate on it, topped it with another cracker, and popped it in my mouth.

"Mmm, delicious."

"You've got it all over you." He traced my mouth with his finger, wiping away the sticky mess.

I closed my eyes and imagined what it would feel like to kiss him again. After our close encounter during the summer,

I didn't dare. But I had to admit I liked his company. He was thoughtful and fun to be with.

I still had my eyes closed when I felt his lips brush the back of my neck. His breath sent a shiver through me. He wrapped his arms around my waist and pulled me against him. My imagination wasn't going to have to wonder for long. If he kept it up, I'd turn around and lay one on him.

"You smell nice," he whispered in my ear.

"You smell like smoke."

He kissed my neck again.

"How about that wine?" I asked, pulling away.

He laughed. "You're playing hard to get."

"Yes, sir. Now fill my glass."

He removed the cork and poured two glasses of wine.

He raised his for a toast. "To the beginning of a beautiful friendship."

I sighed and clanked my glass against his. "Yes, friendship."

"Is that all it is with Hunter? Just friendship?" Alder tipped his glass and drained it.

"Yes, it is. Grant isn't pushing for anything beyond that. We have an understanding. I thought you and I had one too. Honestly, Alder, I'm not ready." Not only wasn't I ready, I was confused. I had two men in my life, two wonderful men, and a not-so-wonderful almost ex-husband. I didn't even know if I could commit, didn't know if I could trust anyone with my heart after what Phillip had done.

I thought I knew what I wanted. Tonight had moved me closer, but I still wasn't there. I wondered if the time finally came when I was, whether Alder would still be waiting. I didn't know if I had the guts to be honest with Grant. We'd left our relationship squarely in the friendship zone, but I knew he wanted more. He'd been widowed long enough he was ready to be in a committed relationship. I didn't think I could live with hurting him.

"Grant, Grant, Grant," Alder mimicked. "Can we talk about something other than that baboon?"

I laughed. "You brought him up." I knew he was joking. He and Grant were fast friends, agreeing to disagree about me. "What did you have in mind? Baseball's over and the Cardinals didn't make it to the series."

Alder leaned back. "Now that you mention it, what's the status of the divorce?"

"Still on track." Not that I was counting, though I suppose I was. According to my lawyer, we were set for court Tuesday. All the paperwork was in order. Phillip had agreed to pay for Michelle's living expenses and college. He'd also agreed to bring the mortgage payment current and pay half of it until Michelle graduated from college. After that I was on my own. Unless something major happened, come Tuesday, I would no longer be bound to Phillip by marriage.

"Ah." Alder walked over to the fire, added a log, and stared into the flames. I went to stand next to him. Not as close this time. In the firelight his expression looked serious.

"What about you? Do you still have divorce regrets?" I asked, knowing I was treading on ground we'd already covered.

"Some days I kick myself for even getting married in the first place. We weren't ready. But it was what all our friends were doing, so we did it too. But if I hadn't, I wouldn't have Becca. And you know how amazing having a daughter is. No regrets over the divorce. Just regrets that I trusted my best friend and my wife."

"But you never married again? That's sad."

"Sad? Why so? You were married thirty years and it's ending in a divorce. Now that's sad."

"True, but all those years you were by yourself."

"I had Becca on weekends and a couple of weeks during the summer. Besides, I never said I lived a monk's life. There've been other women. I've stayed unattached for a reason. Being a cop makes me reluctant to burden someone else with the worry." He sighed. "A cop's life isn't easy. If I had known I was going to become a cop, I would have never married Joyce. My dad worked the eighth precinct in St. Louis, and I watched my mom get down on her knees every night after he went to work and pray that he'd come home. I also saw panic in her eyes every time the phone rang. It's not something I have a right to inflict on someone else."

I leaned into him and rested my head on his shoulder. The emotions I'd been feeling withered inside me. He wasn't looking for forever, and I didn't know if I could risk getting hurt with someone who didn't see a future.

He touched my cheek. "Hey, are you crying?"

"No." I sniffled. "I'm just cold."

He wrapped his arms around me and pulled me in close.

"Let's talk about something else. We're kinda pathetic," I said.

His eyes twinkled in the firelight. "I'd prefer not to talk." He took my glass and led me to the blanket next to the fire. In the glow of moonlight and the flickering flames, he pulled me to him. His mustache tickled my lips. My resolve crumbled, and I kissed him. One last bittersweet kiss, I told myself. One last amazing kiss. Which led to another. I had seen movies where the heroine almost fainted after receiving a toe-curling kiss from the hero. I had never thought it possible. But here it was.

Then an image of Phillip filtered through my brain, followed by one of his mother. *Only a couple more days.* I wiped those images from my brain and concentrated really hard on not passing out.

Then I felt a burning sensation near my feet and wondered if I was self-combusting. "I think I'm on fire."

"Me too," Alder mumbled into my neck.

"No!" I screamed when I really felt the heat and pushed him away. "The blanket's on fire."

Alder scrambled to his feet and stomped on the flames. I raced around, grabbing our supplies, trying to get them out of the way, because if they didn't catch fire, they would surely get smashed the way he was jumping around.

After he'd extinguished the fire he said, "Well, crap. So much for cuddling on the blanket. Did you do that on purpose?"

I could see the wicked grin on his face. "Umm, saved by the flames."

"We're not through. I'll just bring another blanket next time."

"Who said there will be a next time, mister?"

He grabbed my hand and pressed his lips to it. "There will be a next time. I promise you that. And the blanket won't be the only thing on fire, if I have my say."

My insides turned into jelly. "Come on. Let's get this mess cleaned up. I have to work tomorrow."

"Spoil sport. It was just starting to get interesting."

I punched his arm. "That's why we need to go."

Long after we'd put out the fire and driven home, I could still feel his lips and the way his mustache felt brushing my cheek. My resolve had almost caved tonight, but the fire had brought me back to reality. He wasn't the marrying type—he'd just said so—and I wasn't the casual fling type. The logical solution was to keep my distance.

———

After getting a late-night phone call from Liz promising news, against my better judgment, I was sitting at the bottom of the driveway to her palatial home. The home where she was currently hosting her annual sleepover for the wives of the deer hunters—my former friends. Thankfully, I didn't see my mother-in-law's Mercedes.

Cece Cavanaugh, you must have rocks in your head. This is the last place you need to be. Whatever news Liz has can wait until morning.

Before I could put my car in reverse, a tap on the window jolted me from my misgivings. Liz stood next to my car wearing a designer PJ set, holding two glasses of champagne.

She said something I couldn't hear and held out one of the glasses.

I put the window down. "What?"

"Come on up and join us." She slurred her words, and by the fact that she wore no coat over the thin night clothes, I assumed she'd had too much to drink. "There's plenty of bubbly to go around."

I frowned. "Not a good idea. What did you want that was so important it couldn't wait until tomorrow?"

"Don't be a party poop." She thrust a flute at me. "I've got all kinds of goodies from Oppenheimer's Bakery and plenty of alcohol."

That was obvious. I put the van in reverse. "This was not a good idea. I'll call you tomorrow."

"No." She ran around the front of my van, sloshing champagne as she went.

Liz rarely drank, but on occasions such as this, she could not hold her liquor for anything. One drink made her tipsy and slurred her speech—a stark contrast to sober Liz. I knew from past experience, she would be nursing a killer hangover tomorrow.

I slid down the passenger side window. "Liz, go back to your party and enjoy the evening. I'm going home."

"Wait. I need to show you something." She pushed both flutes through the open window. "Hold these a minute."

I pushed the gear shifter into park and took the champagne. *This better be good.* If the wives got to missing her, they would come looking, and I didn't want to be here when they did.

She shoved her hand into the pocket of her pajama pants and withdrew a small object. "Here."

She grabbed her drink back and pushed the object into my hand.

I held it under the map light. "It's a flash drive. So?"

"So? Don't you see?" She tipped the flute and drained it.

"I see you've had too much to drink."

A car slowed, its lights illuminating my van. I was all too aware of how my fluorescent pink van stuck out like a sore thumb in Liz's driveway.

"Oops. Don't look now, but I think Hazel has arrived. I'm out of here." Liz wiggled four fingers in a wave and stumbled up the driveway.

Great timing, you schmuck! I dropped the flash drive in the cupholder, reminding myself to give it to Liz the next time I saw her. Then I wondered if Liz had set it up for me to be here when Hazel arrived.

Before I could back down the driveway, Hazel pulled in behind me, blocking my exit.

She barreled toward my van like a bull charging a matador. "What are you doing here in th-that ridiculous vehicle? Surely Liz did not invite you."

"Spare me your lecture. I was leaving until you blocked me in." My final day in court could not come soon enough.

"If you persist in smearing the Cavanaugh name, I will have a talk with my attorney."

"As much as I regret it, it's my last name too," I said. "And if I want to hire a billboard for Cavanaugh Cleaning, I will. Your threats don't work with me."

"You wouldn't dare."

"Don't tempt me. I don't have a lot of patience with you or Phillip lately. Now move your car before I back into it." My heart pounded. In the entire time I'd been married to Phillip, I'd never spoken to his mother that way. I'd been too scared, but if I had known how liberating it would feel, I might have given it a shot years ago.

Hazel sneered. "Get that heap out of here before Liz's neighbors see you."

After Hazel had moved her car, and I'd backed out of the drive, I breathed in a deep breath and exhaled. I felt empowered by my boldness.

CHAPTER THIRTEEN

"Nancy is okay for a priss. She's got moxie and will be a handful for Cece."
Gigi Evans

My heart wasn't in heading back to school for another round of cleaning. After Alder had dropped me off last night, I'd made a decision that it was best to put the brakes on our relationship for good. Finish it before either one of us got hurt—namely me. If he didn't see himself getting married and I didn't see myself in a casual fling, then I didn't need to keep torturing myself. Even though the emotional scars from Phillip's deceit were starting to lessen, I didn't want to take a chance of opening myself up.

Then there was my purse and the note. Alder might have been right about me staying away, but my reputation was at stake, not to mention my finances. I needed the money from this job, and I didn't need word getting out that I didn't finish what I started. But I had misgivings because of the note.

Nancy had insisted on driving herself. Said she had something to do at noon. We met up at school. I dragged Gigi along so I wouldn't be cleaning alone when Nancy left. I was surprised to see other cars in the parking lot, and that made me feel better about being here. I parked next to Zella and Tommy who were getting out of their car.

"Morning," Zella said.

"What are you guys doing here?" I asked.

"Boss man insisted," Tommy said. "Said 'all hands on deck' until this mess is cleaned up. All hands except Liz. She got special permission to miss out on the festivities."

Yeah, because she's hungover and has a house full of hungover houseguests.

Marni and Keith were standing near the front door. I was too far away to hear their conversation, but from their posture it was clear they were arguing. Marni, acting like a little bulldog, was shaking her fist in Keith's face even though he hovered almost a foot taller than her. He didn't appear to be backing down either. And Liz had told me she was timid. The Marni I saw had some spunk.

"Grab the supplies, ladies." I lifted the backdoor of the van, hoping to catch up to them before they went inside. "We have a long way to go before this mess is cleaned up. We've got today and tomorrow."

"Ugh," Nancy said. "I'm already sick of this place. The mud is disgusting."

"A little mud never hurt anyone," Gigi said, pulling a pack of cigarettes from her pocket. "Don't be a wimp."

"Oh, can I have one of those? Cece made me throw mine away." Nancy watched my mother with hungry eyes.

I snatched the pack away. "Really? This is a tobacco-free campus. You want to get us fired? Nancy, you haven't smoked in three months. Why start now?"

She stuck her lip out. "You're right. Some days I just get to craving one."

"Ned hates it when I smoke." Gigi's tone was wistful.

I hoped that meant she missed him and would soon be on a plane home. Better yet, maybe he'd come get her.

Gigi slung her backpack over her shoulder, and I heard glass clink. Gigi winked at Nancy.

Nancy giggled.

"What?" I asked.

"Never you mind, nosy," Gigi said.

I ran a hand over Gigi's backpack and felt the outline of bottles. "Are you kidding? Did you bring alcohol?"

Nancy's shoulders sagged. "Busted."

"Open it up."

Gigi sat the pack on the ground and extracted two wine spritzers.

"I'm not even going to ask. Leave them in the van and let's go." Nancy had come a long way in the few months she'd been living above my garage. I sure didn't need Gigi influencing her.

"Seriously. What's going on with you?"

"Nothing." Gigi pulled her shoulders back and trotted off, leaving me and Nancy staring after her.

"Man trouble," Nancy said. "She's acting like she don't need that man of hers. But you can tell by how she talks that she's missing him big time."

"But she left him."

"And he hasn't come after her or even called. She's got her feelings all in a tiff and she's too proud to call him."

Nancy gave me an idea. "Go on inside. I have something I need to do."

When Nancy was out of sight, I pulled out my cell phone and called Gigi's home number. It went to voice mail, so I left a message inviting Ned to Thanksgiving dinner. If Gigi really missed him, maybe a reunion was just what she needed. I hoped Ned felt the same way and hadn't given up on her.

Alder was concerned about my safety, but with the faculty and staff here, I felt we'd be okay splitting up. It's not like someone would kill us in front of the employees.

By the time I made it to the front door, Marni and Keith had already gone inside. I found Gigi in the east wing.

"You okay?" I asked.

"Never better. Now what do you need me to do?"

"Have you talked to Ned since you left?"

"No, and I don't intend to. He knows where to find me, and he hasn't bothered." She sniffled and picked up a mop. "Now what do I need to do?"

"Maybe he's giving you some time to cool off."

Gigi held her hand up. "Stop. Don't make excuses for him. I'm done talking. Let's get to work."

I slowly shook my head. "You're one stubborn woman."

"And proud of it," Gigi said. "Proud of it."

I showed her the tasks I needed her to complete then headed back to the center hallway. When I rounded the corner, I saw Keith go into Marni's office. Their argument had piqued my interest, especially since Marni had just argued with TJ the day before. I found a good vantage point across the hall and slid between a break in the lockers. Marni's office had a large window with blinds. Through the half-open slats, I saw Keith rummaging through the file cabinet. I couldn't see the entire room, but he appeared to be alone. Which begged the question, where was Marni? I thought it pretty gutsy of him to be so bold with Marni in the building.

He searched through her file cabinet, then rifled through her desk. Finally, he removed several books from her bookcase and slid his hand along the back of the shelves.

When he finished, he headed to the door. I was in the hallway leading to his classroom. If he turned left out of Marni's office, he'd see me. The girls' restroom was more than twenty feet away. There was no way I could slip in unnoticed. If he was innocent, there'd be nothing to worry about, but if he were up to something, I'd have to think fast, because it was pretty obvious I had no business standing between two lockers, and he stuck out like a sore thumb in her office.

I was saved when I saw Marni barreling down the hall. Keith must have seen her at the exact same time, because he froze in place.

Marni almost tripped over her feet when she saw him. "What do you want?"

I took the opportunity to scamper to the restroom. Once inside, I held the door open a sliver and watched their interaction. I felt a bit like Jessica Fletcher spying on the bad guys.

"Looking for you," Keith said.

"Well, I'm busy, and I don't have time to rehash your problem." Marni pushed past him. "I don't know what Steve was up to. You and TJ need to put your heads together. Apparently, you both were on Steve's radar for something."

"What did he tell you?" Keith asked. "We need to talk."

"I'm through talking." Marni made a shooing gesture. "Get lost."

He took the hint and left, and she slammed her door.

I eased the bathroom door shut and waited until he'd had ample time to get to his classroom.

Everyone in this school—maybe with the exception of Ed—was acting suspiciously.

———

I headed to the cafeteria hoping Zella might have a stash of chocolate chip cookies. Ed waylaid me before I got there.

"Looks like you're making progress," he said.

"We're getting there."

Ed paced back and forth. "Any chance you can wrap it up today? I need to give a report to the superintendent."

It was annoying trying to talk to someone who wouldn't stand still. "I wish. We've still got some classrooms that we haven't touched."

"Can you give me a rundown? Nothing fancy. A list of what you've accomplished and what you still need to do with an estimate of when you plan to finish."

"Sure, that seems reasonable. I'll send you an email after lunch. I've brought in extra help. At the rate we're going, we should be able to finish up tomorrow."

———

Tommy cornered me near the janitor room.

He was pushing a large roll-around fan. "You got a minute?"

I hesitated and started to tell him no, but he had been so much help. I couldn't risk getting on his bad side. With Ed pressuring me to finish tomorrow, I needed Tommy's help. "Sure," I said, peering into his tiny space. Just like thirty years ago, this place was neat as a pin. Tommy had installed a pegboard on the back wall where he kept all his mops, brooms, and handyman utensils. Every tool was neatly outlined with magic marker, so there was no mistaking what went where. "This place hasn't changed a bit. You're still just as organized as ever."

"Nope, not me. This is the janitor's domain. I have maintenance. But he's a good guy and keeps this place as neat as I used to. Neither one of us can stand clutter. We make a good team. Too bad he's laid up with his back."

I imagined Tommy's RV having a pegboard with every pot, pan, and cooking utensil being outlined and hung neatly.

Only thing was, the kitchen was Zella's area, and I highly doubted she'd given him free rein to organize her tools.

He brushed aside a stack of catalogs and motioned for me to have a seat at the desk. "It's clean. You don't have to worry about that. He's not the sort to keep a messy work area."

Not that I had anything to worry about. I had on an old pair of jeans and looked downright grungy. If anything, Tommy might have to clean the place after I left. I imagined I might leave a dust cloud on my way out.

Tommy pulled a chair from the corner, swung it around backward, and eased himself onto it, peering over the top like a kid. "It's good to see you hanging around the school again. It's been a few years."

I laughed. "Yeah, just a few. But we're almost done here, and it will be back to business as usual. Except for you and Zella, you lucky dogs. I can't imagine taking off for parts unknown."

He rubbed a mangled hand over this stubby gray hair. "I don't know if I'm doing the right thing here. Zella's always said this is what she wants to do, but lately her mood has changed. I can't read her anymore. Dang women, why do y'all have to be so aggravating?"

I laughed. "It's our job to keep you men on your toes."

Tommy sobered. "Naw, there's something going on with her. I'm used to her having mood swings. Ever since she went through the change. But lately there's something else. It's like she's there, but she's not. Like she's hollow." He rubbed his head again and sighed. "I can't explain it. She just ain't my same old Zella. She's going through the motions of getting ready to take off in the RV, but I can tell her heart ain't in it. It's like there's a sadness in her. Danged if I know what's eating her."

"Have you tried talking to her?"

"Oh hell, us men aren't much for talking feelings and all

that squishy stuff. But I have, and she just tells me it's my imagination. I swear, I ain't imagining it. We been living together way too long for it to be my imagination. I know that woman like I know my own self, and there is something wrong. Something she's festering over by herself."

I envied Tommy. Not that he was watching his wife go through something she wasn't willing to share with him, but the fact that he recognized it. How many married people knew enough to see when something was bothering their partner? There'd probably be fewer divorces if couples had a sixth sense in the relationship department. Having that intuitiveness might have saved me a lot of grief.

"She seems okay to me, but then I don't live with her." But what did I know? We crossed paths in the grocery store now and again, and at church. It wasn't like we saw each other on a daily basis, and we sure didn't share the details of our lives. Mostly just passed pleasantries when we saw one another.

"Naw, living with her these days is a whole 'nuther thing. If she ain't mad at the world, she's blubbering in the bathroom and pretending her allergies are acting up. Hell, as much as she's blowing her nose lately, I think I need to buy some stock in tissue."

"Have you talked to your kids about her? Maybe one of your daughters could get her to open up."

"Darn girls are too busy with their own families. They wouldn't notice an earthquake unless it opened up the earth and swallowed up one of their SUVs. Between running their kids to soccer, dance practice, and Tae Kwan Do, they barely have time to squeeze in a pedicure." He laughed, but his mouth quickly retreated to a grim frown.

"Gee, Tommy, I feel horrible. Maybe she's having second thoughts about retiring. This school has been so much a part of her life. You two have worked here so long. Your kids even went to school here. I'm sure once you get on the road, she'll get so involved that she won't have a chance to worry." Easy for me to say. I wasn't the one having to deal with whatever it was.

"Maybe you're right. I probably just have to back off and leave her alone, but I can't. It hurts to see her so miserable." He paused and cocked his head to the side. "You wouldn't have a talk with her, would you?"

I gasped. "Me? I don't know why you think she would talk to me if she won't even talk to you. Doesn't she have a girl-friend who could talk to her?"

"Her best friend is Delores Redmond, and you know she's got the Alzheimer's, and her daughter moved her out to North Carolina. Delores and Zella were like sisters. They were like getting together a couple of old hens. You couldn't get a word in edgewise for them gals. But now, she's got no one 'cept me, and she's not talking to me. She always thought a lot of you, Cece. You and Angie. Always left them cookies out intentionally hoping y'all would sneak in and grab a handful."

I smiled at the memory. But that had been more than thirty years ago. Could I get Zella to talk to me?

"Wow, I don't know," I hedged, not ready to tread into this quagmire. "Do you think she'd even talk to me?"

Tommy frowned. "Well, not if you march in the kitchen and tell her I want you to talk to her. She'll clam up tighter than a scrooge. You gotta go in there and just get her to talking like you women do. Talk about your kids or your trouble with us men. Don't spring it on her. Give her a chance to open up. If I know my Zella, she'll come around. She just ain't gonna come around with me, 'cause I been pressuring her to tell me what's wrong. It's the principle of the thing now. It's kinda like when your kids do something to spite you.

They know it's wrong, but they ain't gonna admit it for nothing. That's my Zella."

I found myself nodding in agreement.

"So, you'll do it?" he asked.

"I guess I could try. But I have to warn you, if she does tell me something, it's confidential. I'm not running back to you. I won't betray her friendship that way."

Tommy frowned. "What the hell good will that do?"

"If there's something that's bothering her, I'll try to convince her to tell you, but if she doesn't, it ends there. I'm not going to go behind her back."

"You drive a hard bargain. But I need to find out what's eating at my wife. Whatever you decide, that's how we'll do it." He reached out, grabbed my hand, and shook it. "We got a deal."

I had a deal all right. I'd dealt myself right into a big old mess. *Cece Cavanaugh, how can you get yourself into these predicaments? And better yet, how can you get out of them once you step in them?*

———

Zella was arranging boxes in the walk-in freezer when I came in.

"Do you need some help?" I asked, picking up a box.

"Sure thing. Normally I unpack them, but let's just put them up so I don't trip over them. I can't abide stuff lying around on the floor. It's a safety hazard. I can unpack everything tomorrow. Didn't get to it yesterday."

I placed my box on a shelf in the back of the freezer next to three she'd already stacked there.

She scooted two more cartons around. "Watch that utility knife." She pointed to a tool lying on the shelf. "I forgot to put the safety on." She reached around me and retracted the blade. "Don't want you getting hurt."

After we finished, she switched off the light and closed the door. "How about a cup of tea?" she asked. "Putting away stock always chills me to the bone."

"Sounds good to me." I looked around, hoping for a freshly made batch of cookies but was disappointed. Normally there would be a tray on the counter, but not today.

"Since when do you get deliveries on Sunday?" I asked.

"This was scheduled for Friday, but with the flood I postponed it. The delivery came last night, and all I had time to do was shove it in the freezer. I had too much produce to take care of. The frozen stuff can wait."

I seated myself at the work counter while Zella heated two cups of water. She pulled a box of tea from over the stove and slid it down to me. "Pick out what you want. There're several kinds. I'll have the chamomile."

"Sounds good to me." I plucked two bags from the box.

Zella set the cups on the counter. "Can I interest you in a cookie?"

"I thought you'd never ask. And it seemed rude to go poking around looking for them."

"Never stopped you before, young lady." Zella's voice sounded gruff, but her smile gave her away. She produced an overflowing plate from under the counter. Removing the plastic wrap, she said, "Baked these yesterday, but they're still mighty good."

I took one and broke it in half. "I love your cookies. No one makes them quite like you do."

"Old family recipe, only I had to increase everything twenty-fold to get enough for all these ankle-biters around here."

"Good job," I said around the cookie in my mouth.

"What brings you to Zella's kitchen today besides cookies? I know you got too much work on your plate to be sitting around drinking tea with me."

I choked, and cookie crumbs spewed from my mouth. "Am I that transparent?"

"Always were. I suspect you haven't changed much as an adult. You used to sneak in here on the pretense of a cookie when you really wanted to talk about boys or problems you were having with a teacher." She blew across the top of her mug. "Or your mom. What's on your mind today?"

I measured my words before I spoke. "You."

She gazed across the top of her mug, eyes narrowing. "Me."

"Yeah, here you're getting ready to retire and go on the road, and you'd think you'd be chomping at the bit, but you don't seem so happy. Is everything all right?"

"Have you been talking to my Tommy?" She set her cup down and folded her arms across her ample chest. "And don't fib to me, young lady. Did Tommy put you up to this?"

I met her gaze. "Yes, he did. Zella, he's worried about you."

"Well, the old fool needs to mind his own business." Zella turned her head but not before tears started to puddle in her eyes.

I pushed my plate aside and walked to where she sat. "What's wrong? I know you need someone to talk to."

She didn't say anything but slipped her hand into her pocket and produced a business card, which she handed to me.

ARLENE DELGADO, ONCOLOGIST

"I don't understand," I said.

"It's cancer. I have cancer." The tears broke loose and streamed down Zella's cheeks.

That was a word no one ever wanted to hear, but coming from sweet Zella the word was even more heart-wrenching.

Saying I was sorry didn't seem adequate. I hugged her and held on tight, patting her back and making soothing sounds. When her tears subsided, I sighed. "Tommy doesn't know, does he?"

She pulled away and shook her head. "No, and don't go getting any ideas. You aren't going to tell him either."

"Why haven't you told him?"

Zella inhaled a deep breath and helped herself to a cookie. "You don't have time to be listening to my problems. Be off with yourself."

"Don't be silly. Of course I have time." Zella had always been so partial to Angie and me when we attended Wickford High; there was no way I could turn my back on her.

"You are a dear. If you don't mind, I really do need someone to talk to. It'll be nice to get another opinion. My own kids are too busy trying to run their kids' lives to listen to the problems of their mama."

"So, what's up?" I asked, eyeing another cookie but not acting on my impulse.

"When Tommy first came home from the war, it was a horrible time. You know all the protesting and name-calling. Those poor boys didn't stand a chance."

I remembered how I'd actually seen a man spit on a returning veteran. Gigi and I had been at the bus station, heading on one of our many midnight trips to see my grandpa Earl. I was a small child, and Gigi and I were living with Freddy Falcone. Freddy was a used-car salesman with a penchant for drinking too much and beating up on women. When my mother walked in and caught Freddy smacking me around, off we went.

"Anyway," Zella said, pulling me back to the present, "it took Tommy a while to find himself a decent job. In the meantime, he found the corner bar and spent his afternoons sweeping the floor in return for liquid refreshment. One thing led to another and before long, Tommy was a full-blown drunk."

I slid my hand across the counter and patted Zella's. "Oh, Zella, I know it was rough for those guys coming back. People were so polarized by the war, they took it out on the easiest targets."

"Tommy took it hard. It was rough times for him. Years later, when he finally got hired by the district, he still had a rough patch or two, but he went into treatment. Afterward, he was like a new man. Joined AA and put the bottle away." She sighed and ran a hand through her snow-white hair. "It took a while, but when I was finally convinced he was sober, I agreed to marry him. I loved him even before he went to Vietnam, but afterward, after everything he'd been through, I wanted to heal him so badly."

She was worried that Tommy might start drinking again. That's why she wouldn't tell him. But if he had managed to kick the habit for all these years, he surely could resist.

"Are you afraid retirement will drive Tommy back to the bottle? I could understand if he went from working a full schedule to having nothing to do, but it sounds like the two of you will have plenty to occupy your time."

"That and what will happen to him when I'm gone."

I surprised myself by asking, "What can I do to help?" I had way too much on my plate to be worrying about Tommy, but Zella seemed so stricken. With no family to help her, she had nowhere to turn. Kind of made my mother's predicament a little easier to understand. There she was out in Tucson with a man who was driving her up a tree, and she had no friends or family to talk it over with. A fat lot of good I had been. I only called her once in a while, and since my ordeal with Phillip, I hadn't called her at all.

The thought of telling Gigi about my failed marriage made me want to go into hiding. I'd never understood how she lived the life she had and had always blamed her when one of her relationships took a turn for the worst. She certainly wasn't the typical mother, and she sure wasn't the typical wife. I'd always thought if she tried harder to fit the mold of what I thought a wife should be, that maybe we wouldn't always be leaving under the cover of darkness.

The difference between my mother and me was that she ran. I didn't run, but I sure didn't fight. When my husband told me he was having an affair and then I subsequently found out it was more than one affair, I'd just rolled over and let him walk out of my life. Maybe if I'd had my eyes open during our marriage, I would have seen him for who he was, or maybe he wouldn't have felt compelled to cheat on me. Here I readily judged my mother for always leaving so quickly, for finding the worst men, and yet I took too long to realize there was something wrong with my own marriage.

"Help?" Zella said. "I don't know that anyone can help. I feel like I'm right back where I was."

"Have you talked to him? I mean, you don't know he'll start drinking again. I know he's worried about you. Maybe he needs a little nudge to keep him on track." I felt suspended in the middle.

"Nudge? That old man needs a good swift kick in the pants." Zella shuffled over to the sink, refilled our cups, and nuked them.

"Have you talked to his sponsor?"

"Oh, did I ever. Tommy hit the roof."

"Look, it sounds to me like you two are long overdue for a talk."

"Hmph. Maybe."

"You can't keep this from him. He'll find out when you start treatment."

Her shoulders heaved. "I'm not starting treatment. We

can't be RVing all over the country if I'm taking chemotherapy."

"What? You aren't going to get treatment. Zella, that's just plain crazy. What kind of cancer?"

"Breast cancer."

"How bad?" I asked.

"I don't know. I got the results of my mammogram a couple weeks ago and this referral for a biopsy."

I relaxed a bit. "You haven't had the biopsy yet?"

"No." Zella bit down on her lip.

"Get the biopsy, then you'll know what you're dealing with," I said. "What did the mammogram show?"

"A suspicious mass." Tears came to her eyes. "My only sister died of breast cancer."

I got up and put my arm around her. "You have every right to be scared, but don't make a decision until you know what you're dealing with. Mammograms are not definitive. That's why your doctor referred you for a biopsy."

"Does Tommy know?" she asked.

"No, that's why he's so worried. If you haven't told him, how would he know?"

Zella's face hardened. "Steve."

"I don't understand." Then I remembered what Liz had told me about Zella being so angry with Steve. "Steve knew, didn't he? And he threatened to tell Tommy."

"He came in one day while I was talking to my doctor on the phone, and before I knew he was standing there, he overheard my whole conversation." She pulled a tissue from her pocket and dabbed at her eyes.

"But he never told Tommy," I said.

"Because he blackmailed me." Zella spat the words with a fury I had never seen from her.

She was the third person in as many days whom I learned Steve had threatened with blackmail. Four if I counted Liz. I wondered how many more were on the list and what his motive was for doing so. Would Zella kill to keep her secret?

Zella went to the pantry, and I heard her moving boxes and rearranging stuff. She returned and slid a sealed envelope across the counter to me. "He asked me to hide this. When I questioned him, he just said it was something very important and under no circumstance should I give it to anyone but him when the time was right." Fresh tears appeared in her eyes.

"He was going to go to Tommy if you didn't hide this?" I asked, holding the envelope.

Zella nodded. "So, I did what I had to do."

"I'm so sorry he put you through this. Do you mind if I take it? It might help Detective Alder. It may hold a key to why Steve was killed."

"Take it. I don't want no part of it."

I hugged her again and held on tight. "Promise me you'll get that biopsy. And you'll tell Tommy. He loves you, and it's not fair not to let him help you through whatever you're facing. That might help you understand what he's going through."

"I will. On both accounts," Zella said.

I tucked the envelope under my arm and went in search of my mother.

CHAPTER FOURTEEN

"Is it bad to say I'm counting the days until Phillip's divorce is final? Good riddance, Cece."
Hazel Cavanaugh

I slid the envelope in my purse and decided to take Gigi to lunch. Nancy had already cut out for whatever she had going on. I tried to call Alder, but my call went to voice mail and I left a message.

Gigi and I had just fastened our seat belts when my cell rang. I retrieved it from my pocket and answered.

"What do you think?" Liz greeted me in a less-than-chipper voice.

"I think you tied one on last night." I couldn't help myself. I heard voices in the background and pictured the women in various stages of hangovers in their designer sleepwear downing aspirin, orange juice, or in some cases a brunch cocktail. Parties like Liz's tended to bring out the party animals in Wickford's country club set.

"I mean about the flash drive."

It took me a minute to digest what she meant, then I remembered the device she had shoved in my hand last night right before Hazel arrived and distracted me. I glanced at the drive in my cupholder and noticed the Wickford Wildcats logo on it. "What about it?"

"Cece, I think Steve may have hidden it at my house the morning he was killed."

I picked up the drive and turned it over in my hand. "So?"

"So, it's weird is all," she said, lowering her voice. "You know how I have that little herb garden in the window over my sink?"

"Yes." I rolled my eyes. I wasn't sure if Hazel arriving last night was a planned event or not, so Liz's latest revelation didn't register on my curiosity meter.

"When I went to water the basil, I found it. The flash drive, just lying on top of the dirt."

I started the car and flipped the heater on. "What makes you think Steve hid it?"

"What makes me think Steve hid it?" Liz repeated. "I watered my herbs that morning before Steve came over and it wasn't there, or I would have seen it. Bill hasn't been home since then. I didn't put it there. How else would it get there?"

She had a point. "Well, why'd you give it to me? What's on it?"

Liz inhaled sharply then blew out the breath. "If I knew that, I wouldn't be asking you. My laptop's at school. I couldn't go traipsing over there with all my guests here, now could I?"

More like she couldn't go *traipsing* over there and risk getting pulled over and handed a DWI. "What do you want me to do with it?"

"See what's on it, of course. The way I see it, there's one of three things. It's either something that got him killed—"

Liz covered the phone and I heard muffled conversation. "Sorry. I'm back. Apparently, we're out of champagne."

I noticed Gigi wringing her hands, getting antsy. I needed to move this along and get us to lunch so we could get back to school. I was wasting time on this nonsense. "You were saying?"

"Right. Or something he wanted Bill to find about taking me to court, or best-case scenario just school stuff."

"Well, *A*, if he wanted Bill to find it, why put it in your herb garden? *B*, if it's school stuff why even bother to hide it? And *C*, if it's something that got him killed, why would he leave it with you?"

"I don't know. That's why I gave it to you. I gotta go, these gals are getting restless. Need to get some food on the table before I have a mutiny. Let me know what you find."

Before I could respond, Liz disconnected. "Well great." I pulled out of the parking lot and headed for Café du Soleil.

"What was that all about?" Gigi asked. "This about that guy who got himself killed?"

"Most likely not. I think Liz is still tanked from her party last night." I thought about that flash drive and checking it to see what it contained. Jessie had warned me repeatedly—like I was an idiot—not to open strange files on my laptop. So, stopping by my house to get my laptop was a no-go. The last thing I needed was a virus on my computer and my daughter saying *I told you so.*

When we passed the library, I had a brainstorm. I could look at the flash drive there. If it contained anything related to Steve's murder, I'd give it to Alder when I gave him the envelope Zella had given me. I couldn't justify opening the envelope since it was sealed, but the flash drive begged my attention. My inner snoop just needed to know.

I pulled into the library lot and parked the car. "Can you wait a bit for lunch? I need to run in here a minute."

Gigi's eyes brightened when she saw the winery gift shop, which had recently opened next door to the Wickford Library. "No problem. You go do your thing and come get me when you're done. I'm going to check out the goodies in there. Maybe they'll have some wine samples."

And as luck would have it, Liz's mother-in-law Mavis Blevins and my mother-in-law walked out of the gift shop just as Gigi and I stepped onto the sidewalk.

"Well, if it isn't Georgie. Heard you married—again." Hazel let the words roll off her tongue like sweet, sticky syrup. "Mavis, have you ever had the pleasure of meeting Cece's mother?"

Mavis looked me up and down, then did the same to Gigi. We were both dressed in our cleaning clothes since we'd just come from the school and were headed back as soon as we grabbed a bite to eat.

"I remember her. You can certainly see the mother-daughter resemblance."

"Must be old crone's day. The shop must have had a BOGO sale on brooms," Gigi said to me. "I see Wickford hasn't changed one bit."

I stifled a giggle and remembered what I loved most about my mother—her snark. I would put her one-on-one with Hazel or Mavis any day. Gigi could take it, but boy could she dish it out too.

"Liz said she was out of champagne," I said to Gigi. "Must have sent these two to fetch the booze."

"You go do your thing," Gigi said. "I can take care of myself."

I almost felt sorry for Hazel and Mavis—almost.

"Cecelia," Hazel called. "Don't even think for a minute that the girls will be spending Thanksgiving with you. Cavanaugh tradition is Thanksgiving at my house. This year will be no different."

I bristled. "That's where you're wrong. First off, Michelle and Jessie are old enough to make the decision where they spend Thanksgiving, or any holiday for that matter. They've already made plans with their father for an early breakfast Thursday. But they both decided to spend the day with me since their grandmother is here visiting." I had to get a dig in about Gigi being their grandmother too. Hazel thought she had sole ownership of the title.

"Maybe they'll alternate next year. But it's their decision. Not mine and not yours." I turned my back and headed down the sidewalk, certain that Gigi would dish out a ration should Hazel tear into her.

Inside the library, I headed to the main desk.

"Can I help you?" asked a dreadlocked teen who didn't bother to look up from his phone.

Probably not, I thought. "Just need to use a computer to check out a flash drive."

"Over there." He pointed to a row of computers near the windows.

"I'm familiar."

He grunted in response.

I found a vacant spot and inserted the flash drive. A password box appeared on the screen. I removed the device and tried again. Same result. With patience not being my strong suit, I grabbed the drive and trudged over to dreadlock.

"What's the password?" I asked.

"Huh?"

"The password. It's asking for a password."

"Shouldn't be."

"Well, it is. Can you help me?"

"No," he said.

"What do you mean no?" My cheeks grew warm. "You work here, don't you?"

Dreadlock scrunched his face. "Umm. I'm just here 'cause

I have to do community service. You have to talk to one of the library ladies."

Of course, why else was he manning a desk? I looked around but only saw other teens about his age. Were they all "doing time"? What was our town coming to? And why would you turn a bunch of juvenile delinquents loose in a library, for goodness sake. Make them pick up litter or plant flowers along the roadways. Don't let them work some place where they can influence the minds of our youth.

"And where would I find a library lady?"

He looked up and shrugged. "Dunno. I think they're in a meeting. They just told me to sit here and if anyone came up to the desk to try to help them."

Uh-huh, and some help you are. "Is there anyone who might be able to help with a computer?"

"See that girl in the denim jacket?" He pointed to a slender girl with black spiked hair.

"Yes. Can she help?"

"She's pretty smart," he said.

"Thanks."

I approached the girl. "Excuse me, the young man up front told me you might be able to help me."

She scowled. "Of course, why would he want to do any work. I'd like to take that video game and—"

"Can you help me or not?"

"Probably. What do you need?"

I showed her the flash drive. "I need a password."

She followed me over to the computer I had vacated. "Let me see it."

When I had given her the drive, she inserted it into the slot and got the same password message. "Oh, it's protected. Do you know the password?"

"Well duh, that's why I need your help."

She chuckled. "No, I mean do you know the password for the drive? It's not the computer."

"Oh. Well, no. I don't. Didn't even know you could put a password on one."

She handed me the device. "Unless you know it, you can't get access to the files."

"Crap. How do I do that?" I pocketed the drive.

"Who does it belong to?" She gave me an eye roll like I was a doddering old fool. "You'd have to find out from them."

Think fast. "My kid. It belongs to my kid."

"Spying, huh? Shame on you." She blew out a breath and huffed off.

Figured, but now I was more curious about what was on the drive. "Ugh!"

"Ugh, what?"

I turned and Gigi was standing beside me holding a paper bag that looked like it might contain a bottle of wine.

"Oh, nothing. Is Hazel still breathing or did you take her out?" I asked, kind of hoping for the worst.

"Naw, you can't kill the mean ones." Gigi laughed. "She'll live to see another day. But next time . . ."

"Let's go get lunch." I linked arms with my mother and we breezed out the door.

Gigi had never been to Café du Soleil. Even though I'd been there yesterday with Liz, I figured it would be a quick lunch. After my library detour, we needed to get back to the school.

The hostess seated us, and Gigi made a show of paging through the menu. "What is it with these places? How many pages of food do you need?"

Before I could say anything, I realized Nancy was sitting at a table in the far corner with a man. He had his back to me. I couldn't see his face, but he had a build similar to Grant Hunter. Nancy was chattering like a magpie.

"Hey, isn't that your helper?" Gigi asked. She raised her hand to wave, but I grabbed her arm and pulled it down.

"Leave her alone," I said. "If she's got a boyfriend, I need that relationship to flourish. She needs to find a new place to live. If she's involved with someone, maybe she'll move in with him. Working with her is bad enough. Living with her is making me nuts."

"I'm starving. Are we gonna gawk or eat?" Gigi never was one to mince words.

I shut my menu and got up. If Nancy had a new man in her life, she didn't need me or my mother butting in and making it uncomfortable. "Let's go to Weezie's. The lunch rush should be clearing out by the time we get there." I grabbed Gigi's arm and led her out the door.

Gigi's mouth dropped open. "Why? We're not bothering her."

"Oh, come on. Let's let her be," I said.

When we got to the street, I scanned the area. Sure enough, Grant's truck was parked at the curb two storefronts down. Nancy wasn't having lunch with a boyfriend. If she thought she was going to steal a good cleaning job out from underneath me, she'd better think twice.

Gigi rolled her eyes. "Let's go before I wilt from hunger. But you're paying."

CHAPTER FIFTEEN

"If this amateur detective is so smart, she'll point the finger at TJ or Liz or Marnie. Who didn't have a motive to kill Steve?"
Keith Preston

After lunch I sent Gigi back to finish up what she'd been working on. Nancy arrived soon after, never hinting that she'd had a lunch date. I kept my mouth shut, because I wanted to talk to Grant first. If Nancy was making a play for my job, I wanted to find out from Grant before I confronted her.

I noticed Keith heading to the cafeteria with a sack lunch and newspaper. He had just sat down and unfolded the newspaper when I approached. "Mind if I join you?" I asked.

He glanced over the top of the page. "Suit yourself."

I eased onto the bench. "It'll be nice to see the sun one of these days. I'm tired of all the gloom."

"Uh-huh," he mumbled.

Engaging this guy in conversation wasn't easy. I kind of regretted shutting him down the other day, but I didn't need a creeper in my life. Not when I was on the verge of getting rid of one. My fifty-year-old husband was in a relationship with a twenty-something. That almost qualified as a creeper in my book. "How long have you been at Wickford?"

The paper rustled, and I noticed his eyes peering over the page again. "Several years. Why?" He shook the paper and adjusted it with a big sigh.

"No reason. I went to school here, you know?"

"Absolutely fascinating."

A man of few words. Probably why there was no wedding ring on his finger. I guessed my earlier brush off had caused him to clam up. I had to find common ground if I was going to get anything out of him. He was reading the sports page, so I took a chance.

"You a Cardinal fan?" Not many men could resist talking about baseball. Even if they weren't fans, they'd never let a woman know. Like it was an attack on their manhood not to like baseball.

"Cubs," he said without hesitation but added, "The Cards did great this year. Too bad they got killed in the postseason. It would have been great to have the World Series here, locally."

I knew enough about baseball to be dangerous, but if I could get him talking and then start asking a few questions about Steve, maybe he'd take the bait.

"I was looking forward to seeing them play. The stadium is pretty spectacular. Don't you think?"

He laid the paper aside and picked up his sack. "Yep. Guess I better get back to work."

"You haven't even touched your lunch."

"Not that hungry," he said.

"I'm heading that way, so I'll walk with you." I followed him into the hallway.

When we got near Steve's art room I said, "Steve loved

baseball so much, he had season tickets. You ever get a chance to go to a game with him?" Lucky for me, Liz had told me what a fanatic her ex was about baseball. It was another reason their marriage failed. Liz said he glued himself to the television during the summer and fall and didn't move for anything. Well, anything except apparently another woman.

"Nope." He stopped and shifted the paper under his arm.

"Too bad about Steve. I guess it will be hard on the students when they come back."

He frowned. "I'm sure it will."

"Was he well-liked by the kids?" I remembered when my tenth-grade algebra teacher died in a car accident; the entire school had gone into mourning.

"Probably not any more than any other teacher. Maybe the football team. What's with the Q&A?"

I gulped. "Nothing. I didn't know him and was curious to learn more."

"Being a little nosy, huh?"

"Not hardly." I bristled at his comment. "Liz used to be my tennis partner—not that it's any of your business. I knew she had an ex, but I had never met him. Wondered what kind of guy he was."

He shrugged and started to walk away.

Think fast. I scanned Steve's classroom and an idea came to me. "Hey, do you think you could help me for a minute?"

He turned and stared at me. "What do you want?"

"I've been trying to get the blinds in his room open to get some light in and can't reach the cord. Could you see if you can? You might have to stand on a chair. I'm kinda scared of heights."

He scowled. "Why don't you call Tommy and have him bring a ladder. That's what he's here for."

Duh! "I could, except, I don't have a clue where he is, and

I'd really like to get started. The overheads just don't light it up enough."

He tromped into the room and threw his paper on the desk. "Which blind are you having trouble with?"

"That one over there," I said, pointing to one at the back of the room.

He reached up and couldn't quite grasp it.

"You need something to stand on." I scooted over a chair. "See if this will help."

He climbed up and drew the blind open. "There. Anything else you need?"

"No, thanks a lot." I pushed the chair back. The walls were lined with pen and ink drawings. I noticed that while some of them belonged to students, the majority had Steve's name scribbled in the corners. "He was an amazing artist."

"I guess so. I never really noticed. Comes from having my head stuck in a science book too often, I suppose."

I laughed, relieved he was finally starting to open up. "What grades do you teach?"

"Mostly seniors. My classes are all for honors students." He headed to the door, grabbing his paper on the way.

"Thanks for getting that for me. I'll be here forever if I don't get a move on."

"No problem." He started out the door but turned around. "Can I ask you a question?"

I hoped he wasn't going to hit on me again. "Sure."

"Is it true what Marni said about you finding out who killed the Redmond guy?"

"Sort of. It's not like I set out to do it," I said.

"Are you going to get involved with Steve's murder?"

Play it dumb, Cece. "No, why would you think that?"

"You'd done it before, so I assumed with all the questions you were asking, you were doing some snooping. I have something I wanted your opinion on. I'm not sure if I should show it to the police, because it might be nothing. Don't you worry about it though. I'll figure something out."

"I don't mind taking a look. It can't hurt, right?"

"You sure? It might be a ruse to get you alone and have my way with you." He laughed.

I backed up a step.

"I'm teasing. You got pretty upset when I came on to you, and I know when my advances aren't wanted. But I really would like your opinion."

"Maybe it's not such a good idea." *Why did I say that? I need to know what he has.*

"Suit yourself. But seriously, I'm harmless. You can ask anyone," he said.

"Okay, then. Don't make me regret my decision."

I followed Keith to his classroom where he pulled an envelope from his desk and handed it to me.

I pulled a paper from the envelope. In big, black letters the words TJ HAS A SECRET THAT IS ABOUT TO BE EXPOSED!! were scrawled along with a smear of ketchup posing as blood. Just like the warning I had received.

"Where did you get this?"

"Found it on my desk the evening before Trupeli was killed. I stayed late to set up some experiments in the science lab, and when I got back, it was propped up on my stapler." Keith folded the letter and slid it in his drawer.

"What does it mean?"

Keith pulled out a chair for me and then slumped into the one behind his desk. "What do you think it means?"

"How would I know? I don't know TJ."

"For a snoop, you're pretty naïve."

I thought about what Liz had told me. "Does this have anything to do with the argument you had with Steve on Thursday?"

He whistled softly. "Now you get it, don't you?"

Beads of perspiration gathered at my neckline, and I tried in vain to fan away a potential hot flash. "Not really. What prompted the argument?"

"Isn't it obvious that Steve was holding something over TJ's head? Something he threatened to expose hoping to get TJ fired."

"The two of you argued about TJ?"

"Look, TJ is an all right guy. Steve just had a chip on his shoulder and was looking for revenge. All I did was try to get him to back off."

"And what happened after your argument?"

Keith grimaced. "Did I take it a step further? No. I confronted him. He told me to mind my own business. When I told him to lay off TJ, he came at me. If Tommy hadn't been coming down the hall at that exact moment, I have no doubt that Steve would have punched me."

I mulled over what he had told me, trying to make a connection between Steve's death and the note. A note that had similarities to the one I found in my purse. A purse that I found in Keith's classroom.

"What do you think I should do?" Keith asked. "I haven't shown that to anyone but you. Not even the cops. I'm afraid it will put a big target right on TJ."

"My advice is to show the police. I understand about you not wanting to point fingers at TJ, but by holding on to the note, you're impeding the investigation."

Keith gave his ponytail a tightening. "I was afraid you'd say that. Are you sure you can't keep it to yourself and just keep an eye out for what's going on around here?"

"It's not my story to tell, but I really do encourage you to be up front with Detective Alder. The more pieces he has to put together, the sooner he can solve this."

Nancy stuck her head in the door. "We about ready to wrap up for the day?"

Gigi stood next to Nancy, tapping her toes. "Yup, I'm ready to get the heck out of here."

Oh, if only she meant get the heck out of Wickford.

"Sure thing," I said to both of them. To Keith I said, "Think about what we discussed. I know you'll come to the right decision."

CHAPTER SIXTEEN

"Best friends like Cece don't come along often. I'm lucky to have her as mine."
   Angie Valenti

I dropped Gigi off at home and headed to Angie's with a little gift I'd picked up on the way. I clutched the paper bag in my hand as I climbed the stairs to Angie's bedroom. This was the third day that Angie had been in bed feeling miserable. I had a hunch I knew what was wrong, and it wasn't something a little antacid could take care of. That's why I'd stopped at the drugstore.

When I walked in, Angie was hunkered down in bed, moaning. I rapped on the doorframe. "Anybody home?"

She threw the blanket back and pushed up on her elbows. "I feel horrible. I swear my twenty-four-hour bug has turned into a thirty-six-hour bug."

"Did you make a doctor's appointment yet?" I'd sworn that I'd drag her to the doctor if she didn't make one. As a former nurse, I hated it when people were sick and just complained about it instead of taking action and doing something. Get a pill, do something, but don't lie around groaning.

She slumped against her pillow. "No, I get to feeling better and then, wham, it hits me again. I figure if I make an appointment, by the time I get in to see the doctor, I'll be better. Yesterday, I felt fine all afternoon, then this morning, it's like I have aliens in my stomach."

I held up the paper bag and wiggled it. "I don't think it's aliens, and I don't think it's your stomach that's giving you fits."

"What are you talking about?"

Angie and I were the same age, give or take a few months, so what I was about to tell her was going to give her a scare. But someone had to break the news to her, so I figured it might as well be her best friend. "I had exactly the same symptoms you're having."

"You did? I didn't know you'd been sick. Why didn't you tell me? Are we passing the same bug back and forth? If so, you need to get out of here. Maybe we need Beatrice to disinfect both our houses." Angie jumped from the bed and raced to the bathroom.

After I heard the toilet flush, I stuck my head in the door and pulled a pregnancy kit from the bag and opened it. "Pee on this," I said, pushing the plastic stick into her hand.

Her eyes grew wide. "Are you freaking kidding me? You want me to take a pregnancy test. I'm forty-eight years old and haven't gotten pregnant in thirty years—even when I tried."

Angie had taken birth control the first couple years after she and Dave got married, but when she quit and tried to get pregnant, nothing. They'd tried everything to have a baby and nothing worked. She'd been tested, had her tubes blown out, taken fertility treatments. When those didn't work, Dave had been tested. None of the tests had ruled out having a baby, but it never happened. They'd stopped short of in vitro. Angie was of the firm belief if they could not have a baby the old-fashioned way, then it wasn't going to happen.

"Pee on the stick," I said. "There's only one logical reason to explain your sickness. If it looks like a duck and quacks like a duck, it ain't no chicken."

Angie eyed the stick and then motioned me out of the bathroom. A few seconds later, she emerged, stick in hand. "What now?"

"Now we wait for the results." I sat down on the side of the bed.

Angie covered her eyes with one hand and thrust the stick at me when the time had passed. "You look. I can't do it."

I stared at the result, checked the instructions on the pamphlet, and then stared at the result again. "You aren't going to believe this."

Angie peeked through her fingers and took it from me. "Ohmigod. I'm pregnant. I cannot be pregnant." She dropped the stick. "It's a mistake. I can't get pregnant. I tried for thirty years to have a baby." She grabbed the box off the nightstand and gave it the once-over. "Did you get this out of the bargain bin? How reliable are these things?"

I nodded. "It says these have a 99-percent accuracy rate."

Tears formed in her eyes. "I'm forty-freaking-eight years old. I cannot be pregnant. How can I be pregnant?"

I smiled and rolled my eyes. It didn't take an ob-gyn to tell her how it had happened. It also gave me pause. If Angie could be going through menopause and get pregnant, so could yours truly. I thanked my lucky stars that I hadn't thrown caution to the wind the other night with Alder. It had been a close call. Good thing the blanket had caught fire.

"I know how it happened. I mean why? After all these years, how could it happen now? You'd think by now that all my eggs would be dried up." She buried her head in her hands. "What am I going to do? I'm too old to have a baby."

I put my arms around her and patted her back. "It'll be okay. You just need some time to adjust. Once the shock wears off, you'll see it as the blessing it is." Ha! There was no such thing as a pregnancy at forty-eight being a blessing. What would I do if I found out I was pregnant at forty-eight? But I needed to maintain a positive attitude for my friend. There had to be an upside to late-life pregnancy, but I couldn't think of one. Then again, I already had two kids.

"Blessing—are you kidding me? Thirty years ago, it would have been a blessing. Twenty years ago, it would have been a blessing. Ten years ago, maybe a minor inconvenience, but now? Now it's a freaking disaster."

"Think about how excited Dave will be. He's always wanted a baby. Maybe it will be a boy."

Angie sobbed. "I . . . can't . . . be . . . pregnant. Dave is going to have a fit. He's been talking about cutting back on his practice and phasing into retirement. He can't retire if we have a baby. And me, how can I work if I have a kid? Have you ever seen a pregnant cop? I'll have to quit and just when I'm up for promotion."

I heard the front door slam.

"Hey, anybody home?" Dave called up the stairs.

"Ohmigod, it's Dave." Angie gathered up the stick, pamphlet, and box and shoved them back into the paper bag, which she pushed into my hand. "Don't you dare breathe a word of this to him." She nudged me off the bed and straightened the blankets. "We're up here."

"I won't, but you have to tell him."

"You pinky swear right this minute." Angie snatched my hand and wrapped her pinky finger around mine. "You swear to me you won't say anything. I have to think about this."

"I swear, but I don't like it."

Dave stuck his head in the bedroom. "What are you two up to?"

I smiled. "Just checking to see how the patient is doing."

Angie glared.

"I keep telling her she needs to see a doctor, but does she ever listen to me?" Dave laughed and kissed her on the forehead. "Probably shouldn't do that. Don't want to catch your bug."

"I don't think there's any chance of that happening." I couldn't help myself, but sometimes my evil twin just worked her way out.

Angie shot me another look and promptly gagged, racing to the bathroom again.

"Better get her back to bed, Dave. She needs all the rest she can get." Again, evil Cece couldn't resist.

I left swinging the little paper sack, humming a lullaby.

CHAPTER SEVENTEEN

"I don't know what my mom is up to, but I'll bet she's up to something."
Jessie Cavanaugh

Jessie and Brad came staggering through the door with canvas bags overflowing with groceries for our holiday meal.

"I think I got everything on the list," she said, dropping the bags on the counter. "The store was a madhouse. You'd think people had never cooked a Thanksgiving meal before."

Brad laughed. "You won't believe it, but there were two women actually fighting over a turkey. The one had it in her cart and while she was getting butter out of the dairy case, another woman took it right out from underneath her nose. I swear, as long as I live, I won't understand women."

Jessie slugged him on the arm. "Hey, I'm a woman and I resent that remark."

"Not you, baby. I got you all figured out." He dropped onto a barstool and pulled her onto his lap.

"Stop it, you two. We've got food to put away. No PDA in my kitchen."

I unpacked the bags while Jessie put away the canned goods.

"Brad, will you get a roaster from over the fridge and put the bird in it and stick him in the fridge in the garage? He's going to need some time to thaw."

I continued pulling out groceries.

"Hey, where are the cranberries?"

"You didn't have it on the list."

"I most certainly did. It's not Thanksgiving without cranberries."

Jessie rolled her eyes. "It won't kill us not to have them."

"Never mind, I'll stop tomorrow on my way home from work and pick some up." I folded my canvas bags and stuck them in the pantry. "Thanks for getting this stuff. There never seems to be enough time in the day."

"No problem. It was kind of fun, dodging all the blue hairs and their motorized carts. I've never seen so many old ladies at the grocery store in my whole life."

"Speaking of old ladies," I said, "how'd Hazel take the news that you were eating dinner here?"

"Gran wasn't happy, but I told her the alternative was having you come to her house, and she backed down pretty quickly. She's doing another meal on Saturday, so we'll go then. Except I think Michelle has to work, so Gran will probably go ballistic over that."

"Who'll go ballistic?" Brad asked, returning from the garage.

"My grandmother. The one we're eating with Saturday."

"My sympathies," I said. "You'll need them."

Jessie tossed a loaf of bread at me. "Don't start, Mom."

"Sorry, I'll behave myself." I finished putting away

groceries while Jessie and Brad checked their phones for all the important stuff they'd missed.

Jess was a wiz on the computer. Before she'd decided to become a nurse, she'd taken several computer classes at the community college and knew all about bytes, bits, RAM, and all things computer. "Jessie, while you're on there, will you take a look at something for me?"

"What did you screw up now?" She constantly had to get me out of jams when I forgot to back up my work. She'd even made me a spreadsheet to track my income from cleaning. If it was computer-related, Jessie knew how to do it.

"Nothing, smarty pants. I'm looking for something for my friend Liz."

"Liz that you used to play tennis with? I didn't know you two were still friends." Jessie swiveled around in the chair. "Didn't she get another partner after you dropped your membership at the club?"

Dropped my membership was a nice way to put it. The minute Phillip served me with divorce papers, Hazel had the membership committee vote me out. I received a formal letter telling me that due to the circumstances, my membership was no longer valid. The snobs! I had been tolerated due to my marriage. Once it was in jeopardy, I was kicked out like day-old bread.

"She teaches at Wickford High and asked me to help her find some files on her flash drive."

Jessie curled her lip. "She asked *you*? Does she know that I've just about had to take your laptop into protective custody to save it from you?"

"Ha ha. Funny girl. Just look on the drive and see if I am missing anything. All I can find are class schedules, tests, and school stuff." I leaned over her shoulder.

"What exactly are you looking for?" Jessie asked.

Good question. I remembered the old Sesame Street song

about one of these things not looking like the other. "Something not school-related. She put some personal files on there and now she can't find them. Look for something that doesn't look like school stuff."

Jessie shook her head. "What's the deal, really? Are you on another one of your snooping escapades?"

"No, why would you ask that?" I straightened.

"Because you have a track record of getting involved with police investigations, and there's one going on at the school right now. And it just happens to be Liz's ex-husband."

"Oh, good grief. It's nothing like that. Liz lost a few files and I was trying to help her." I snatched the drive from Jessie and shoved it in my pocket. "Never mind. I'll try something else."

"Am I going to have to rat you out to Angie?" Jessie pushed her chair back. "The last time you got involved with a friend of yours, you almost got yourself killed."

"For your information, if I hadn't gotten involved the last time, you would have never met Brad. So there."

"I'm serious. Whatever you're involved in, you need to quit. I will call Angie, and she'll sic that detective on you."

"Fine, I'll tell Liz I can't help. But you leave Angie out of it. She's been sick, and the last thing she needs is you whining to her." So much for Jessie helping me. I'd just have to figure it out by myself.

CHAPTER EIGHTEEN

**"I'm a doctor. How could I have missed all the signs?
Dave Valenti**

I was waiting on the patio when Nancy came down the steps headed for Hunter Springs.

"Can we talk before you go to work?" I wrapped my jacket around me. It had turned colder overnight, and even though it was November, I wasn't prepared for it.

Nancy eyed me with curiosity and fished the wad of gum from her mouth. "Didn't expect to see you." She started to flick the gum into the lawn, but when I cleared my throat, she rolled it around in her fingers.

I pulled a tissue from my pocket and handed it to her.

"Thanks." She wrapped the gum and shoved it in her purse.

My stomach clenched, but I didn't say anything. Lord only knew what was in her purse. I didn't want to see.

"Hey, what's up with Angie?" Nancy asked. "She's grouchy as a bear."

Alert. Alert. Angie has enough on her mind without Nancy bugging her to death. Handle this quick and then change the subject.

"When did you see Angie?"

"I didn't. I called her this morning to see what she was bringing to your house for Thanksgiving. I'm making coleslaw, and I didn't want her bringing it too. She told me to get a life and hung up."

Coleslaw? That goes well with turkey.

"She's been down with some kind of virus that's going around. Caught it at work, I imagine. If I were you, I'd stay away from her. We can't afford to get sick, not with all this work and the holiday coming up."

Nancy grimaced. "Ew, I hate sick people. I hope she gets better before Thursday. I'm not eating whatever she brings." She reached in her purse and pulled out a box of Vitamin C. "You want one?"

I shook my head. If she'd put chewed gum in her purse, no telling what else was in there.

"Nancy, do you know anything about flash drives?"

"Sure, I used them all the time when I worked for Bonafide. Fletcher had backups for each client." Nancy blew a bubble and let it pop.

I dug the drive out of my pocket and handed it to her. "This one apparently has a password. I tried to open it on my laptop, and I keep getting a message that it can't read the drive. I hope I haven't screwed it up. It worked the other day at the library, but I couldn't get past the password protection."

Nancy took the drive and turned it over in her hand. "Where's your laptop?"

"In my office," I said.

Nancy took off down the hall. "Let's check it. What's it got on it that's so important, and why don't you remember the password?" She stopped and turned around. "Does this belong to Michelle? Because I'm not going to help you spy on her. I have my conscience to think about."

I almost burst out laughing but contained myself since I needed her help. "No, nothing like that. Michelle and I have no secrets."

This time Nancy laughed and didn't try to control herself at all. "Right. If it's not Michelle's diary, then what's on it?"

I needed her help, and the only way to do it was to come clean. "Liz found it in her herb garden. She thinks Steve may have hidden it there the morning he was killed."

She tapped her lip with a fuchsia fingernail. "And you're not giving it to the detective why?"

"I plan to. I want to see what's on it first."

"I love intrigue," Nancy said. "Smart thinking."

I told her my main suspects.

"Why would Steve hide it? That seems stupid," I wondered out loud. "Why not just give it to Liz? Wait, Keith told me Steve had something on TJ. Maybe this is what he was holding over TJ. You know, TJ showed up late the morning Steve died, and he admitted to bringing Steve a coffee from Café du Soleil. The same kind of cup that was next to Steve's body."

Nancy's eyes rounded. "Maybe he planted it to incriminate her."

"He's the victim. He has no reason to incriminate her."

"Maybe he knew the bad guy was wise to him and he needed to ditch the evidence."

"There's a thought. Marni had a motive that everyone knew about. But that doesn't explain the note TJ received in the mail from Steve. Or the note that Keith got. Or the note I got. It's like the killer was pointing to everyone."

"To confuse things."

"Anybody home?" Angie called from the vicinity of my

kitchen. No doubt she had crossed between the hedges that separated our houses and let herself in my backdoor.

"Ugh, she can't see this." I started to grab the drive from Nancy, but she shoved it down her bra.

"I'll take your laptop and see if I can work my magic."

"Go out the front door. I'll come up when she leaves. Do not damage that thing."

"Okie dokie, but give me some credit."

I pushed her out the door and crossed my fingers.

"I'm in here!" I yelled as I ran down the hall to the laundry room. "Why are you up so early?" My dirty wash had been piling up, and with my mother here, I had four loads. Michelle could change outfits two or three times a day and never wear the same one twice, and she went through bath towels as if we had an endless supply: one for the floor, one for her hair, and one to dry off with. The child didn't know the meaning of *conserve*.

"Nancy woke me up ranting about coleslaw. Seriously, she's got a screw loose."

"Tell me something I don't know, Einstein," I said. "You look chipper."

"I'm feeling better. Not sure how long it will last, but I figured I better make the most of it." Angie peered around the doorframe. "You in the mood for a cup of tea? I'll even make it."

She did look better, even somewhat perky. I still didn't see the usual sparkle in her eyes, but with an unplanned pregnancy, she had a lot on her mind. "Give me a minute to get this load going."

I shoved a pile of jeans and dark clothing into the washer, added detergent, and closed the lid. I punched the appropriate controls and joined Angie in the kitchen.

"It's good to see you upright and not hanging over a toilet."

She retrieved two mugs from the microwave, dunked the teabags, and followed me to the great room.

"The mornings are the worst. I'm good until I get out of bed, and then my insides turn over. By the afternoon, I'm pretty much my old self. But once in a while, an odor will do me in. Yesterday it was coffee. Dave made a pot when he came home. The minute the smell hit me, I was off to the bathroom."

"With Jessie it was anything mint. I even had trouble brushing my teeth. Ever tried to find toothpaste that isn't mint flavored? Even thinking about it makes my gag reflex kick in. When I was pregnant with Michelle, anything vanilla-scented churned my stomach."

Angie grimaced. "Let's quit talking about it. I'm getting queasy."

"How did Dave take the news?"

"Shocked, disbelief, denial. Just like me." Angie sank onto the sofa. "We never dreamed this would happen. I mean, obviously, it hadn't happened all these years, so who'd imagine I could even get pregnant. And of all times."

"When are you going to make an ob-gyn appointment?"

Angie's face clouded over, and I noticed she was picking at her nail polish, a habit she had long since kicked.

Before she could answer, Nancy burst in the door. "I need to talk to you."

"Can it wait?" I nodded to Angie. "I'm kind of busy."

Nancy was so oblivious; it wouldn't have mattered if the Queen of England had dropped by for tea. Much less that my dearest friend appeared to be in distress.

"I really need to talk to you. It's important."

"Okay." I took a deep breath. She'd better have a good reason for interrupting. "I'll be upstairs in a minute."

She shifted her eyes toward Angie without moving her head.

"What?"

She leaned in and whispered, "It's about the thing we talked about."

Crap! Angie might be feeling off, but she was still a cop and had a sixth sense about her in all things cop related, and Nancy was acting entirely too suspicious.

I tried to act nonchalant. "We can talk later."

Nancy's mouth twisted into a little circle. "But you don't understand. It's important. It's about the you-know-what that you asked me to look for."

I hustled her to the door and lowered my voice. "Oh, for Pete's sake, will you get a grip on yourself? As soon as Angie leaves, I'll be up."

Nancy scuttled through the door and climbed the stairs to her apartment.

"What was that all about?" Angie asked.

"Oh, you know her. She probably broke a nail and is in denial about it."

"You gotta admit, she was acting strange, even for Nancy." Angie narrowed her eyes. "What's the you-know-what you asked her to look for?"

I had to think fast. Angie could smell a con. Too many years of working with criminals. "A surprise, so don't spoil it."

Angie shrugged. "Don't even think about a baby shower."

"Never in a million years. Now, where were we?" I asked. "Oh yes, you are going to see your doctor, aren't you?"

"Maybe not for the reason you're thinking. Dave and I have been talking about not having it."

I closed my eyes and took a deep breath. "Oh, Angie, you and Dave have waited so long. Are you sure this is the right decision for you?"

"I'm not sure about anything." Angie shifted so she faced me. "On one hand, it's a baby. When I think about it, I feel like a monster for even considering not having it. But then I think of everything that could go wrong. I'm forty-eight. What baby deserves to come into this world to parents who are old enough to be grandparents?"

"Any baby who gets you and Dave as parents would be lucky. Sweetie, don't you see, it's not the age. It's the love you have to give to this child. You two are so overdue for this." I set down my tea and took her hand in mine. "And as far as anything being wrong, there are all kinds of tests. Your doctors will stay on top of everything."

Tears filled her eyes. "What would you do, if it were you?"

My heart thudded in my chest. What would I do? "Ang, I can't make this decision for you. Neither of my kids came at opportune times, but the thought of not having one of them is something I can't even fathom. But, regardless of what I want, this has to be a decision you and Dave make. You two need to sit down and have a heart-to-heart. List out the pros and cons."

She rubbed her eyes with the heel of her hand. "You're right."

As if on cue, Dave tapped on the patio door. I motioned him in.

"There you are. I've been looking everywhere. You okay?"

Angie sniffled and nodded. "I think so."

"Hey, enough with the tears. You got your eyes all puffy." He wrapped her in a hug. "Let's go see what we can do about breakfast. You haven't eaten much the last couple of days. Then let's figure out what we're going to do today. I'm thinking it might be a good day to veg and stream some of those sappy movies you like to binge watch."

Angie grinned. "What about your appointments?"

"Boobs can wait. I got a wife I need to take care of. Besides, I didn't have any surgeries scheduled so I called the office and told them to reschedule everything else."

He wrapped his arms around her and led her home.

Watching the two of them walk across my back lawn gave me renewed hope. Maybe I would be ready for a relationship one day.

I slid the door shut. Their relationship was strong enough to get them through this, regardless of their decision.

CHAPTER NINETEEN

"I could make more money working someplace else, but I have to admit I'm starting to feel at home in Cece's little apartment."
Nancy Lustbader

After my neighbors left, I hightailed it up to Nancy's apartment. She must have heard me stomping up the steps, because she met me at the door.

I had barely crossed the threshold when she thrust my laptop at me.

Her shoulders slumped. "We need to find another computer."

"What? I thought you'd found something."

"Your USB port isn't working," Nancy said. "I can't do anything."

"Brilliant, but the library isn't open yet."

"We're headed back to school. We can use a computer there."

I had to give her credit. Every once in a while, she came up with a plan.

"Good thinking." I took stock of her outfit. "You need to change. We still have cleaning to do."

"Nope, I have plans this afternoon, so as soon as we're done, I gotta leave. I'll just have to be extra careful not to get messy."

"Seriously." It was on the tip of my tongue to ask her about Grant, but I still hadn't talked to him. "At least take along some decent shoes. We need to finish up at the school today. How are you coming at the condos?"

"Umm, I'll be there until Thanksgiving and possibly after. Grant's people released several more. And that's if I stay with it. If I help you at the school or get sick, I'll be behind. There's a whole slew of condos that will be waiting for us next week. Grant said it's gonna die off after that. Probably won't have any more until spring." Nancy cocked her head. "Does Angie have that flu that's going around? That stuff is bad. I heard that some people have died from it."

I shivered. "No, it's just a bug. Don't worry about it. She's not contagious. How do you know about the condos? Why didn't Grant call me?"

"I can tell him to call you if you want. He just didn't want to bother you."

I wondered if it was more than that. Surely, he wasn't pouting because I'd turned down his invitation to the ballet. But if Alder had mentioned the bonfire, that could definitely be the cause.

"Let's go downstairs," I said.

Nancy grabbed my laptop, followed me to my kitchen, and sat down at the breakfast bar. "You got any coffee? I didn't have time to make a pot this morning."

I shook my head. "You know I don't drink the stuff. I've got tea."

She scrunched her face. "Kill me now. I need hot, black coffee. I'll stop on my way to work."

"About that," I said. "I'm thinking we could put Gigi out at Hunter Springs while we finish up the school."

Nancy hiked an eyebrow. "Are you going to can me? I need this job. How can I ever start paying you rent if you fire me?"

"Oh, good grief, no. I'm just trying to keep my mother busy until she comes to her senses and goes home."

"I heard that." Gigi shuffled into the kitchen in my green Ralph Lauren robe. "I'm not going home. You can put me to work permanently. I'll earn my keep."

Nancy laughed and pulled a stick of gum from her purse.

I shot her a look, and she dropped it back into the abyss. "You know I'm kidding, Gigi. You can stay as long as you need to figure out what you want to do. But you can't stay here indefinitely. You need to iron things out with Ned."

"Not going to happen," she said. "He's history. So, about this job."

"I was asking Nancy to let you take over at Hunter Springs, and Nancy can break off and help me finish at the school."

Gigi let out a whoop. "Are you serious? I enjoyed helping you girls. I'm not meant for sitting around on my duff all day. I swear Cecelia, I don't know how you used to do it. And with you having a housekeeper and all." Gigi poured herself a glass of orange juice and joined us at the bar. "Honestly, didn't you just want to gouge your eyes out? Boring!" She rolled her eyes.

Okay, so I didn't have a patent on the eye roll. I'd learned it from my mother.

"As long as I'm not fired, it's cool," Nancy said. "You gonna make her work by herself?"

I shot Nancy a look and mouthed, "Shut up."

Gigi saw me. "Oh, it's all right. I don't mind working by

myself. Gives me time to think about things." She pulled an iPod from the pocket of my robe. "I bought me one of these things when the girls took me shopping, and Michelle helped me load it with music last night. I can't wait to try it out. Where is my granddaughter anyway?"

"She left for school already. Why don't you go up and change? Nancy can drop you at the condos and meet up with me at school."

"This will be fun." Nancy scooted off the stool and hugged Gigi. "We all make a great team."

Why did that worry me? Sounded like a catastrophe waiting to happen. But I had no choice. I needed Nancy's help at the school, and Gigi couldn't get into any trouble at Hunter Springs. At least I hoped she couldn't.

"Didn't you work in Tucson?" I had never known her not to work. She had sometimes held down two or three jobs when I was growing up mostly out of necessity, but still she wasn't the type to sit idle.

"Not since I married Ned. It seemed silly. He had more than enough money to take care of us, and any little piddling job I could do wouldn't amount to much."

"Gigi, that's it!" I said rather forcefully.

"What?" She looked around confused at my outburst.

"A job. You need a job."

She narrowed her eyes. "You want me to get another job." She put her hands on her hips and looked around. "You don't want me working with you?"

"No, that's not what I meant," I said. "I mean in Tucson. Maybe that's what Ned and you need."

"Too late for that. He hasn't even bothered to call since I've been here. If he missed me, you'd think the least he could do was check on me."

"But you left him. What's he supposed to do? Did you even tell him where you were going?"

"Well . . ." She blew out a breath. "It should have been pretty obvious. You're the only family I have. It's not like I have a mother to go running home to. And if I did, she'd probably be in a nursing home. I'm almost sixty-five, you know."

"Gigi, you're seventy."

Her eyes filled with tears. "If the old fart really loved me, he wouldn't have let me leave."

"You left with all your luggage. If I know you, you either left in the middle of the night or waited until Ned was gone and then took off."

She stuck her tongue out. "You're such a smarty pants. You don't know everything about me."

I grinned. "Which was it? Middle of the night or when he was gone?"

Gigi looked down at the floor. "Middle of the night. The old man snores like a foghorn."

"See," I said. "You sneak off while he's sleeping. What's he supposed to think? Probably thought you took off with another man."

"Oh, get real Cece. Why would he think that?"

"Umm, let's see. How about your track record? How many times have you been married? It's not like you've lived a solitary life."

"Apparently, you either."

"What's that supposed to mean? Phillip cheated on *me*. He's the one who left, not me."

"What about that cop?"

"What? What do you even know about Detective Alder?" I had a sneaking hunch that Nancy had opened her big mouth.

"Just that he's sweet on you."

"I don't know what Nancy told you, but she doesn't know anything."

"Oh," Gigi cooed. "Don't get your panties in a knot. Maybe I'll call him and invite him to Thanksgiving. I've never gone out with a man in uniform. Maybe he'd like to date an older woman."

"Don't you dare. I don't need you making a move on him. Besides, you're married."

"You are too, but it's just a technicality. Ned probably already has a lawyer drawing up the divorce papers." She sighed and ran a hand through her tumbled hair. "Poor old Ned. I really thought he was the one."

"You need to call him. That's all there is to it."

"I can't," she said. "Once I leave, I never go back. It goes against my very grain. Never have, never will."

"Do you still love him?"

That must have surprised her because she spun around. "Of course I do. But the man drives me batty." With that declaration she flounced out of the room.

"Your mom is a mess," Nancy said. "If I ever found me a good man, I'd hang on for dear life."

"You got one in mind?" I crossed my fingers and said a silent prayer. If I could get Gigi and Ned back together and Nancy found a love interest, I could get my house back.

She stared wistfully into space. "I could only hope."

I poked my pointer finger in the air. "Ha! There *is* someone."

"No, just dreaming."

Apparently, she wasn't ready to share. "You sure you don't want some?" I held my cup out to Nancy and wiggled it. "I make a mean cup of English Breakfast."

Nancy shuddered. "No thanks. I'll be having to use my pinky, and that goes against all I stand for. You got any diet pop? That'll get my engine going if you don't have coffee."

I pointed to the fridge. "Help yourself."

Gigi made it back in record time, wearing a pair of jeans

and a University of Arizona sweatshirt. She performed her best *Cover Girl* pose.

"Ta da. Am I fit for duty?"

"Perfect," I said. "I'll head over to the school. Gigi you got the condos."

"Can do." Gigi tried to high-five me and missed.

"If you get done before one of us comes to pick you up, give me a call. I'll have my cell phone with me."

Nancy slung her arm around Gigi. "Come on girl. We've got some chatting to do. See ya in a little while, Cece."

I cringed. No telling what those two would cook up.

———

Nancy arrived at the school about two hours later.

"What took you so long?" I asked.

"We stopped for coffee. Then I showed her the new section. Guess I lost track of time. She was eager to get to work. But don't get any ideas." Nancy laughed. "You're not getting rid of me that easy."

"Like I could," I said.

"Did you find anything?"

"Not yet. Too many people around. They've cleared out for a breakfast meeting, so I was getting ready to take a look. Head on down and get your supplies ready. I'll take this flash drive to Steve's classroom and check it out."

Nancy frowned. "Didn't the cops take his computer?"

I thought for a minute. "Sure thing. I didn't see it yesterday. I'll go check Marni's."

I fired up Marni's computer and inserted the flash drive. When I clicked the correct icon, a password box came up. "Drat! The dreaded password."

I typed different combinations of passwords. Liz and Steve's kids' names. Their grandkids' names, even the dog's name that Liz used to always complain about. I even tried the word password, then Wickford High. Nothing.

In a fit of curiosity, I picked up Marni's keyboard and was rewarded with a pretty pink sticky note stuck to her desk.

"Eureka!" I shouted.

Nancy pushed her bucket into the room and stood in the doorway. "You find something?"

I moved the keyboard farther away so she could see the piece of paper.

Nancy shook her head. "I don't get it."

"Password. I found the password. Well, *passwords* actually. It was so easy. If it were a landmine, I would have stepped on it."

Nancy produced two bottles of water from her jacket pocket and handed one to me.

"Thanks!" I twisted off the cap. "I can't believe it took me so long to think of this."

"Are you going to tell me or am I going to have to sit on you?" Nancy giggled.

"I went through all the common stuff people use for passwords, like password and other dumb words." I stopped to take a long swig from the water. "Then I thought about my own passwords and how I have dozens of them and can't keep them all straight, so I have a piece of paper taped inside my desk drawer. You did not hear that, by the way. I better not catch you in my desk."

"Like I'd want to see what's in your dumb old desk," Nancy said.

"Whatever!"

"I don't get how Marni's passwords will help you with Steve's flash drive."

I rolled my eyes. "Not Marni's passwords, Steve's."

Nancy hiked an eyebrow. "Marni has his passwords?"

"No. If I have a list of my passwords in my desk, and

Marni has a list of passwords at her desk, maybe Steve does too."

The imaginary light bulb over Nancy's head suddenly illuminated. "Oh! But I still don't get why he would hide a flash drive. Why not give it to the police? Why not toss it in the river? Smash it with a hammer. Pour glue into it. Drop it in acid. Break it into a bazillion—"

"I get the picture!" I yelled. "Tell me where you are going with your train of thought."

Nancy jumped up and down on her heels. "I know. I know. You told me that Liz thought someone was trying to set her up, right?"

"Yes."

A big grin spread across Nancy's face. "What if that someone was pointing the fingers at all of them to fake everyone out?"

"We talked about that. So that brings us right back to TJ, Marnie, Keith, Liz, or even Steve," I said.

Nancy scratched her head. "Why would a dead guy try to set anyone up?"

"Who knows. Several people have indicated that Steve was having money problems. Maybe he was holding stuff over their heads to extort money."

Nancy scrunched her face. "I don't get it."

"TJ got a threatening note. Keith got a note pointing to a secret coming out about TJ. Steve was going to take Liz to court. Who knows who else might have gotten a note? Let's go check around Steve's classroom."

Nancy followed me down the hall, her loony spike heels tapping against the tile.

"Can't you walk quieter?" I whispered. "Why can't you wear normal shoes like everyone else?"

Nancy caught up with me and jiggled her leg out in front

of her like a Rockette. "They make my legs look nice. Who wants to look like a frump?"

I frowned and picked up the pace. Talking with her was like talking to a ten-year-old, except you could discipline a kid for being sassy.

"I didn't mean you look frumpy," she said. "You don't think that, do you?"

Correction, she was like talking to a mynah bird. She never shut up. Here we were getting ready to break into a computer, and she was clacking down the hall in hooker shoes, chattering away.

As we approached Steve's class, movement inside caught my attention. I held my finger to my lips and clamped a hand around Nancy's arm. "Shh!"

The hair on my arms prickled.

"I thought everyone was at breakfast," Nancy whispered.

I shrugged. "Me too. I watched them leave." Then it dawned on me who hadn't been in the group. "It's got to be TJ," I mouthed. "I don't remember seeing him."

"O-m-g, is he the killer?" Nancy's voice quivered.

"Shh," I warned. "Let's get out of here before he sees us."

Nancy took a step backward and tripped on her heel and fell into me, sending us both crashing to the floor.

TJ stuck his head out the door. "Ladies, are you okay? What happened?"

He shoved something under his shirt and rushed over, reaching out a hand to Nancy. "Here, let me help you."

Nancy gave me the side-eye but took his hand. When he reached out to help me, a CD slid out of his shirt and landed at his feet. His face pinked up as a blush spread across his cheeks. "Guess I've been caught red-handed."

Nancy slapped her hands over her eyes. "I didn't see anything. I swear. Please don't hurt me."

TJ's brows closed in on one another. "Hurt you. Why

would I hurt you? Oh, wait. You think I killed Steve? No! No, no, no." He shook his head vigorously as he retrieved the CD.

I scrambled to my feet. "Then what were you doing in his classroom?"

"Yeah." Nancy still had her hands clamped over her eyes but was peeking through her fingers. "What Cece said."

TJ chuckled then waved the CD. "These are training videos for the team. I told you about them. It's what Steve and I argued about. I've been begging him for them since I got here."

I wasn't sure I was convinced. "Why all the cloak and dagger? Why wait until everyone was gone to rifle through his room?"

"I'm not sure I need to explain myself to you ladies, but I will because you apparently think I'm capable of murder." He drew in a breath and exhaled. "I talked to Ed about the videos and he gave me the go-ahead to look for them. I worried the police had taken them, so I talked to the detective this morning. He assured me they were still in the classroom. I didn't go to breakfast with the others because I have a blood test in a couple hours and needed to fast. Nothing nefarious going on."

Nancy uncovered her eyes. "You sure had us fooled, didn't he Cece? We thought for sure you'd done the guy in and were in there covering your tracks."

Nancy continued to ramble, digging herself deeper.

"Whoa," I said to Nancy. "Take a breath."

I turned to TJ. "Look, we're sorry. Everyone's on edge about this. But before you leave can I ask you one more question that's been bothering me?"

TJ pulled his cell phone out and glanced at the screen. "Make it quick. I've got to be at the lab in twenty minutes."

"A couple days ago, I overheard you tell Marni about a note you received that you suspected Steve had sent."

"I don't know for a fact that it was Steve, but it was pretty suspicious considering how he felt about me replacing him. I'm not proud to admit it, but I got in trouble back in college. Sports-betting, and I figured he intended to take that information to Ed. Only thing is, Ed already knows. I came clean when I hired on." He glanced at his phone again. "I really do have to go. Apologies for scaring you."

After he was out of sight, Nancy pursed her lips. "Waddya think? Did he do it?"

"I don't know. Maybe he's lying about coming clean to Ed to throw us off. I don't know. We don't have time to speculate. We've wasted too much time already. Let's get this over with." I stalked into Steve's room and began my search.

Nancy eventually joined me.

"You keep a lookout. The staff should be back soon. I'll see if I can find anything."

Nancy swiveled her head toward the hall. "Okay. What's our code?"

I glared at her. "Code?"

"You know in case someone comes. Do you want me to whistle or sing a song or something, so you'll know to hurry up?"

I shook my head. "I think you can just engage them in conversation. If I hear talking, then I'll know you aren't alone. Think you can do that?"

Nancy nodded her bobble head. "I should have thought of that. Duh!"

Exactly. Heaven help me. It bothered me to snoop into a dead man's classroom. I sent a little prayer heavenward that Steve would understand my invasion of his privacy. If I was going to bring a killer to justice, I needed to check every possible source.

Nancy started whistling. I crossed over to the door and peeked out. "Everything okay?"

She jumped. "You scared the crap out of me."

"You were whistling. What's going on? Did you see someone?"

"Sorry, guess I was just nervous." She drew her finger over her lips like a zipper. "I'll concentrate harder."

As I suspected, Steve's computer was gone. The keyboard remained, but there was nothing taped under it. Most of his desk had been cleared too, save for a couple art pads and a cup of pencils.

There was no folder marked passwords and nothing taped in his desk drawer. If Steve had password-protected the flash drive, he had taken the password to his grave or the morgue since he wasn't buried yet.

"Ugh, this isn't getting me anywhere," I said. In a last-ditch effort, I ran my hand under his desk drawer. It took only a second for my fingers to find the edge of a piece of duct tape. I peered under the drawer and found what I was looking for. A one-inch square sticky note. I peeled it back and pulled it free of the tape. It contained a code I was sure would unlock the flash drive: Renior*7#Matisse. Never in a million years would I have guessed that.

I heard a door slam down the hall. "What's that?"

"Sounded like a door." Nancy trotted into the room.

"I know it sounded like a door. We're supposed to be alone. They must be back from breakfast." My arms freckled with goosebumps. "Go stand lookout while I finish up."

Just as I slid the sticky note into my pocket, Nancy's voice startled me.

"Hi Detective," she said at the top of her voice.

I raced over to the bookshelf and pretended to work. When Alder walked in the door, I was straightening books.

"I saw your van in the parking lot and thought I'd check on you. Everything okay?" Alder leaned up against the desk.

"Classes are back on tomorrow, and we're just putting the finishing touches on the place."

"Makes sense." When he was quiet, I glanced at him. "You got big plans for Thanksgiving?" he asked, smoothing his mustache, which made my stomach do a little dance.

"Just family and Angie and Dave," I said. "How about you?"

"Becca's spending the day with me. She promised to cook a traditional dinner while I watched football."

Becca was Alder's daughter. In April, I'd seen the two of them together and jumped to the conclusion that Alder dated younger women—much younger women. It had been ugly and provided my first inkling that I had feelings for him. Unfortunately, I'd acted like a schoolgirl and made a fool out of myself.

"Sounds like fun. Wish someone would cook for me." I sighed and thought about the meals we'd had at previous holidays at Hazel's. Though, it was so worth not having to spend the day with her.

"Isn't your mother still here?"

"Ha, she can't cook. Angie can't cook and Michelle won't cook. That leaves Jessie and me. And if you can believe it, I haven't cooked Thanksgiving dinner since I was eighteen."

"You'll do fine. There are tons of websites where you can print off menus and recipes. That's what Becca did. She sent me a grocery list with strict orders not to deviate from it."

"We gotta get back to work," I said, pointing to the clock. "Only so many hours left before we turn this school back over to Ed, and I don't want to be here all night."

"I can take a hint. If I don't see you before Thanksgiving, enjoy the time with your family." He hesitated. "Maybe after the holiday we can plan another bonfire."

My heart leaped at the thought of being alone with Alder

with my divorce behind me, but my head knew it was a dead-end street. I bit my lip. "We'll see."

He winked. "Don't think you're going to give me the brush-off. We've got lots of bonfires in our future."

Now was as good a time as any to rip the bandage off, even though I knew it would hurt like crazy. The longer I let myself think there was a future with him, the more it would hurt when he walked away, or worse just wanted to shack up. With Nancy right outside, Alder wouldn't be able to try to talk me out of my decision.

"I don't think we can make this work, Alder." My heart was breaking as the words came out of my mouth. I felt tears well up behind my eyes. Who knew letting go of someone I really never had would be so hard?

Alder stared at me, disbelief in his gorgeous blue eyes. "What are you talking about? I thought—"

"You thought wrong." My chin quivered. I needed to get him out of here before I lost all my nerve. "Go on, get out of here and let me get to work."

"I'm not going anywhere until you tell me what's going on." He crossed his arms over his chest. "I gave you all the space you needed. Your divorce is almost final. You can't deny there's a connection between us. Now you're pushing me away. Is it your independence you're worried about?"

"I can't talk about it now," I said. "Please just go."

"We are going to talk about it because I need to understand where you're coming from. I'm holding back words that I need to tell you because I'm worried I'll scare you off."

Nancy walked in the door. "We got more company."

Alder cursed under his breath. "We're not done with this."

"Oh, I have something for you." I dug into my purse and handed him the envelope Zella had given me. I had wanted so badly to open it, but I knew better. If it wasn't sealed, all bets would have been off. But it was.

"What's this?"

"Something Steve Trupeli had given to Zella for safekeeping," I said. Alder opened his mouth, but I cut him off. "I know what you're going to say, but Zella would have never given it to you. She trusts me."

Alder pulled a pocketknife out and slit the seal. He scanned the papers and slid them back in.

"I've got to go." He brushed past Nancy and stalked down the hall.

I rubbed my eyes. "Who's here now?"

"Breakfast must be over. They're all back."

I shut the lights off and pulled Steve's door shut behind us. "Let's get back to work."

Nancy said, "That detective is a real pain in the butt. We're never going to find anything if he keeps showing up."

I grinned and pulled the sticky note from my pocket. "Don't be so sure," I said, dangling it in front of her face.

"Is this what I think it is?" Nancy asked.

"Yep, found it taped beneath Steve's desk. Let's just hope it works."

CHAPTER TWENTY

"I knew Steve would never marry me. He was still hung up on Liz."
Marni Caruthers

Nancy and I each grabbed a bucket and mop and headed our separate ways. An hour later she glided into the room looking like she hadn't even broken a sweat. Me, I looked like a pig. Between the sweat stains and muddy splatter, I looked like I'd been working on a farm.

"Hey, I finished in the front office. What do you want me to do next?" she asked.

"Just in time. I'm gonna head to Marni's office and give it a final mop. While I'm there I'll check out the flash drive. How about giving the east wing one last mopping? Then we'll do a walk-through together to make sure everything looks good."

"Sure thing."

"We still got company?" I asked. With other people in the building, I felt a little less uneasy.

"I think so. Tommy just helped me change the water in my bucket, and I didn't see the science guy. He's kind of attractive in a hippie kind of way," Nancy said.

"Don't even think about it, Nancy. We're here to do a job, not find you a date."

"Okay," Nancy said. "You want me to check and see if the science guy is still here?"

"Might not be a bad idea, just so we know who all is in the building," I said. "Don't disturb him though."

"Don't worry." She took off down the hall, swinging her hips and humming.

Poor Keith.

———

Gigi called just as I sat down at Marni's computer, and she said she was almost finished at Hunter Springs. I could hear her huffing and puffing. The one thing about her was that she worked like a champ. Not an ounce of laziness in her. She was probably on her hands and knees scrubbing those subfloors while I had been content to do them with a mop.

"Sure thing. Give me about thirty minutes to tie things up here, then I'll pick you up." I thought about checking the cafeteria for a couple cookies for Gigi as a reward but figured I'd just eat them in the car on my way to Hunter Springs. *Sorry Gigi, but my hips can't afford it.* At least not until I forced myself to get back to the gym and actually start doing a few workouts a week. Even though I was using muscles that I hadn't used in ages, it wasn't like an honest-to-goodness workout on the elliptical or stair machine.

After I disconnected, I placed my phone on the desk and fired up the computer. Luckily it didn't have a password. I inserted the flash drive and pulled out the sticky note. When prompted for a password, I crossed my fingers and typed it in.

Ack! INCORRECT PASSWORD glared at me from the screen.

I tried again with the same result.

Think Cece!

I tapped the icon to show what I had typed. I had hit the * and $ instead of a #. I retyped the password, RENIOR*7#MATISSE.

Voilà!

Two folders appeared. I clicked the one labeled INVESTI-GATOR NOTES. A series of documents lined up on the screen. I clicked one, and a profile of subject number one opened. As I read the notes, they appeared to be profiling a murder suspect, grad student mid-twenties. Under motive, insurance beneficiary was listed. Subject, estranged spouse of victim. I scanned the rest of the documents. The final one contained witness reports, detective statements, DNA evidence.

I wondered why Steve was compiling information on a murder. And what about the private detective? Who was he investigating? Steve's estranged spouse, now ex-wife, was alive and well. Did he have another estranged spouse who was not alive and well?

I opened the second folder and images of newspapers filled the screen.

The headlines—all from a newspaper in James City, Missouri—were dated thirty years earlier, and they all referred to the murder of a local woman. The first article said the victim, Phyllis Preston, was found dead in her residence strangled with the cord of her hair dryer. The next indicated her husband, Keith, a graduate student at the university, was a suspect.

My insides turned to jelly. I did a bit of math and deter-mined that the grad student could definitely be about fifty-five now, give or take a few years. About the same age as—

"We're going down to the cafeteria for coffee," Keith said. "Want to join us?"

Nancy's eyes were wide like she'd been spooked, but she didn't say anything. She blinked her eyes rapidly. That's when I saw the bulge in Keith's pocket, and I didn't think it was because he was happy to see her.

"I'm just finishing up." I reached for the off switch on the monitor but not before Keith saw what was on the screen.

"I knew you were trouble the first time I saw you." He jerked the flash drive from the computer and shoved it in his pocket. "Get up."

When I didn't move, he yanked me out of the chair so quickly I stumbled over my feet, finally righting myself.

"You're both coming with me. Now get moving."

I started to pull away, but Nancy's eyes pleaded with me. "Just do what he says, Cece."

"Come on, ladies. We're going to have a little conversation, and then the two of you are going down for a long winter's nap."

My mind reeled with possibilities. I remembered reading about being abducted and the warnings not to get in the car, because if you did, you were dead for sure. Certainly, between the two of us, we could take this guy out. Though Nancy would probably run screaming from the room and get away. Then I'd be stuck with him. On the other hand, I could run screaming from the room and leave her with him. Decisions. Decisions. Or if I could somehow get it across to her maybe we both could run screaming from the room in opposite directions. I wondered if any of the others were still in the building. But I didn't want to put any of them in danger.

I looked over at Nancy. Her eyes were closed, and I'm not Catholic or anything, but it looked like she was mouthing a Hail Mary.

I willed her to open her eyes and focus on me. She didn't.

Keith pulled a bag of plastic zipper ties from his pocket and tossed it to me. "Wrap a couple of these around her wrists and make them secure."

Here we go again. Why had Alder shown up earlier and not now when I needed him? Scratch that. I didn't need a man; I needed to take charge of this situation.

Nancy's eyes fluttered but remained shut.

I didn't move, and the bag hit the floor and slid into the hall.

"Pick it up and do what I told you, or I'll knock her into next week." Keith tugged Nancy's arms around her back and held her wrists.

I picked up the ties, pulled one out, and wrapped it loosely around Nancy's wrist.

Keith nudged me. "Tighter."

I grabbed the tie and did as instructed. "I'm sorry, Nancy."

Her mumbling was so loud, there was no way she'd heard me. Who would've taken Nancy for being religious? But at a time like this, I probably should have been praying too, instead of worrying about my next move. How did I manage to get myself into these situations? And better yet, how was I going to get myself out?

"Loop another one through it and wrap it around her other wrist," Keith commanded.

If only I'd listened to Alder. Once again, he was right. You'd think I'd learn by now.

"Now you turn around and put your hands behind your back," Keith directed.

I did, and he pulled the tie so tight, I thought my wrists were going to be severed. "Jerk," I said under my breath. Secretly I hoped he'd hear me, but in truth, I was afraid he would. I needed to feel like I had some control, if nothing else but over my words.

"Now, let's line up and march to the cafeteria like good little children," he said.

I didn't budge.

He placed his hand in the center of my back and pushed. "I said move."

Nancy and I started walking. I glanced over my shoulder and saw my cell phone lying on the desk where I'd laid it earlier. Terrific. How stupid could I get?

"Why are we going to the cafeteria?" Nancy asked.

Now she decided to pay attention to what was going on. If my hands weren't tied, I would have reached over and slapped her, but instead I just prayed that she had a little pull with the guy upstairs. With two of us praying, it might help. Finding Zella or Tommy in the cafeteria wouldn't hurt either.

"I'm gonna put you ladies on ice while I figure out what to do with you." Keith chuckled. "On second thought, I don't have to do anything with you. The freezer will take care of that. By the time Zella gets here in the morning, you'll be two frozen pops."

He prodded us into the kitchen past the counter where I'd been eating Zella's chocolate chip cookies yesterday. The room still bore the fragrant scent of vanilla. What I wouldn't give to see Zella puttering around. But there was no sign of her or Tommy. The peg by the backdoor where she usually hung her coat was empty.

"Yep, they're all gone. Just the three of us." Keith stopped in front of the walk-in freezer and pulled the door open. "Get in."

"Are you serious? We'll freeze to death." I backed up a step.

"That's pretty much the idea, blondie. Now get in."

"This is so unfair," Nancy whined. "I didn't do anything."

"You're both too nosy. I never dreamed there was a flash drive. Old Steve really did his homework. Only wish I had found it first." He patted his pocket. "I have it now. That's all that matters."

My mouth dropped. "Steve hired a private investigator to check out your past."

Keith smirked. "In the beginning, he wanted justice, but he got greedy. Stuck his nose in the wrong person's business."

"He was blackmailing you." All the pieces of this puzzle fell into place. I screwed up my courage. "And then you started laying clues to make other people look guilty or deflect the attention off of you. Like putting my purse in your classroom. No one would ever suspect you, would they?"

Keith pushed us in the freezer and slammed the door.

I stood on tiptoes and watched as he secured the handle. "You won't get away with this!" I screamed.

He looked in and gave a little wave before leaving the kitchen.

CHAPTER TWENTY-ONE

"Here we go again. How do I get myself into these situations?"
Cece Cavanaugh

I rubbed my shoulder around the door, feeling for the internal plunger that I'd seen when I was helping Zella. I pushed my body weight into it to release the door, but nothing happened.

"He's fixed the handle so we can't get out." I pushed the plunger again and again, hoping to release whatever had it stuck. "It's not working."

With the little bit of light coming in the tiny window in the door, I could see that Nancy had shuffled to the back of the freezer. Her sobs echoed in the space.

"Nancy, don't cry," I said. "You want to freeze even faster? If you hadn't been so busy saying all your Hail Marys, we might have been able to get away from him. But no, you had your eyes all squeezed together like you were making a wish or something."

"You're the one who snooped around," she shot back. "It's not my fault. You started this whole thing. He's right, you're just plain nosy."

"It doesn't matter. We're in this situation. Now what? You got any big ideas?"

"No."

I remembered helping Zella put away supplies the previous day. "I think there's a light switch somewhere on the wall by the window. If I can just figure out where it is."

Edging myself over, I slid my shoulder along the wall until it grazed the switch. I rubbed up and down until I finally made contact and the light flickered on.

The room wasn't more than six feet by ten, and with shelves on both sides, only a narrow walkway remained down the middle.

Nancy huddled against the back wall, teeth chattering. "I'm so cold."

"I know. Me too. We can't think about that. Let's try to get the ties off our wrists, then we'll figure out a plan."

"Okay. What should I do?"

"Turn around," I said.

I bent over and tried to get the edge of her plastic tie between my teeth, but I was chattering so badly, I could barely get a hold of it. Finally, I caught it and started tugging.

"Yow, you're making it tighter. Stop!" Nancy yelled.

I slumped against a shelf. "Now what?"

"I'm so cold I can't think."

"Wait, Zella had a knife in here the other day. Let's hope she didn't take it out. Help me look. It's a little gray tool about the size of a stapler." I checked the shelf where I had seen it yesterday. "Not here."

Nancy stood against the back rack of shelves, shivering.

"Hey, if you want to get out of here, help me look for the knife," I said. "I can't do this by myself."

Nancy mumbled a curse word.

"I heard that," I said.

She shuffled toward me and made a show of craning her neck and looking around.

"You're going to have to move some of those cartons," I said.

"And how do you propose I do that with my hands tied behind my back?"

"Use your head. Literally." I nudged a box on the shelf. "Like this."

The carton I'd just moved dislodged the knife, and it fell between boxes on the lower shelf and stuck there.

"Now what?" Nancy asked.

"Now I have to figure out how to uncover the blade without cutting my fingers off." I slid to the floor. "Tell me when I'm close to it. I need to be able to push that silver slide to get the blade out."

Nancy bent over and watched as I scooted backward toward the crevice where the knife had fallen. "Keep scooting. It's about three inches away."

"How's that?" I asked.

"A little to the left. No, I mean my left."

My fingers brushed the knife and it wiggled. "Ugh, it's too loose. I'm going to try to wedge it tighter in the crevice before I push the blade out."

When it felt secure, I found the slide and pulled it toward me. "Is the blade coming out?"

Nancy squealed. "You got it. You got it."

"Stop it. I don't want to cut my hand off." I gritted my teeth and prayed I could trust her. "Now help me position my hands so that the blade is under the plastic tie. Then I can saw it back and forth until it cuts through."

"Okay." Nancy kneeled and leaned in closer.

"And use my left and my right. Not yours," I said. "If I

slice a wrist, you're going to freeze to death after you watch me bleed out."

Nancy's lower lip quivered. "Don't put so much pressure on me."

"Oh, for crying out loud. Stop acting like a baby and tell me which way and how many inches I need to move my hands."

"Left about two inches."

"My left?" I asked just to double-check.

"Umm." Nancy bit her lip. "Yeah."

"You sure?"

"Yeah."

I slid my wrists left and stopped. "Now what?"

"You're right on top of it. If you go about an inch lower you should feel it."

I eased my wrists lower and felt the blade scrape the heel of my hand.

"You're okay. A little bit more and the tie will be sitting right on the blade."

I moved lower and felt contact. Sucking in a breath, I looked up at Nancy. "If I start sawing, am I going to cut myself?"

Nancy scooted closer. "No, you're good. Go slow."

I started moving my arms back and forth, which was no small feat when I couldn't see what I was doing, and I had to rely on a dingbat to keep me from dismembering my arm. "Is it doing anything?"

"Maybe. Keep going," Nancy said.

After what seemed like forever, my arms felt trembly. "Need to rest before I make a mistake." I raised my arms away from the blade, scooted around, and stood up. "Take a look at the tie and see if I'm making progress."

"O-M-G, you're almost there. Give it a tug and see if you can pull it apart. It's like hanging by a sliver."

I jerked my wrists apart, but all that budged were my upper arms. A white-hot pain shot through my shoulder sockets. "Jeez Louise, not a good idea." Tears sprang to my eyes. My arms were on fire, but the rest of me was freezing. I needed a good hot flash now, just not one that felt like my arms were being ripped from my body. "Give me a couple minutes, then I'll try again."

I knew time was of the essence, but my arms ached so badly, I stretched those couple minutes into more, waiting for the pain to subside.

"Come on," Nancy said. "You can do this. You have to do it."

When Nancy started shivering again, I knew I had to get back to work. She hadn't asked for any of this, and I owed her big time.

"I'm sorry for making you wear those ugly sneakers," I said. "If we get out of this, you can borrow those boots. And the handbag you liked."

Nancy squared her shoulders. "Let's get back to work."

I lowered myself to the floor, followed Nancy's instructions to position my wrists over the blade, and promptly sliced my palm. A few curse words later and despite what I knew was blood flowing from my hand, I gave it three more attempts and the plastic broke free.

"Now, do mine," Nancy said and turned around.

"Give me a minute." I checked the cut, which didn't look too deep, then clenched and unclenched my hands trying to get the feeling back. Once I could feel my fingertips and trusted that I wouldn't saw Nancy's hands off, I cut her free.

"Awesome job," Nancy said.

I gave her a quick hug. "You give good directions. Give me your phone so I can call someone to get us out of here."

Nancy blinked rapidly, then her lower lip quivered. "I don't have it."

"What do you mean?" I slapped my arms trying to warm them up. "Where is it?"

"He took it. I was trying to send you a text to warn you, but he saw me and grabbed it out of my hand." Nancy's eyes narrowed. "Where's yours?"

The sleuthing business wasn't everything it was cracked up to be. "I left it on Marni's desk."

Nancy groaned. "We're going to die in here!"

"Stop it. Come on. Pull it together." I glanced at my watch. "How long do you think we've been in here?"

"It seems like forever," Nancy said through chattering teeth.

"I'm serious. Try to think. When was the last time you checked the time?"

"I don't know. You took probably an hour with that knife and having to rest 'cause you were tired," she mocked. "What does it matter anyway?"

My feet were freezing, and we needed to insulate ourselves. "We need to worry about hypothermia." I glanced at the thermometer hanging from a shelf. It read zero. If we didn't find a way to save our body heat, we'd freeze to death. Or worse, if we didn't freeze, we could use up all our oxygen. I didn't know how well the unit was sealed, but I suspected there was a good possibility it was pretty leak-free.

The large boxes Zella had stored earlier were stacked on the shelving toward the back of the unit. "Let's unpack those."

Nancy curled her lip. "You wanna stock the shelves? Don't we have more to worry about than how this place looks?"

I rolled my eyes. "I want to put the cardboard on the floor. If we can get enough down, it might keep us from getting our feet frostbitten. Then we can worry about the rest of us."

Nancy shrugged. "If you say so."

We pulled open the boxes and dumped the contents on the shelf.

"Flatten them out and stack them one on top of the other."

After we'd lined the floor, Nancy started jumping up and down, flapping her arms to keep warm.

"Stop it," I said. "We have to conserve our energy. Besides you're going to breathe in the remaining oxygen quicker."

"If I stand still, I'll turn into a block of ice."

As much as I hated to admit it, she was right. The only solution was to make sure all our exposed skin was covered and then huddle together to share our body heat. I said a silent prayer of thanks that the weather had taken a turn to the chilly side. Nancy actually had the foresight to dress in layers, and instead of skimpy, she had chosen skintight. At least her limbs weren't exposed. Well, her feet were practically naked in her stupid-looking hooker shoes.

Unfortunately for me, I'd let my hot flashes rule. I had started out the morning in jeans and a sweatshirt but had quickly peeled down to a thin T-shirt. My sweatshirt was slung over the back of a chair in the cafeteria.

"What have you got on under that sweater?" I asked.

"A long-sleeved Henley." She narrowed her eyes. "Why?"

"Take it off and give it to me."

"Are you crazy? I'm freezing. It's not my fault you don't have on long sleeves." She patted her arms and started hopping again.

"Stop the jumping and give me your shirt. If one of us freezes, we're both going to freeze. We need to be on an even playing field if we're going to try to keep one another warm."

She relented and slipped out of the sweater. I pulled it over my head. I felt like a stuffed sausage, but it didn't matter —my arms were warmer. "Now we have to get close and huddle together, so we can share our body heat."

"What difference does it make? We're just prolonging it. We're going to die. No one is going to find us." Tears rolled down her cheeks.

"Stop it, right now." I sounded like a broken record. I put my arm around her and pulled her to me. "We can't think negative. Gigi or Michelle will start missing us and come looking."

"Sure," Nancy whined. "By then, we'll be ice cubes."

"No, we won't. Let's take a couple of those boxes and build a shelter. We can leave two or three on the floor to insulate our butts. Then we can sit down and put the others over us to hold in our body heat."

Nancy started shivering. "I just want to go to sleep."

I hugged her closer. Her shivering continued.

When she yawned, I started to panic and nudged her arm. "Snap out of it. We need to get busy." I pulled three of the biggest boxes off the floor, made Nancy sit down, and scooted next to her. I used the box knife to slit two of the boxes and pulled the cardboard around us. The third one I pulled over the top of us, creating a small, cramped shelter. "Now use your imagination and pretend we're camping." I thought about the bonfire Alder had built and longed to see the flickering flames and feel his arms around me. Why was I so stupid?

Just because Phillip turned out to be a dog, didn't mean that all men were cheats and liars. I knew two who treated me like a queen. Neither had ever shown anything but the utmost respect. I didn't like it so much that they'd become friends, but even in their rivalry over me, they managed to stay civil to one another. So what if Alder didn't want to get married. Why was I being such a prude? It's not like I'd never had sex.

Then I thought about Dave and Angie. She'd found a great guy. They didn't come any better than Dave Valenti. He worshiped Angie and she, him. I didn't know how their baby issue would turn out, but I knew Dave would support Angie in whatever decision she made.

And Jess. Just when I thought she would never find a soul mate, along came Brad. I could tell by the way he looked at her, she was the one he wanted to spend the rest of his life with. The two of them might not know it yet, but they were destined for one another.

Nancy slumped against me.

"Wake up. Don't you fall asleep on me. We're in this together." I pulled her tighter. "Come on, Nancy. Stay awake. Focus. Let's think about what we're cooking for Thanksgiving."

It took a while, but she started talking. She talked about last year, I tried to talk about how I hadn't cooked a turkey in years, and we rambled for a while about our childhood Thanksgivings.

"One of my favorite memories is my grandmother's coleslaw. It was legendary," Nancy said. "That's the recipe I'm making for our Thanksgiving, if we get out of here. It always reminds me of my Nana and how much she meant to me."

"Ah, that's a sweet memory. Mine is games. Our family always has board game challenges the whole day. Everyone brings their favorite game and we square off for tournaments." I smiled at the thought and wondered if Jessie would tell Brad to bring a game.

"Sounds fun. We were never much for games." Nancy's voice faded.

"Okay, tell me another memory."

"I can't think." Nancy stretched out her legs and knocked over one of the cardboard sections, causing our makeshift roof to collapse. She listed to the side and lay down.

I shook her. "Nancy, get a grip. Come on, sit up." I pulled her into a sitting position and repositioned the cardboard.

"Hold on to me. We've got to keep our shelter around us. That's the only way we're going to hold in our body heat."

I was shivering so badly I considered skin-to-skin contact since it was a good way to share body heat, but the thought of being found frozen and naked made me nix the idea. I tried to pull the cardboard tighter around us, but my arms and fingers felt like lead when I reached for the boxes. Nothing seemed to be working. I tried to remember the stages of hypothermia, but all the symptoms muddled together. Panic rose in me. Why wasn't Gigi looking for us? I'd lost track of time, but it had to have been two or three hours since I'd talked to her and told her we were almost finished. Surely, she'd call Michelle and the two of them would start to worry about me. But even if they thought to come to the school and saw my van in the parking lot, they'd never find me in a stinking freezer.

But if I had a couple of chocolate chip cookies, it would take my mind off of everything. Or Alder. Now, he could take my mind off anything. I felt all warm and tingly just thinking about him. I remembered I needed to pick up cranberries before I went home. It wouldn't be Thanksgiving without cranberry sauce. Hazel never served it, and I always had to bring it. I even had a new recipe that called for Grand Marnier and grated orange peel.

What was wrong with me? I was freezing my butt off and thinking about cranberry sauce and chocolate chip cookies.

I laid my head against Nancy's shoulder and closed my eyes.

Maybe a little nap would clear my head.

CHAPTER TWENTY-TWO

"Cece always managed to get herself into predicaments in school but getting locked in a freezer by a killer—that is something else."
Zella King

I roused when I heard a noise. The light inside the freezer was dim, and being inside the cardboard shelter didn't help, but when the light went out, I screamed.

"What in the world?" a voice said, and the light came back on. "Oh, my goodness."

I felt the boxes move around me.

"Lordy be, Cece. What in the world are you doing in here?" The voice was warm and syrupy.

Warm, mmmm.

I tried to blink, but my eyelids felt heavy, and Nancy was a dead weight in my lap.

Hands tugged at my arm. "Come on, honey. Let's get you two out of here."

I stumbled to my feet and followed the voice.

"Come on over here and sit down." The voice belonged to Zella. I'd never been so glad to hear her in all my life.

She had helped Nancy to a chair when I finally managed to open my eyes and keep them open.

Nancy and I sat shivering while Zella heated water in the microwave.

"I called 911, and I've got you some hot cocoa. Give me a minute to get some blankets from the nurse's office."

She placed two steaming mugs in front of us and shuffled out the door.

I tried to lift the mug, but my hands were too cramped. Instead, I bent over it, inhaling the steam.

Zella returned with blankets and wrapped them around me and Nancy, pausing to rub us gently to help our circulation.

I heard the wail of a siren approaching and felt nothing but relief. Things were happening in a straight line now, and I was starting to grasp time again. "How did you find us?" I finally ventured.

"I took your advice and told Tommy. When I went to look for the card the doctor had given me, I couldn't find it. The last place I'd had it was on the counter, so I came back to look for it." She shuddered. "That's when I saw the locking bar had been engaged and the light was on in the freezer. I didn't remember locking it, but I figured I'd left the light on so I must have locked it by mistake." She sank onto a chair. "What were you doing in there? If I hadn't come back for the card . . ." She shook her head.

Alder flew through the door with Gigi, Michelle, Angie, and a string of paramedics.

My heart soared when I saw him. How had he gotten here so quickly? How had any of them gotten here so quickly? It didn't matter. They'd found us. Alder would gather me in his arms and tell me everything was going to be okay.

"What happened?" he asked.

Zella filled him in on how she'd come to find us in the freezer.

I finished the story with details about Keith, and the flash drive, and how Steve had hidden it in Liz's herb garden.

"What the hell were you thinking?" he demanded.

I blinked. I guess no hugging for me. "What?"

He kneeled and grasped both my arms, bringing his face so close I could have kissed him. Except he was yelling at me. I almost froze to death and he was yelling.

I pulled out of his grip. "Stop it. Why are you yelling?"

"Did I tell you not to get involved with this case?" He nodded. "Yes, I distinctly remember telling you to leave it alone. Listen, yes, but not get involved. I knew it was a bad idea. And you get yourself locked in a freezer. Running down leads, questioning suspects, I swear if I didn't care so much, I'd . . ." He shook his head.

Gigi and Michelle were staring open-mouthed. Angie was leaning against the wall looking a little green. The paramedics had laid Nancy on the floor and were working over her.

Tears sprang to my eyes. "I'm sorry. It's just that . . ." I rubbed my eyes with the blanket and hiccupped. "You needed my help." That was what I was sticking with. It wasn't like I could tell him I enjoyed unraveling mysteries. Though, I didn't like the part where the killer caught on to me.

Alder's face softened. "This is all my fault." He stroked my hair.

I shrugged and leaned in to him.

We were interrupted by the paramedics who wanted to check my vitals. They had loaded Nancy on a stretcher and were wheeling her outside. My heart pounded against my chest. I had not only put my life at risk, I'd involved Nancy—again. "Is she okay?"

The female paramedic nodded. "We just want to have a

doc look at her to make sure, but she'll be fine. You ladies were smart to fix those boxes up to help keep in your body heat. That's key in holding off hypothermia."

Michelle broke loose from her grandmother and ran to me. "Mama, are you okay? Gigi called me when you didn't come. We tried your cell, but you didn't answer."

"I left it in one of the offices I was cleaning. I'm so glad to see you." I caressed her face.

"We got here just as the ambulance drove up. Mom, I was so scared." She nuzzled into my neck. "I don't want anything to ever happen to you."

I pulled her down in the chair beside me. "Nothing's going to happen to me."

Alder rubbed his mustache. "I hope so. One of these days you won't be so lucky."

Michelle frowned at Alder. "If you're finished chewing her out, I'm taking my mom home."

Alder nodded. "We can talk later."

My daughter helped me to my feet. "You don't have to do anything tomorrow, Mom. Me and Jess will do everything. You just sit around with your feet propped up and give us orders."

Sounded good to me. Though I doubted seriously that I'd get off that easily. My daughters took after me. Our cooking skills were severely lacking. Michelle could make meatballs and spaghetti, and Jessie excelled at grilled cheese. My best dish was scrambled eggs. None of those were on our Thanksgiving menu, so we were in for an adventure in cooking.

I hobbled down the hall, with Michelle on one side and Gigi on the other. "I need my phone and my sweatshirt." I felt my pocket for my keys and pulled out the sticky note. "Will you go get them for me? I need to say something to Detective Alder."

Michelle stiffened. "I'm staying here."

Gigi must have read the look in my eyes because she put her arm around Michelle. "Come on, sister. I think your mom needs some privacy."

I waited until they were out of sight and went back to the cafeteria in search of Alder.

He looked up when he saw me dragging the blanket across the room. "I thought you left. You need to get home and get some rest."

I held the sticky note out in my hand. "I had a flash drive with everything Steve had collected on Keith, but he took it away from me."

He took it and turned it over in his hand. "What's this?"

"It's the password to the flash drive Keith took."

Alder exhaled and slipped the note in his pocket. "This is the end of it. No more. Okay?"

"I know. But everything you needed to go after Keith Preston was on that flash drive. I'm really sorry."

"You need to learn to trust me. We're picking up Preston even as we speak. We got everything we need to put him away for a long time."

"But, how did you know? Everything was on that drive," I said.

"We started getting anonymous tips about Preston a couple days before Trupeli was murdered. After he died, they stopped. We followed the trail he left. The envelope you gave me had all the news clippings of Preston's wife's murder. Plus, a report from a private detective. I checked the lead you gave me about the investigative firm. Apparently, some new evidence had come to light and the detective was running down leads on Preston's wife's murder. Everything he compiled made the locals up there in James City reopen the case."

CHAPTER TWENTY-THREE

"I'm doing everything in my power to get Cece and Alder together, but she's going to have to make a move before it's too late."
Angie Valenti

Once I had thawed out, Angie hustled me over to Weezie's—our favorite hangout. Weezie's was a bar and grill on the outskirts of town run by our friend Louise Weezie Hopkins. It was not much more than an overgrown café, but an addition a couple years ago had added ambience. Weezie had found an antique wooden bar at an auction and remodeled the whole restaurant around her find. It looked like an old-fashioned saloon bar with its heavy dark grain, curled edged, and wood that had a patina from many years of bellying up to the bar. If wood could talk, this piece would be able to spit out a novel of epic proportions.

We threaded our way through the crowd of casually dressed patrons. The happy hour and appetizers at Weezie's were legendary. The minute the five o'clock whistle blew in Wickford, throngs of customers filed in for chicken wings, skewered shrimp, and dollar longnecks.

When Angie had arrived at the school with everyone else, it had come as a surprise. I expected her to be hanging over the toilet and not ready for public display. I hoped it meant she was feeling better, and really hoped it meant she had come to a conclusion about the baby.

Weezie waved and met us at the table with beers and a plate of assorted appetizers.

Angie pushed the beer back. "Can I get an iced tea?"

That bode well.

"What's gotten into her?" Weezie asked, wiping her hands on the apron she wore around her ample middle. "Never known her to turn down a brewski."

I glanced at Angie.

"I'm just getting over a bug. Can't mix my meds with alcohol," she said.

"Yeah, no mixing alcohol and drugs," I said. "She's one smart copper."

Weezie shrugged. "Hope you aren't contagious. Business has been great lately. I don't need my customers coming up sick, and I sure don't need to get the creeping crud. Got too many holiday parties booked." She backed away from the table and disappeared into the crowd.

"You're looking better." I picked up a shrimp and dipped it into the container of cocktail sauce that Weezie served on the side.

"Once I get myself going, I'm okay. Even managed to go to work today for a bit." She eyed the shrimp longingly. Angie loved seafood, especially the crispy shrimp Weezie served.

I noticed I'd been hogging the plate and pushed it toward her. "Sorry, you want one?"

"Umm, no. Don't know if my stomach will tolerate it. Just watching you is about to make me sick." Angie groaned and pulled a package of crackers from her purse. "If it wasn't for these things . . ." She tore into the package and stuffed a square into her mouth.

"Jeez, I'm sorry." I laid my napkin over the plate and pushed it off to the side. "I'll ask Weezie for a to-go box."

"Thanks." Angie continued to munch on the cracker. "Tell me what's going on with you and Alder."

I choked on my beer and started coughing.

"Umm, hit a nerve, huh?"

When I recovered, I put on my nonchalant face. If Alder had told Angie about our bonfire activity, I'd never speak to him again. In fact, not speaking to him again was already on the agenda. I needed to stay as far away from that man as I could. "What are you talking about? There is nothing going on with Alder."

"This is your best friend you're talking to, or rather not talking. You've never held back the important stuff with me." Angie's green eyes bored into me.

I leaned in and hissed, "What has Alder been telling you?"

She slapped the table. "Ah-ha. I knew something was going on between you two. Alder hasn't said a word. He's a gentleman. Now spill the beans."

I scowled. "If Alder hasn't been talking, how did you know?"

She smiled. "Can't sleep at night. I saw him bring you home the other night. You two sat in his truck a long time before you finally went in."

My mouth dropped. I thought I had been discreet. Leave it to my nosy neighbor to get the scoop.

"Don't look so shocked. Not my fault."

"You're a little too snoopy for your own good," I said.

"Look who's talking, Miss Marple. At least I have an excuse. I'm a cop. Investigation is my job. Unlike you who goes around sticking her nose in where it doesn't belong." Angie motioned to Weezie.

I finished off my beer and held up the bottle. Weezie arrived promptly with Angie's tea and my replacement.

"You girls gonna eat or just drink?" Weezie picked up my empty.

"I'm good," Angie said. "Just keep the tea coming."

I considered ordering a salad, but in deference to Angie's stomach, I shook my head. "Nothing for me, but can I get a doggie bag for the appetizers?"

Weezie frowned and left, shaking her head.

"You were serious about that? You know those aren't for takeout," Angie said.

"I don't care. It's not like I order seconds. She brought them over to our table. I don't want them to go to waste." I took a swig of my beer and smirked.

"They'll go to your waist all right. Enough about finger food. Tell me about Alder." She crossed her arms over her midsection and leaned in. "Don't leave out any details."

I caved and told her everything, including how a flaming blanket had saved my virtue.

"You are such a tool," Angie said. "Every woman at the station would love to be in a secluded spot with him. Much less curled up on a blanket getting ready to do the deed. You need to have your head examined."

Yeah, and then I might be in the same position she was—pregnant. "He's not ready to settle down, just like Phillip. I'm not ready for another man with a revolving love life."

"You idiot. We've been over this. He's not a player. You know how many women he could have slept with at the station? Probably all of them except Bertha. She's over seventy, wears combat boots, and still lives with her sister.

And she's probably a virgin. On second thought, she's flirted with him a time or two."

"And how many of them has he slept with?"

"As far as I know, he has never dated anyone from work. It's not his style." Angie frowned. "I can't believe you're making such a big deal out of this."

"Ang, you of all people know I'm not the casual fling type of person. Just because people fall into bed with one another for indifferent sex doesn't mean it's the right thing for me. Phillip is the only man I've ever slept with."

"Lot of good that did you," she mumbled. "It's time you quit living like you're still married and find out what life is all about."

"I'm not about to start adding notches to my belt at this stage of my life," I said.

"Nobody's telling you to go out and start sleeping with every man who looks at you twice. I'm talking about starting a relationship with someone you care about and who obviously cares about you."

"He's not in it for the relationship," I said. "He told me that Saturday night."

Angie shook her head. "I don't believe that."

"He did. He said if he'd known he wanted to be a cop, he would have never married. He's been divorced almost as long as I've been married to Phillip, and he's never remarried. That says something. The man doesn't want commitment."

"So?"

"He never remarried because his dad was a cop, and he used to watch his mom go through agony wondering if her husband was going to come home after a shift. Once Alder decided to become a cop, he married his job. He doesn't want to get involved with anyone who will worry about him like that."

Angie sighed. "People change, you doofus. Maybe he just

hasn't found the person he's willing to share his life with. Besides, he's getting older and maybe he's ready to settle down. It won't be long before he starts thinking about retirement. Why else would he consider building that house? Did you ever consider that?"

"You know about the house?" I asked.

"The whole department does. He's been eyeing that piece of property for years. As long as he works for the force, he can't live outside of city limits. If he's considering building, then he's thinking about his retirement."

I hadn't thought about that. But still.

Weezie returned with a to-go box and sack. "Don't get used to this," she said. "I'm only letting you take this stuff home because you already started eating on it. Next time, I'll throw it in the trash." She scraped my plate and packaged up the leftovers.

"Thanks Weez," I said.

She shrugged her shoulders and headed back to the bar.

"Tell me again why we come to this place," Angie said.

"Cut her some slack. She's just having a bad night." I downed my beer and thought about ordering another one, but I figured I'd had enough alcohol for one night.

"Ah, good advice. Now cut Alder some slack. He's not the enemy. Hell, if it weren't for Dave and now this"—she patted her midsection—"I might even go after him."

That would be the day. Dave and Angie were like chocolate and peanut butter—meant to be together. "I'm sure you would. Speaking of that," I said, gesturing to her stomach, "have you made a decision?"

Angie didn't meet my gaze but picked at a thread on her sleeve. "No."

I reached across the table and touched her hand. "You've got plenty of time, but please do me a favor and at least make an appointment with your doctor."

"I called Dr. Weaver's office." She flicked a cracker crumb from the table. "Looks like we both have decisions to make."

Not that I'd get a chance. Not the way I'd treated Alder the last time I saw him. What man in his right mind would give me a second chance? Make that a third chance.

CHAPTER TWENTY-FOUR

"I never thought I'd see the day that Cece would actually go through with a divorce. We'll see if it sticks."
Phillip Cavanaugh

Low, heavy clouds hung over Wickford as I nosed the car into a parking spot outside the courthouse. Angie, friend that she was, offered to accompany me to court, but I knew this was something I needed to do solo.

Considering everything that had happened, the district suspended classes until after the holidays. I dropped Gigi off at school to do the walk-through for me that Nancy and I had intended to do yesterday before the incident with Keith. I told Nancy to stay home and get some rest. We were both still feeling the effects of our freezer ordeal, but with my court date, I had no choice but to get it over with.

Initially, when Phillip had filed the petition, I hadn't wanted a divorce, but when I realized my husband was a habitual cheater, I knew freeing myself would give me the life

I deserved. It wasn't easy to untangle thirty years, especially when Phillip later decided he didn't want to go through with it. I'd finally convinced him it was our only solution and he agreed, reluctantly.

Barring any unforeseen circumstance, today was merely a formality. I'd sign a few papers and be a single woman. Our attorneys had worked everything out in advance with finances and provisions for Michelle.

Phillip parked his Porsche next to my Cavanaugh Cleaning van and met me on the sidewalk.

He wrinkled his nose. "How long are you going to drive that eyesore around?"

I looked over my shoulder at my hot pink van. "Long as I need to."

"You know it drives my mother nuts?"

I laughed. "Partly why I do it. Hazel needs to learn that she doesn't control everything."

Phillip slung his arm over my shoulder and pulled me to him. "It's not too late to stop this, you know."

I shrugged out of his embrace. "It was too late before it got started."

"Is that cop still hanging around?" Phillip's tone turned sour.

"You still boinking Willow?" I shot back. "Let's not drag this out. After today it doesn't matter what I do or who I do it with. And you sure didn't think about me before you started in with your endless affairs."

"Answer me one thing," Phillip said. "Have you slept with him?"

"None of your business." I wouldn't give him the satisfaction of knowing he was the only man I'd ever been intimate with. "Our prenup dies a quiet death today. So you needn't worry yourself."

Phillip started walking toward the courthouse but

stopped abruptly and turned. "I know I have no right to ask this, but—"

"But what? You want a *nooner* for old time's sake? Don't even."

His face softened. "No. I was going to ask if we could have Thanksgiving dinner one last time as a family. Just the girls and you and me."

"Hazel would have her panties so twisted she'd never get the knot out."

"Leave her out of this. I'm asking for us. Our family."

I adjusted my purse on my shoulder. "There is no us, Phillip. That's why we're here. Let's go get this over with."

———

By the time I left the courthouse, snow had started to fall—big, wet, gloomy flakes. Nancy was resting, Mom was at school, and Michelle still had classes at Lakeview. I had no desire to go home, so I decided to treat myself to lunch at Weezie's.

I dialed Liz's number.

The police had picked Keith up a little after midnight and charged him with Steve's murder. It had been all over the news this morning. The news had also confirmed that the James City police had reopened the case on Keith's wife.

My call went to voice mail. "Liz, it's Cece. I guess you've heard the news about Keith. At least I hope you have. Anyway, I just finished up at court—my divorce is final. If you're not doing anything, how about some lunch at Weezie's, my treat."

After waiting ten minutes for Liz to either show up or call, and suffering through Weezie giving me the evil eye for taking up a booth, I ordered an iced tea and called Gigi to see if she wanted to join me. I could zoom over to the school, check in with Ed, pick up Gigi, and be back before Weezie gave my booth away. She liked me despite always giving me a hard time.

Gigi said she was finished and would be waiting in the front hall. I called Liz one more time. When I got her voice mail again, I hung up.

"Hey, Weezie. I'm going to run by the school and pick my mom up. Be right back. Don't give my booth away. Throw us on a couple of grilled chicken wraps with side salads."

She flipped me off, but at least she had a smile on her face.

CHAPTER TWENTY-FIVE

**"The Cavanaugh women are something else. I'm not
sure if that's good or bad."**
Brad James

Gigi—bless her heart, for all her shortcomings meant well. I'd
heard her puttering around in the kitchen long before the sun
came up. But truth be told, the woman could not cook, so
who knew what kind of mess I'd find when I made it
downstairs.

Yesterday, I'd made a list of stuff we needed to do. There
was plenty she could do to help me get ready. There were
veggies to chop, cornbread to make, and eggs to boil. I'd
gotten home too worn out even to begin.

But I needed to call Liz.

She would have to be feeling relieved. She didn't have to
worry about being a suspect, and she no longer had to worry
about Steve coming after her retirement. I had even begun to
wonder if we could revive our friendship. I'd left messages for
her for two days and she hadn't returned my calls. I assumed

Bill was back in town and they were preparing for the holiday, just like me.

I drummed my fingers on the table while waiting for her to pick up.

"Hello," she answered with a stiff voice.

"Hey Liz, it's Cece. Guess you've seen the news."

"Yes."

"So, I was wondering . . . I know you have a new tennis partner, but I could really do with some exercise. Would you be interested in some recreational tennis once in a while?" I paused when I heard a sharp intake of breath on the other end.

"I'm not sure how that would be possible," she said. "Didn't the club suspend your membership?"

I laughed. "Yes, thanks to Hazel. I thought maybe we could check out the rec center at the park. It's free for Wickford residents."

"Umm, it's not really a good time. With the Christmas holiday coming up, my weekends are pretty much booked, and the thought of doing anything after school wears me out. It gets dark so early, I just want to go home and put my pajamas on and watch TV."

"I totally understand," I said. I totally understood all right.

"Maybe in the spring when we can get outside and get some fresh air," she offered.

"Sounds good." I disconnected and slid my phone in my pocket, knowing I would never call Liz in the spring. I wouldn't have to worry about waiting around for her to call me either. So much for that.

When I walked into the kitchen, Gigi was at the stove, pots and pans on all four burners. "Good morning, sunshine."

I shuddered. No telling what she had going. I was glad I had the ingredients on hand for a breakfast casserole. If her breakfast turned out inedible, at least we'd have something to eat.

"I've got a big breakfast planned. There's fried potatoes." She lifted one of the lids. "And sausage. I also did my Grandma Buchanan's egg gravy and made-from-scratch biscuits." She pulled a towel from a tray on the back of the stove to reveal flaky, golden brown biscuits.

I blinked and stared at the food. Martha Stewart must have dressed like Gigi and whipped up this feast, because the Gigi I knew could not boil water without instructions and even then, she'd boil the pan dry and possibly set the kitchen on fire.

"As soon as Jessie and Brad get here, I'll scramble up some eggs." She shoved a fork full of potatoes at me. "Here. Open up and tell me what you think."

I braced myself and allowed her to feed me. "Umm, these are good. Where'd you learn to cook like this?"

"Ned is a wonder in the kitchen. He taught me everything he knows. And he built me a kitchen to die for. It puts yours to shame. Though yours isn't anything to sneeze at." Her voice held a hint of sadness. "Guess I'll have to learn to make do."

Not if I had anything to do about it. I'd called Ned seven times, and he hadn't returned my phone calls. He must have been good and mad at her, but I still held out hope that he'd accept my invitation for dinner. I knew Gigi missed him and was homesick. I hoped he was feeling the same thing. I prayed he was feeling the same thing. Ned was the best thing that had ever happened to her, sanders I wasn't about to let her screw it up.

"How are you going to make do? Hiding out at my house? Mopping display homes?"

"It works for you," Gigi said. "I'll get a job. A real one. And an apartment. I've been on my own before."

"Call him. It's Thanksgiving. I can tell you're missing him."

She sniffled and turned her back. "No. It's up to him."

There was no use talking to her. I pulled the turkey from the fridge and prepared it for the oven. It had been years since I'd prepared a Thanksgiving meal. In truth, I'd never prepared a real-deal Thanksgiving meal, just the slap-together meals Gigi and I had done when I was a kid.

Ever since I'd married Phillip, we'd celebrated the holidays at Hazel's house. All we had to do was arrive, sit at the table, and wait for her servants to bring in the platters of food, which had been prepared by her cook.

Don't get me wrong, it was always wonderful. But I'd never gotten to man my own stove or bond with my daughters over the preparation. In fact, truth be told, I probably would have liked my mother-in-law more if we'd been able to bond while slaving over a hot stove together. On second thought, probably not. Hazel was not the bonding type. She preferred to be waited on and pampered. Something she had drilled into her staff.

Speaking of bonding with my daughters over preparations, where were they? They'd conferred with their father last night and decided not to have breakfast with him.

"Gigi, why don't you call Jess while I go see if I can rouse Michelle from bed? The day is awastin', and those girls need to be in here enjoying the festivities." I tossed the phone to Gigi.

Just as I reached the stairs, Jessie and Brad bounded in the front door, bringing a stiff wind and a flurry of autumn leaves. I kissed them both on the cheek. "Gigi's in the kitchen with enough food for an army."

Jessie frowned. "Oh, Brad, I'm so sorry. Maybe we should have had breakfast with my dad. My grandmother can't cook."

A dish towel sailed through the air, landing on Jessie's shoulder. "I heard that, young lady, and I'll have you know I've been taking cooking lessons," Gigi said with an indignant look.

Brad suppressed a grin. "I bet you're an excellent cook, Mrs. Evans."

The smile on my mother's face couldn't have gotten any bigger. "He's a sweet-talker, Jess. You need to hang on to this one. And you, young man, may call me Gigi."

Michelle descended the steps in sleep pants and a much-too-small T-shirt, wiping the sleep from her eyes. "You guys are making so much noise down here. What's going on?"

When she saw Brad she yelped, did a quick about-face, and ran up the steps mumbling.

Brad turned ten shades of red and yelled, "Sorry, Michelle."

"Don't worry about her." Jessie shrugged. "She'll act like a prima donna all day."

Gigi retrieved the towel she'd thrown at Jessie, and I took their coats to the hall closet.

"How about you two set the table in the dining room, while I put the eggs on," Gigi said as she turned and plodded down the hall.

"Sure thing." Jessie gave me a questioning look. "Can she really cook?"

"Beats me, but it all looks edible." I closed the door and joined Gigi in the kitchen.

While she scrambled the eggs, I shoved the turkey in the oven and prepared the cornbread dressing, which I decided to cook outside the bird. Everything I'd read said it was safer that way, and since I didn't want any of my guests to get food poisoning, we'd have no stuffing in the turkey.

Gigi did an excellent job on breakfast. Even Michelle went back for seconds, which she never did. Brad reached for a third biscuit with a guilty look on his face, and Jessie actu-ally unzipped her pants. And this was just breakfast. We still had the big meal with our guests.

After the breakfast mess was cleared, Gigi and I continued to put together our dinner menu. It was kind of fun, working side-by-side in my kitchen. The girls and Brad retired to the great room to play a board game. So much for me putting my feet up. Score one for old-fashioned Thanks-givings. I wondered if we'd be caroling and drinking eggnog for Christmas.

Angie and Dave came in the backdoor around one. Dave had two paper bag–sheathed bottles, one in each hand. Angie hugged me. I searched her eyes to see if she'd made a deci-sion, but she had on her blank cop face.

The kids made a place for Dave and he joined in their game. He was a big kid, anyway, so he fit right in. Angie donned an apron and went to work making mashed potatoes. I supervised because she couldn't cook worth a lick either. Though, after I saw her trying to figure out how the mixer worked, I took away the kitchen utensils and sent her in to supervise the game tournaments.

At two, the doorbell rang. I froze. The time had totally gotten away from me. I'd wanted to ease my family into Grant coming for dinner and hadn't thought about it since I'd asked him. After I'd thawed out, I felt guilty about him spending the holiday alone. When I called with the invita-tion, he'd jumped on it. I mean, what could I do. He was single with no family. There was no way I was going to make him go to some restaurant for Thanksgiving or worse, eat a frozen dinner in front of the television. I did the only friendly thing I could think of. But now I had two seconds to clue in my family.

"Hey everybody, I've been meaning to tell you," I said,

wiping my hands on a towel. "I invited Grant Hunter to dinner."

Brad grinned and nudged Jessie in the side. Jessie frowned and twisted away from him. Grant was Brad's boss, so he had encouraged Grant's interest in me. His thought process was if Grant was keeping me busy, it left me no time to snoop into what he and Jessie were doing.

Angie had just taken a drink of water and gasped, choking on what she'd inhaled. Dave jumped to her rescue, patting her back.

Michelle glared at me, and my mother just smiled. Gigi loved a crowd. The more the merrier. In fact, if she could have invited the homeless from down at the mission, she would have loved every minute of it.

I threw the towel on the counter and headed for the door.

"Umm, Cece, I think there's something I need to tell you." Angie followed close on my heels.

Now she was ready to tell me her decision about the baby. The doorbell chimed again. "Let me answer the door, and then we can talk."

"You don't understand," she said. "I might have screwed up just a little."

"Umm, no you screwed up a lot. That's how you found yourself in your little predicament." I reached for the door handle.

"I invited Case Alder to dinner," she said as I pulled open the door.

CHAPTER TWENTY-SIX

"Grant Hunter and Detective Alder at Thanksgiving dinner. What else can my mother do to humiliate me?"
Michelle Cavanaugh

Standing on my front porch were both Alder and Grant. Grant carried a pie container and Alder held a paper bag.

I stole a glance at Angie and whispered, "Tell me this is not happening."

She smiled sheepishly. "I'm afraid so."

I planted on my best hostess face. "Gentlemen, come on in. Dinner is almost ready."

Grant stepped over the threshold first and thrust his pie at me. "I baked it myself. Pumpkin."

"Of course he did," Alder said with a smirk. He held up his package. "I brought pumpkin pie too. Marie Callender baked mine."

"That's lovely. We can't have enough pie, now can we?" I made myself a mental note to kill Angie as soon as everyone left. I also hoped I could disappear before we made it to the kitchen. Talk about a pickle. I didn't know how I'd gotten myself into this situation, but it was bound to get worse before it got better.

I retreated to the kitchen, not much caring if anyone followed me or not. How was I going to explain this to my mother or my kids?

Angie caught up to me. "You didn't tell me Hunter was so attractive."

"That makes us even. You didn't tell me you'd invited Alder to dinner."

"Technically I did tell you. Just now, but I did."

Leave it to Angie to mince words. If she wasn't pregnant, I'd take her out right now, and I didn't think anyone would blame me.

"Hey, you didn't tell me you had a big screen," Hunter said from somewhere behind me.

"Huh?" I turned and he was focused on the giant TV in the great room.

Alder pushed his paper sack into my free hand. To Hunter he said, "You thinking what I'm thinking?"

Grant grinned and slapped him on the back. "If it involves football, you better believe it."

The two headed to the TV, leaving me with a pie in each hand and my mouth hanging open. "You thinking what I'm thinking?" I said to Angie mockingly.

"That you hate men," Angie said.

"I was thinking that you're pretty high on my doo-doo list right now. Why'd you invite Alder?"

"I could ask the same question about Hunter."

Touché. "Grant has no family in the area. I didn't want him eating alone."

"Same thing with Alder. His daughter canceled out at the last minute because her mother is in town, so he was hanging around the station looking pathetic. You two seem to be hitting a rough patch, so I thought maybe I could spark things up."

As we passed the dining room, I stuck my head in. "Set two more places, will you? We've got more company."

Jessie cocked her head to the side. "Who else is here?"

I cringed, but the truth would come out the minute our company stepped foot in the dining room. "Detective Alder."

The frown on Jessie's face only made matters worse. "Who wants him here?"

At the same time, Angie and I pointed to each other and said, "She does."

"Why are you pointing at me?" I asked. "This one is on you. Inviting Grant is all I'll own up to."

Brad tried to stifle a laugh, but I heard it loud and clear. "This should be interesting."

I still hadn't heard from Ned. And the closer we got to dinner, the more I'd given up hope on him actually showing up.

I called everyone to dinner and introduced Alder and Hunter. The looks going around the table ranged from shocked—Dave—to angry—Jessie and Michelle—to ecstatic —Gigi. Angie had given up the right to any sort of look after pulling her stunt.

Jessie had penned name tags and placed them around the table. She seated Dave at the head of the table since he was carving the bird. On his right sat Angie, then Brad, Jessie, and Michelle. I was at the other end of the table, and to my right sat Gigi, Grant, Nancy, and Alder. It was pretty obvious that Jessie had placed Alder as far away from me as possible, but she hadn't done Grant any favors either, since she sat him between Gigi and Nancy. Poor guy.

Brad poured a nice Merlot for everyone except Michelle. I raised my glass for a toast. "Welcome to Thanksgiving at the Cavanaughs'. Here's to a wonderful afternoon."

Glasses clinked around the table. I noticed Angie did not drink from hers.

"While we're in the spirit of Thanksgiving, I'd like to say that I'm thankful for my family and friends." I raised my glass again. "To all of you who add meaning to my life."

Jessie wrapped her hand around Brad's arm and said, "I'm thankful that Brad is in my life. I know my mom is grateful for that."

Brad stroked Jessie's hand and said, "And I'm thankful that Cece introduced me to Jessie. This is the best Thanksgiving ever."

"Well." Alder cleared his throat. "I'm thankful for bonfires and moonlit nights."

I gulped and tried to keep the heat from inching up my neck. At the moment I was thankful for turtlenecks and would be even more grateful for men who kept their mouths shut.

Angie shot me a look that said, "You go, girl," and all but pumped her fist in the air. If she had cheered, I wouldn't have been surprised.

Grant curled his lip. "I am grateful for blossoming friendships and long walks along the river."

My stomach tightened. It was a good thing we hadn't eaten, or I probably would have tossed my cookies. These two guys were unbelievable. Their pointed jabs did not go unnoticed.

Angie looked from Alder to Hunter to me. Dave's mouth opened and closed as if he were a fish. Jessie and Michelle both rolled their eyes—in unison. I could tell that after our guests left, I would be interrogated to the nth degree.

To break the awkwardness, I said, "Anybody else want to share?" Nothing worse could come out, so maybe we could get this over with and eat.

Dave wrapped his arm around Angie's shoulder. "Shall we?"

Angie took a deep breath. "We're finally going to have a baby."

My chest warmed, and I fought a cheer of my own. That was the best news I'd heard all day, but before I could offer my congratulations, Michelle blurted, "Oh gross. You guys are, like, old."

When I saw the defeat on Angie's face, I wanted to shove a dish towel down Michelle's throat. Angie sank in her chair, big tears rolling down her cheeks.

I shot Michelle the mom-eye—the look that said she'd screwed up big time. "Michelle Suzanne Cavanaugh, that was a horrible thing to say."

"Whoa, can't believe I said that out loud. That's *totes* not what I meant." Michelle went to Angie and hugged her. "I'm sorry. You guys aren't old. It's not like you're toddling around with canes and walkers."

"But we are old," Angie said. "Or at least we will be by the time this baby is your age. People will think we're the grandparents. Why did this have to happen, now of all times?"

Dave planted a kiss on her cheek. "Don't be silly. We've been given a gift. Who cares what people think? Sure, it would have been nice thirty years ago, but Angie, this is what we have always hoped for. Some couples never get the opportunity to know the joy that a child can bring. Now we get to have the experience. We're going to embrace it."

By the time Dave finished, I was almost in tears. Jessie's eyes glistened. Michelle offered to be the designated babysitter. Alder and Grant stood stock still, probably glad it wasn't them. I wondered if Alder had a wee bit of a tinge after our almost encounter the other night. Maybe he'd think twice about bonfires and moonlit nights, especially where I was concerned. And I hoped it dampened Grant's spirits as well.

Gigi burst into tears. What a Thanksgiving this was turning out to be, and we hadn't even sat down to eat yet. When Gigi's crying didn't sound happy like I initially thought, I frowned.

"What's wrong?" I asked. Though I had a sneaking hunch she was missing Ned. Darn him for not showing up. Maybe he was glad she had left.

"Nothing," she said, swiping at her eyes. "It's just so . . ." With that she fled from the room.

I set down my glass. "If you all will excuse me, I need to find out what's wrong with her."

"She's been a wreck all week," Jessie offered. "I'll go see if you want."

"Me too," Michelle said.

They both stepped away from the table.

"Stop." I held my hand out. "Let me talk to her. I think I know what's wrong. Dave, you cut the bird. I'll be right back." If I had to tie them in their chairs, nobody else was leaving this table.

I knocked on the guestroom door and Gigi mumbled, "Come in."

She was sprawled facedown across her bed sobbing. I sat next to her and rubbed her back.

"It's going to be okay."

She rolled over. "Men! Why do we put up with them? Today, going around the table talking about what we were thankful for made me realize how much I miss Ned."

I said a little prayer. "Then do something about it. Call him. Don't let your pride stand in the way."

The tears began again. "I did," she blubbered. "Only he won't return my calls."

Ugh, he hadn't returned my calls either, but I wasn't about to tell her. Maybe she really had stepped in it this time. I pulled a tissue from the box on the nightstand and handed it to her. "Come on, wipe your eyes and let's go down and eat. The girls have been looking forward to having you at Thanksgiving."

She patted my arm and sucked in a slow breath. "You're right. Ned can go to the devil. I've got my family and that's what matters. You go on down. Give me a minute. Then I'll freshen up and come down."

Umm, that wasn't exactly what I wanted her to take away from this conversation. I'd have to put on my thinking cap and find another way to get her and Ned together. Maybe I could take some time off and drive her to Arizona to make sure they would sit down and talk. If Ned wouldn't come to Gigi, I'd take Gigi to Ned.

As I grabbed the newel post and started down the stairs, the doorbell rang. My heart rose in my throat. If it was Phillip, I would just walk out the door and keep going. Planning this dinner had been a gigantic mistake, one I wouldn't soon forget.

I pulled the door open ready to flee.

CHAPTER TWENTY-SEVEN

"I think Gigi missed me. If I want her to stick around, guess I'm going to have to change."
Ned Evans

An older man stood on my porch, hat in hand. "Is this the Cavanaugh residence?"

"Yes." I eyed him warily. "May I help you?"

He offered his hand. "I'm Ned Evans. You called me."

"Am I ever glad to see you." I clasped his hand and shook until he gently pulled away. "I never dreamed you would come. You didn't call. I just assumed . . ."

He let out a low belly laugh that rose in volume. "Never assume. You know what they say about assuming. Now, may I come in? I'm about to freeze to death."

It was almost forty-five degrees, which for November in Missouri was almost shorts and T-shirt weather. I stepped back and ushered him in.

"I believe Gigi is in her room. Would you like to go up and surprise her?"

"Point the way," Ned said.

"Top of the stairs, make a right, and it's the first door on the right." I hugged his neck. "I'm Cece, by the way, and I am so glad you're here."

"Me too. I wanted to come all week but thought Gigi might need some time to miss me. Is she missing me?"

"Yes, I believe she is. She's been a basket case since she got here. That's why I called you."

"Sorry about not calling you back. All part of my plan to make her miss me. I know I've been a pain, but old men really can change. I'm going to show her that. If she needs her space, well, I'll just give it to her." Ned took the stairs two at a time. Pretty spry for an old guy.

The dining room looked like someone had cast a spell over the diners. It was quiet, too quiet, and everyone just sat motionless. Except for Grant and Nancy. They were engaged in an animated conversation, Nancy giggling and blushing like a schoolgirl. I hoped she wasn't sweet-talking him to get him to give her the condo job.

We'll just see about that Miss Nancy.

Alder had a smirk on his face and seemed amused by the whole scene with Grant and Nancy, probably hoping that Nancy could charm Grant. She did have a way with men. She'd even dressed for the occasion today. I didn't know if she'd been to a resale shop or not, but surely, she'd not purchased the black Victorian lace mini dress off the rack at a department store. She also had black leather boots and fishnet stockings, and the whole look was topped with scarlet lipstick and pale foundation. I wondered if she'd worn her Halloween costume because she sure looked the part of a vampire, and Grant seemed intrigued.

"Let's get this show on the road." I clapped my hands. "We've got food to serve, people to feed, and games to play."

"Games?" Alder and Grant both spoke at once.

"Yes," I said. "It's a tradition. After dinner, we haul out the cards and play a rousing game of spades. If you don't play, you don't get dessert."

"Hey, we brought dessert," Grant said. "You can't withhold pie from the guys who brought it."

"You wanna bet," I said. "My house. My rules. Now let's start passing the food."

"What about Gigi?" Jessie asked.

"I think Gigi will be happy with leftovers." I grinned and felt a warmth spread through my body that for once wasn't a hot flash. "That was Ned at the door."

CHAPTER TWENTY-EIGHT

"I know enough to know there is no such thing as happily ever after. I also know it's up to me to make my own happiness."
Cece Cavanaugh

After dinner, Dave coerced Alder into going next door to see the boat he was building in his garage. Brad's head swiveled at the announcement of a boat, so he and Jessie joined the faction heading over to the Valentis'. Angie followed along like a lovesick puppy. Since she'd made the announcement about the baby, all I could see was love in her eyes. I knew she'd made the right decision.

Gigi commandeered Nancy and Michelle and put them to work in the kitchen doing dishes. She and Ned settled in the great room to talk.

That left Grant and me in the dining room. "How about a brandy?" I asked.

"Point me in the right direction and I'll do the pouring." Grant pulled out my chair and followed me to Phillip's den.

My den. That was a hard habit to break, but it was now my den.

We walked into the leather-clad room with its mahogany furniture and dark green accents. It needed a makeover, but my budget wasn't in any shape to make this room more feminine, so it would have to stay this way for a while. Phillip's personal effects were gone, evidenced by the empty spaces on the shelves and walls.

Grant pulled the French doors closed behind us and ushered me to the sofa.

I gulped and hoped he wasn't expecting a romantic interlude, not with my family down the hall. I guided the situation in another direction. "The liquor cabinet is in that armoire," I said, pointing to the massive piece that served as the focal point of the room.

He took the hint and poured two brandies, taking longer than necessary. "Quite a collection of brandy you have here. Who's the connoisseur?" The minute he said it, he cursed under his breath. "Sorry."

He poured the drinks without further comment and placed them on the coffee table. "Can we have a fire?" he asked. "It'll take some of the chill out of the room."

"Sure, make sure the gas is turned on and just hit the ignition switch near the mantel. It'll take right off."

He played with it a while, then he let out a deep sigh. "This isn't going to work," he said, his back to me.

"Sure it will. Just hit the switch and it should light right up." I took a sip of brandy. "I've never had a problem with it before." Not that I'd made many fires in here, it being Phillip's study and all. But that would change. It was my dominion now.

He flicked the fire to life and joined me on the sofa. "I'm not talking about the fire." He set his snifter on the coffee table and took my hand. "I'm talking about us. We're not going to work."

I took a sip and let the warm liquid glide down my throat. "Grant, what are you talking about?"

"I care about you, Cece. Probably more than I have a right to." He stood up and pulled me up. The next thing I knew he leaned in and kissed me. A soft, tender kiss. When I didn't respond, he pulled back.

"It's not there. No spark," he said.

"What?"

"There's no spark. I've always wondered if we'd have it, but we don't. I watched you and Alder tonight at dinner, and there's something between the two of you." His eyes held a sadness that belied the lilt in his voice.

"There's nothing going on. We're friends. The same as you and me. I've told both of you that I'm not ready for a relationship, but neither one of you can seem to get it through your thick skulls."

Grant rubbed my hand. "Dear Cece, you are lying to yourself. I can see it in the way you look at him when you think no one is watching. He looks at you the same way. You may not be involved physically, but you're involved emotionally. If you could get over your anger at Phillip, you might be able to see that you have an opportunity to be with someone who cares about you."

"But . . ."

He put his finger to my lip. "No buts. I recognize the look. Ellie and I had it for years, and you deserve it. At least you owe yourself the opportunity to see if you can take the relationship somewhere."

"What makes you such a smart man?" I asked.

"Years of experience with a woman I loved more than life. Cece, love like that doesn't come around often. When it does, you have to go for it. I'd be a fool to try to stand in your way.

Besides, Nancy and I seem to be hitting it off, if you didn't notice."

Here I was worried about hurting his feelings, and he was the one letting me down easy. "You and Nancy?" I had noticed that she seemed to be hanging on his every word, but I never dreamed he'd been thinking about her. Go figure. She was a looker but a bit shy in the brain department. Maybe a man like Grant Hunter was just what she needed to straighten up.

"Tonight at dinner when I was watching you and Alder, I got to thinking, here she was paying so much attention to me, and all I was doing was watching you. I can't go on being an observer. It's time I got back in the game, and she seems like a sweet lady. I've dropped by the condos a time or two when she was there, and I took her to lunch the other day to show my appreciation for how hard she'd been working."

"And I thought she was trying to steal my job." I laughed. "I would have never dreamed." I leaned over and kissed him on the cheek. "You're such a catch."

Grant smiled and touched his cheek. "You're a catch too, and I'll tell Alder if he ever mistreats you, he's going to have to answer to me."

"You're a good man, Grant Hunter, and I will always treasure our friendship."

Grant pretended to pull a knife from his heart but laughed as he was doing so.

Nancy and I were going to have to have a talk. I wanted to know what her intentions were with Grant. She'd had kind of a shady past, but it didn't mean she couldn't change if the right man came along.

———

After dessert, Nancy invited Grant up to her apartment for a nightcap. She looked at me for assurance and I nodded. I knew she was in safe hands with Grant, but I worried about him. He was a grown man and had a way of reading people. I'd also learned that Nancy, even though she was a bit of an airhead, had a good heart. The two of them would be just fine.

Dave and Angie left arm in arm. It was nice to see Angie smiling. She had a long road ahead of her, but I'd vowed to help her out in any way I could. After all, she'd been my rock for the past thirty-plus years. If I had to pull a little diaper duty or babysitting, I guessed that was a small payment for everything she'd done for me.

Jessie and Brad had retired to the great room for a bit of privacy, but Michelle finally pulled out The Game of Life and coerced them into playing. Jessie said if she had to play then the rest of us needed to join the game. Alder declined, saying he'd left his reading glasses at home.

"I guess I better be going," he said.

"Don't wait for me," I told the game players. I knew once they started, they'd be oblivious to everything else that was going on, even if I left for a while.

"You sure you don't want to hang around?" I said, following Alder to the door. "We can have a second dessert."

He waggled his eyebrows. "I could use dessert, but pumpkin pie isn't exactly what I had in mind."

"You ready for another bonfire out at your place?" I winked and reached for his hand.

"Are you serious?" Alder stroked his mustache, and I felt my stomach tighten. "I thought after our conversation the other day, you were giving me the boot."

"That was the old Cece. This is the new Cece," I said. "One who isn't afraid of the future. This happened yesterday."

I placed a manila envelope in his hand. Inside it were papers that read DISSOLUTION OF MARRIAGE.

"Is this what I think it is?" Alder asked, a sparkle in his eyes.

I nodded and took the blanket I had stashed in the hall closet after my talk with Grant and tossed it to Alder. "Let's get out of here."

If you enjoyed Pensions, Tensions, and Homicide, follow Cece's journey by reading Book 4 - Mimosas, Magnolias, and Murder. Find out what happens when Cece plans a day of self-care and mother-daughter time but winds up as an uninvited guest at Phillip and Willow's wedding.

ALSO BY TRICIA L. SANDERS

Grime Pays Mystery Series

<u>Book 1 Murder is a Dirty Business</u>

Between hot flashes and divorce papers, a middle- aged woman reconsiders her outlook on life when she butts heads with a hot detective during a murder investigation.

<u>Book 2 Death, Diamonds, and Freezer Burn</u>

An unwelcome visitor, an unrequited love, and a dead body create chaos in Cece's plan for a productive summer.

<u>Book 3 Pensions, Tensions, and Homicide</u>

A former friend, a runaway mother, and a dead body threaten to spoil Cece's low-key family Thanksgiving.

<u>Book 4 Mimosas, Magnolias, and Murder</u>

Cece wants a day of self-care, mother-daughter time... and anything but her ex-husband's wedding.

The Mattie and Mo Mysteries

<u>Hark! A Homicide (Prequel)</u>

When a dead elf threatens to spoil Pine Grove's Christmas, being on Santa's naughty list is the least of Mattie's worries.

<u>Book 1 Flea Market Felony</u>

These new retirees have just hit the road. Will their first campsite's shenanigans land them both in handcuffs?

A Tropical Cozy Mystery

<u>Candy Canes and Culprits (Prequel)</u>

Financially strapped, Shelby agrees to photograph the wedding festivities for her rival. Will a murder at the posh event land Shelby's mom in jail?

Women's Fiction

<u>Dandelion Summer</u>

Annie Chisholm led the perfect life for more than 30 years -- at least that's how it seemed to everyone around her. But she and her husband, Michael, knew the truth about their shattered marriage.

RECIPE - BEATRICE'S CORNBREAD DRESSING

Ingredients
Cornbread (make a day or two ahead)

- 1 1/2 cups cornmeal
- 1 cup all-purpose flour
- 4 teaspoons baking powder
- 1 teaspoon salt
- 2 cups buttermilk
- 1 large egg beaten
- 6 tablespoons unsalted butter, melted and divided

Directions:

1. Preheat oven to 425 degrees F. Heat a 10-inch cast iron skillet in the oven.
2. Combine cornmeal, flour, baking powder and salt in a large bowl
3. In a separate bowl, add and stir the buttermilk, egg, and 3 tablespoons melted butter. Pour mixture over dry ingredients and stir until combined.

4. Remove skillet from the oven and add remaining 3 tablespoons melted butter.

5. Pour the mixture into the hot skillet. Place into oven and bake for 25-30 minutes until golden brown.

Dressing

- 8 tablespoons butter (1 stick)
- 3 medium onions, chopped
- 4 stalks celery, chopped fine
- 1/2 cup shredded, cooked turkey (optional)
- 1 teaspoon poultry seasoning
- 1 1/2 teaspoons dried sage
- 3/4 teaspoon salt
- 1/2 teaspoon pepper
- 3 pieces day old bread, crumbled
- 1/2 cup milk
- 3 eggs, lightly beaten
- 2 eggs, hard boiled and chopped (optional)
- 2 to 2 1/2 cups turkey or chicken stock
- 2 tablespoons butter

Instructions

1. Preheat oven to 400 degrees.
2. Crumble the pre-made cornbread. Set aside.
3. Melt stick of butter in a large sauté pan.
4. Add celery and onion and cook until soft.
5. Add poultry seasoning, sage, salt, and pepper to onion/celery mixture.
6. In a large bowl combine crumbled cornbread and bread.
7. Beat together milk and eggs and add to bowl.

8. Stir in 2 cups of turkey or chicken broth.
9. Stir in onion/celery mixture. Mixture should be very moist. Add more broth if not.
10. Add in shredded turkey and chopped eggs. (optional)
11. Transfer to a greased baking dish.
12. Cut remaining butter into tiny pieces and dot across top.
13. Bake at 350 degrees for 30 minutes, or until it turns light brown on top.

ABOUT THE AUTHOR

Photo Credit: Alecia Hoyt

Tricia L. Sanders writes cozy mysteries and women's fiction with a dash of romance and a sprinkling of snark to raise the stakes. Her heroines are humorous women embarking on journeys of self-discovery all the while doing so with class and sass.

Tricia is a recent transplant to Texas, but she's still an avid St. Louis Cardinals baseball fan, so don't get between her and the television when a game is on.

A former instructional designer and corporate trainer, she traded in curriculum writing for novel writing, because she hates bullet points and loves to make stuff up. And fiction is more fun than training guides and lesson plans.

Visit her website at www.triciasanders.com.

www.ingramcontent.com/pod-product-compliance
Lightning Source LLC
Chambersburg PA
CBHW022124310726
48972CB00007B/2182